PUCK BLOCK

SJ SYLVIS

For all the book girlies who have an overbearing older brother with incredibly hot friends <3

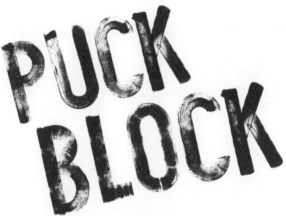

USA TODAY BESTSELLING AUTHOR
S.J. SYLVIS

PREFACE

TAYTUM

I was twelve when I had my first boyfriend. It lasted three minutes.

I was thirteen when I had my first kiss. A rumor started the next day that I had such bad breath he passed out after.

I was sixteen when I realized I wasn't the problem. It was my two overbearing bodyguards instead.

Ford Collins became my brother's best friend when we were in elementary school, and that meant, by default, he was another one of my defenders—and I'm not referring to his position on the hockey team. My brother was—and still is—a bossy, looming shadow that follows my every move, and as soon as Ford practically started to live at our house, he did the same.

That's not to say that Emory and Ford were nice to me, though. In fact, they were anything *but.* I wanted nothing more than to hang out with them and follow their every move, so much so that I'd sit outside for hours, ignoring my own friends, just to watch them practice their hockey drills.

Emory possessed a skill that not many people had. He was quick on the ice, ruthless too, even as a ten-year-old. Ford was right behind him with precision and agility, and to top it all off, he had a knowledge of hockey that was simply unheard of.

I was nine the first time they banded together and rejected me.

My dad had built a makeshift hockey rink for my brother and Ford in our backyard, and of course, I wasn't allowed on it. They'd race to it after school, and I'd follow after them, even with Emory mumbling under his breath for me to go away. The boys were rough and rowdy, and I was docile and fragile. The explanation of, *"It isn't a place for you to play and get hurt; it's a place for the boys to practice,"* was something I'd heard a million times, but still, it only took two weeks for me to gain the courage to step over the side and feel the rush of defiance. Emory threatened to tell our parents, but I knew Ford would cover for me.

Except, things took a turn the moment I slipped backward, and that was the start of Ford becoming my enemy.

The sound my head made when it hit the ice was a pure reflection of my poor choice.

"Taytum!" Ford made it over to me first, sliding onto his knees to come to my rescue.

I gasped with a throb so painful I cried out.

Emory checked for injuries as Ford kept me in his lap. I remember counting the faint freckles on Ford's face to help me calm down, but when Emory pulled his hand away from the back of my skull, his fingers were painted red, and we all froze.

My parents stormed outside, and my pulse raced.

I tried to talk myself out of trouble, even with the sticky blood matting my hair. I looked to Ford for an olive branch, but with his face pale and Emory muttering into his ear, I knew my game of tug-o-war with my brother was over.

He won.

Ford was *his* best friend.

Not mine.

A flash of hurt flickered across Ford's boyish features right before my parents turned to him to get the story straight—like they always did. And sure enough, he threw me right under the bus.

I no longer considered Ford anything but my foe.

He wasn't my friend. He was Emory's.

And every day since, he and my brother have banded together to make my life a living hell.

Or, according to them, they've banded together to *protect* me.

Which is complete and utter bullshit.

[1]

TAYTUM

My body arc is curved to perfection, and my toe points to the sky in the middle of my arabesque. The stretch is a breath of fresh air, and I inhale the moment I touch my foot back to the shiny stage, but it takes a moment to adjust to it.

There's a groove in between my eyebrows with thoughts that send my heart into a bit of a tizzy. *Calm down, Tay.*

"Hey, you okay?" Claire's face comes into sight. I don't answer her right away because, truthfully, I'm not sure, but I know I don't have to lie to my best friend and hide my concern.

"Yeah, I think. I just got a little dizzy."

She holds her water bottle out for me, and I take it with a shaky hand. I tip my head back and swallow a few gulps before handing it back and nodding. "I'm fine. Maybe grab my snack kit just in case."

She hands me my little pink bag with llamas wearing sunglasses all over it. "Should I call Emory?"

I scoff. "Absolutely not."

I know my brother means well, but he, along with my parents, tend to forget that I'm twenty-two and have, on occasion, taken care of myself.

"Tay, are you sure? We don't want a repeat of the incident at The Bex. Where is your glucose monitor? We should check your levels."

I glance at Claire with her hands on her hips and her bottom lip tucked underneath her teeth. She's the shyer one of our bestie duo, but the burn of embarrassment was much more potent to me than it was to her that night.

Nothing like the entire restaurant spinning when your feet are firmly planted on the ground and then, to make matters that much richer, your face meeting the unmoving floor moments later and taking your friend down with you.

That was the start of everyone learning that I have type 1 diabetes, and ever since I was diagnosed before coming back to Bexley U in the fall, I've been riding waves of ups and downs.

I take a deep breath, and the room settles. "I'm fine. Really." *See? Totally fine.*

Coming to Bexley U, even with my brother and Ford in attendance, was a breath of fresh air for me. For the first time, I was able to break away from being Emory's little sister and go off on my own. They still tried to step in and interfere whenever our paths crossed, but it wasn't nearly as demoralizing as when we were in high school.

But this year, I'm back to being in my own version of hell.

After I was rushed to the ER during our yearly summer lake trip, nearly died, and was later diagnosed with type 1, things fell into the same cycle as before.

The phone calls from my parents are borderline obsessive. If I don't answer, they dial Emory next. If he doesn't answer, they move to Ford because they know he will stop anything to take their call.

"As long as you're sure," Claire says.

I nod to her and unzip my bag. I stare at the contents inside. *Candy, glucose tablets, peanut butter crackers.* After I sort through everything, I zip it back up. I feel fine physically, but there's a nagging voice in the back of my head that's making me hesitate.

Professor Petit claps her hands twice, and I push my bag off to the side. Claire and I stand and make our way over to center stage to run through the end-of-year performance again. Dance isn't my one true love like it is for a lot of the dancers in the program, but it's all I've ever known. With Emory and Ford having an all-consuming passion for hockey that dictated their lives from elementary school and on, I decided at a young age that I wanted something like that too. It turned out to be ballet, and here I am, at Bexley U on a scholarship.

"That was a great arabesque, Taytum!" I smile at one of the younger dancers when she finds her position on the stage.

"Yeah, except for the landing. Why don't you go practice instead of trying to make friends with the more established dancers?" Heat burns my neck at the sound of Kate's piercing voice when she reams into the freshman. "And as for you"—she turns to me, and I want to flick her pointy little nose—"we wouldn't want your face to meet the floor again, so maybe you should go practice too."

I bare my teeth. "Shut the fu–"

Claire's face pops into view. Her eyes are wide, and when her hands land on my shoulders, she hisses under her breath, "Taytum!"

4 / SJ SYLVIS

"What?" I shrug. "She doesn't get to talk to me or the other girls like that. This isn't an audition for *Mean Girls*."

Kate rolls her eyes and turns around in a huff.

I may have some areas of insecurity, but that doesn't make me passive by any means.

"She needs a dose of reality," I grumble.

"And you need to take a deep breath," Claire reminds me. Her hand falls to mine, and she gives it a gentle squeeze. "Ballet dancers are supposed to be poised, remember?"

A tight laugh tumbles from my mouth before I back up to prepare for a pirouette. "I only got into ballet because I was jealous that Emory and Ford were good at something. I wanted to prove that I was good at something too. It has nothing to do with my demeanor."

Claire laughs while bending at the waist to stretch. "Obviously." She slowly stands up and says, "It's probably a good thing you're in ballet. You'd be way too intimidating if you were in a highly competitive sport."

"Like hockey?" I ask. "Could you imagine if there were two Olsons on the team?"

My older brother has a temper—much like every goalie there ever was.

Claire does a quick sauté and lands in first position. "It would be terrifying."

We both laugh and practice a few more turns while we wait for Professor Petit to stop correcting some of the younger dancers' form. I step in line to do another arabesque because Kate's little dig irritated me. Determination runs through my blood just as potently as it does for my brother, and if we're given the chance to prove something to someone, we will obliterate it.

I arch my back deeper this time and lengthen my neck.

My focus is stable, and my left foot balances along the floor before I finish and regain my posture. I finally exhale, and that's when I realize the room is spinning again. Black dots swarm my vision, and I become aware of the all-too-familiar tingling in my clammy hands.

Shit.

Like a looming nightmare, I know what comes next.

I was wrong earlier.

I'm not fine.

I make eye contact with Claire, and she knows right away that I'm about to go down. She takes off in my direction, but before I can see if she attempts to pull another heroic move, like at The Bex, everything goes black.

———

"This is totally uncalled for." I'm scowling, and it causes the paramedic to chuckle under his breath.

"Has anyone ever told you that you're a terrible patient?" he asks.

I pause and look away because *yes*.

"Only every single time," another voice says.

I tip my head back and make eye contact with the dark-haired EMT who has unfortunately had me in his care before. He turns away with a smirk and goes back to reading my levels on the monitor. His strong brow furrows, which is never good.

Do you know what else is never good? When the campus EMTs start to recognize you.

I'm beyond embarrassed, and I continue to curse my wonky pancreas all the way to the hospital, where Mr.

Bossy-Pants refuses to let me walk and threatens to strap me down onto the stretcher if I even dare step a toe off.

I fling myself back onto the uncomfortable padding and cross my arms. The other EMT, the one that has a much better bedside manner, pats my arm, but the dark-haired one swoops in and whispers in my ear, "Relax, princess. Let us take care of you."

My stomach gushes with something warm, and my cheeks burn with a blush. *Christ, Taytum.* I'm so deprived of the opposite sex–thanks to Emory and his friends becoming even more involved in my social circle because of Claire dating their captain–that I think the cute paramedic is flirting with me.

He's not.

He's just doing his job.

Kate is likely throwing a party with confetti and cake due to my sudden disappearance during practice. Knowing her, she's probably set up some viewing site where my face met the floor.

When the elevator doors open, I tense. We're headed for the ER, and I hope they don't take me to the MICU. I'm convinced Dr. McCarthy lives there. I imagine him sleeping in the hallway with his white coat as a blanket, prepared for anything and everything. A vacation for Dr. McCarthy is heading down the street for a coffee and back.

"Alright, boys," I say. "Fess up. What was my sugar?"

The two EMTs look at each other before swinging their gazes toward echoing footsteps. I lean forward only to quickly jolt backward to hide. The cute one rolls his lips together to hide a smirk.

Dr. McCarthy walks past us, and I breathe out a heavy breath when he's out of sight, but then he takes one step backward, rolls his head toward me, and blinks once. "Taytum..."

Damnit.

"Sorry, Doctor. I'm not sure who that is." I look behind me and catch a grin from the other paramedic. He stuffs a laugh deep in his throat, but we both pull it together when Dr. McCarthy sighs.

"What happened?"

"She fainted at practice but regained consciousness quickly when her friend checked her sugar. We took over once we got there and finally persuaded her to get on the stretcher."

I cross my arms. "If threatening to call my brother is what you consider persuading, then sure."

Dr. McCarthy clicks his tongue—his usual telltale sign that he's thinking hard, which I picked up on within the first week of being under his care. He isn't the warmest doctor I've met, but he's the top endocrinologist in our area, and he actually takes my opinion into consideration despite my parents' refusal to listen.

"Get her into a room. I want a reading on her levels and what was given by her friend, if anything."

He pulls out his phone, and even though I'm being pushed down the long hallway, I crane my neck back.

"I hope you're not calling who I think you're calling. I'm fine, Dr. McCarthy."

We briefly make eye contact, but he turns his back to me as soon as he puts the phone up to his ear.

I flop back onto the stretcher and cross my arms. It doesn't take long for me to feel like a child again, and I know it's only about to get worse.

[2]

FORD

I'M AN OBSERVER.

A sly one at that.

I've been called many things throughout my hockey career, and though I sometimes clown around on the ice, what I do is a true art. In other words, I'm crafty. When slicing my skates against the ice, moving toward the puck with my witty remarks, my focus is on pinching off the forward, forcing them toward the boards and never even coming close to our goalie.

Coach wants to punch me ten times out of ten when I seem out of position, but he knows I have an unmatched ice awareness and always seem to be exactly where I'm needed when the puck spills out. Emory and I have grown up on the ice together, and at this point, we're a package deal. I defend him, and he defends the net. It's a flawless relationship.

He skates over to me in a rush after talking to Coach for

a quick second. "We gotta go." He pulls his mask off, and his sweaty hair flings off to the side.

"What? Why?" I pull my mask off and grin. "Don't tell me. Coach told you that we're both just so fuckin' good that we don't need practice." I throw my stick up in the air, and our team captain ducks.

"You need practice on how to shut up," Theo snaps, jumping over my stick.

"Ford." Emory is stoic. My smile falls, and I already know what he's about to say. He has his serious face on–which isn't that far off from his regular face, but I know the difference.

"Where is she?" I ask, swiping down to snag my stick. We skate off to the side, and thankfully, practice is coming to an end, so we don't have to persuade Coach that, although I'm not blood-related to the Olson family, I'm still considered as much, which means when there's a family emergency, it also applies to me.

"Hospital."

My heart sinks. I follow after Emory while quickly pulling my hockey gear from my body on the way to the locker room. Emory is too slow for my liking, so after I throw all my shit in a pile, I rush over to him and help him with his pads, even though he tries to slap my hands away. We're in his car seconds later, and he shows me his phone.

I read the text and sigh.

Taytum. Taytum. Taytum.

She has caused so much trouble in my life, and she doesn't even mean to.

Well, most of the time, she doesn't. Other times, yeah, okay...she's well aware. Like the other day, when she tagged along to a party because she knew I'd keep my eye on her instead of following the blonde so I could have five minutes of peace with a mindless puck bunny.

Rude.

Emory is on the phone with his parents when we make it to the endocrinology floor, and I can't pay attention to what he's saying. The sterile scent of alcohol burns my nose and pulls on my usually calm strings, sending my heart flying.

My shoulders are tense, and my skin is itchy.

I loathe hospitals, and anyone close to me knows it. Taytum is pretty much the only person I'd ever make the sacrifice for, which is becoming a nuisance, considering this is happening more and more lately.

By the time her brother and I make it outside her hospital door, he nods to her doctor, who is someone I now know on a first-name basis. Which isn't a bad thing at this point because, in a couple of seconds, he may become my doctor too. My pulse is alarmingly high, and if the annoying beeping sounds in the hallway don't cease, I'm going to snatch his stethoscope and plug my ears so I can hear nothing but the echoes.

"She's sleeping," Dr. McCarthy says, coming up beside Emory.

Doubtful. If I know Taytum as well as I think I do, she's fake sleeping to get out of any conversation regarding her health.

"Let me guess." Emory crosses his arms. "She's refusing whatever you're trying to sell her."

The doctor sighs dramatically. "She's my most stubborn patient. Her nonchalant behavior regarding her diabetes concerns me." He scratches his head. "I want her to wear a glucose monitoring system at all times to track her sugar. Once we can be certain that the insulin is the correct dosage for her body, then she can use an insulin pump, and her forgetful moments will be a concern of the past."

My assumption is that Taytum isn't necessarily being forgetful.

She's in denial.

Emory has his phone in his hand as he's listening, likely typing everything out so he can repeat it back to his parents. "And what will an insulin pump do?"

I answer for the doctor. "Automatically inject the insulin at the right times and with the proper dosage. There is less risk of high and low sugars." Dr. McCarthy stares at me, and I shrug. "I like to do research."

He seems to take my answer with pride and continues, "Until we can be certain her blood sugar is staying in range with the glucose monitor, I don't want her driving. Her levels are unstable, and they really shouldn't be, since her body has reacted to the insulin perfectly fine. I think it's her."

The longer Dr. McCarthy talks, the higher my blood pressure goes.

Part of me wonders if he can see my pulse beating against my neck. He's probably about to call some code so the nice people in the white coats will pick me up and lock me in the psych unit for my near panic attack from being in a hospital.

He steps forward and pats Emory on the shoulder after looking at me for a second too long, in my opinion. "See what you can do. I've always been a big advocate for listening to my patients, but their safety is my number one priority."

Emory nods and dials his parents as soon as Dr. McCarthy walks away. I escape into Taytum's room—anything to put me farther away from the annoying reminders that there are numerous patients hooked up to machines keeping them alive.

The door shuts quietly behind me, and I stop just as it hits me in the back. Seeing her, even in a hospital bed, cools the sweat trailing down my back.

I'll blame it on the rush from practice, but it's very clear that it's due to the anxiety of being here. I'm like this every time I come to a hospital, and every time, I deny it until I'm blue in the face.

Taytum's blonde hair lays in waves around her face, and I drop my eyes to her wrist, seeing the scrunchie there. She must have pulled it down in the midst of being wheeled up here, since she was clearly at practice if her tight, pink leotard has anything to say about it. Her ballet shoes are thrown onto the floor, and I smirk at the hospital gown that is bundled up beside the worn pair.

Refusing to wear a hospital gown is typical Taytum behavior.

"I know you're not asleep," I say, walking closer to her bed.

The faint beeping of the machine she's hooked up to pulls my attention just as Emory opens the door and stomps into the room.

"Shh." I put my hand up. "She's asleep."

I'll throw you a bone, Tay.

She may act like she hates me, but she can't deny that I have her back from time to time.

"Mom," Emory lowers his voice. "Taytum is sleeping right now, but I'll lower the volume and put you on speaker because Ford is in here. He can probably help."

I shoot Emory a look because he knows I hate it when he puts me in this position, mainly because he knows I'll do anything his parents ask of me.

I owe them, even if they refuse to acknowledge it.

"Hi, Ford."

I lean toward Emory's phone. "Hey, Ma."

I have two mother figures in my life: my Aunt Jo, who I call Mom, and then Emory and Taytum's mom, who I call Ma most of the time. Neither one signed up to mother me but they both rose to the occasion anyway, and I know it hasn't always been easy.

"Okay, boys. We are gonna need your help," Mary-Ann says. "Since Dr. McCarthy doesn't want Taytum to drive, you may need to step up."

"We can do that," I discreetly look past the phone and notice the tiniest crevice in between Taytum's eyebrows. I knew she was awake.

"And we need to talk her into the glucose monitoring system. It will automatically track her sugar."

"Maybe then she'll take it more seriously if she knows she can't lie about it," Emory grumbles.

Mary-Ann sighs through the phone. "Emory, have some compassion. This whole thing is a learning curve, and her life has been turned upside down."

The memory of Taytum in the hospital this summer still makes my heart finicky. I blame it on the fact that hospitals are a trigger to me, but that isn't the only reason I get sick to my stomach with the thought.

I take my hand and rub it over my face as Mary-Ann continues on with our new *job*. "She simply cannot drive right now, and I want you to watch her at dance practice when you can..." There's a pause. "Just in case."

Oh, she'll just love that.

The beeping noise that's been faint since the moment I stepped into the hospital room is gaining more traction. I flick my attention past the little divot carved into Taytum's forehead and watch her heart rate join the party. I creep toward the machine and put my back to it. In an attempt to de-escalate the rising tension and Taytum's distress, I crack a joke.

"I can quit hockey and take up dancing. I'll twirl beside Taytum and be the star of the show. That way, I can keep an extra-close eye on her."

Emory rolls his eyes and ignores me–per usual–but the worry line in between Taytum's closed eyes smooths.

Mary-Ann laughs quietly, but then she starts back up again. "Part of me wants to try to convince her to move home for a while. I'm sure the school would understand and put a pause on her scholarship."

The beeping behind my back fires up, and I count backward in my head. 3, 2, 1...

"That is completely unnecessary!"

I turn my head and can't help my smirk.

Taytum is in all her glory, commanding the room with her angry little scowl and flushed cheeks.

I won't admit it out loud, but it's highly amusing.

[3]

TAYTUM

ONE LOOK at my brother from across the room, and my pulse is hovering somewhere in between threatening and deadly.

"You don't get an opinion in this discussion." Emory, who takes up nearly the entire doorway with his wide shoulders and haughty chest, rolls his eyes.

"Excuse me?" I shriek.

I glance at Ford when I hear a chuckle. We make eye contact, and he raises an eyebrow, angling his body slightly before tipping his chin to the machine I'm hooked up to. I can read Ford's mind like it's my own at the moment. *Right, calm down.* If my blood pressure rises and causes some crazy alert on the monitor, everyone will come rushing into my room, and I'm already feeling suffocated.

"Honey, I agree. You're being stubborn, and you make poor decisions. Not to mention, you're still learning about this disease. We all are."

If I were a child, I'd cross my arms and stand up to

stomp my foot just to get my point across. But I'm in my twenties, which is all the more reason why I *should* get a say in the matter.

I hold my hand out, and Emory sighs before walking over and placing the phone in my palm.

"Mom—" I start, but she cuts me off right away.

"No, Taytum." There's instantly a pain in between my breastbone from the concern in her voice. The only sound in the room is the incessant heart monitor behind Ford. "I will not lose you to your own defiance."

"You're not going to lose me. I know my own body," I try to reassure her. "I'm not moving home. I'm fine—"

"You are not fine, Taytum Elizabeth Olson!"

The sound of Ford rubbing his hand against the scruff of his face draws my attention, and I know he agrees, just like my brother. I also know that neither of them will back me up if I refuse to let them drive me around campus like I'm some damsel in distress or watch my every move like I'm a felon trying to escape prison.

It's always them against me.

Always.

"Mom, I don't need the glucose mon—"

The door opens, and in walks Dr. McCarthy with his white coat flying behind him like a superhero's cape.

"What's the verdict?" he asks, ping-ponging his attention around the room. He lands on me, and his mouth immediately turns into a frown.

"I don't want to be watched like a lab rat, and I don't want some monitor placed on me like I'm being tracked. I won't allow this disease to rule my life like this." I'm unable to hold back the snip in my voice. I've been on edge since being diagnosed, and it bothers me to no end that everyone else is on edge too—because of me.

"I see," Dr. McCarthy says, taking a seat on my bed.

Ford clears his throat, and we make eye contact again. His blue eyes widen, and his jaw muscles flicker with a hidden message. My heart is beginning to jump all over the place, and if I don't agree to the stipulations that are being laid out for me, then it's going to be an uphill battle on top of the already demanding battle with my diabetes.

"Let me explain this to you," Dr. McCarthy starts. "If you don't get this under control, those organs that were impacted last summer when you were first diagnosed will continue to be impacted. Today was a high-blood-sugar episode, but last week was a low-blood-sugar episode while you were driving. You have to see how dangerous that could have been for you and others."

I do. Of course I do.

Emory intervenes—as if my brother's hostility regarding my health is going to help matters. "That means you'll die or kill someone else."

"Yes, thank you for clearing that up for me," I snap, flinging myself back onto the hospital bed.

Ford turns his back to our conversation and starts to stare at the machine keeping track of my heart rate. He puts his hand on the top, and from my position on the bed, I can see the furrowing of his facial features, as if he somehow wants to reach inside the device and control the beeping.

"He's right, Taytum," Dr. McCarthy adds. "It is necessary for you to wear the monitor so we can be certain that the insulin is the right type for your diabetes. Once it's stable, then we can move on to a pump."

A pump? *No way.*

I hate this.

I hate being the center of attention.

I hate that everyone is worried about me, as if I'm

purposefully crying out for help. But it's not me. It's the wonky, weakened organ inside my body.

"If you don't agree to this, we're moving you home." I stare at the phone in my lap like it's the devil. My heart pounds, and my entire body heats.

"She'll wear it." We all turn toward Ford, but he's looking at me. "Right, Taytum?"

He knows me too well, and I hate it. It's either move home or wear the monitor, so of course I'm going to wear the monitor.

Emory is staring at me with his eyebrows raised, and my mother is silent on the other end of the phone.

I look to Dr. McCarthy. "Yeah," I say.

Dr. McCarthy stands up and peers down at me on the bed. "No driving, even with the continuous blood sugar reading. Moving home won't benefit you, though. You've gotta come to terms with this sooner or later."

Relief settles my heart rate right away, but it's followed by frustration. I have come to terms with it. That doesn't mean I have to like it or flip over backward when someone snaps their fingers at me.

Emory steps forward. "We have it worked out, then. Ford and I will make sure she doesn't drive, and we will have someone close by at all times until we know that we can trust her."

"Trust me?" I fly upright and glare at my brother. "You act like I'm–"

"Taytum." I jerk my attention to the phone mid-sentence. My dad is the silent type, only speaking up when necessary. "The last thing we want is for you to give up graduating, lose your scholarship, and move back home. You're absolutely right. No one wants a disease like this to control them in the way it's controlling you, so please just promise us that you'll take care of yourself."

I slink back onto the bed and slowly hinge my jaw back together. My lips close, and I'm quieter than a mouse. Dr. McCarthy takes the phone from my lap and moves closer to the door to speak into it. My brother follows and listens intently.

My fingers fiddle with one another in my lap, and I remain silent. Last summer, the doctors said my body was resilient for keeping up with the demands of insulin production for as long as it did, but all I want is to go back to before—when I wasn't under everybody's watchful eye, and constantly worrying about my sugar levels, and secretly injecting insulin into my body.

I thought it would get better when I came back to Bexley U this fall and could figure out how to live with this disease on my own, but I still find myself full of frustration and dissatisfaction. Everyone is just as concerned as they were before, and Emory and Ford's reins have only gotten tighter. They view me as their helpless little sister, creating some gigantic protective bubble around me that they love to inflate. I swear they get off on shunning me from parties and directing any potential guy to the blonde across the room instead, because they think I don't need the distraction right now with everything else going on.

I grit my teeth at the thought of what they used to do in high school when I had a date. And for what reason back then? Did they think a little kissing or dick was going to kill me?

Someone clears their throat, and I snap back to reality. Ford's blue eyes flare when he gestures behind him. I look at the monitor and see my pulse rising. He has somehow silenced the volume, and Dr. McCarthy is too involved in the conversation with my parents to notice.

"Calm down," Ford mouths.

I glare at him because, as always, he's trying to come to my rescue. I don't care if it's needed at the moment or that I follow his hand movements regardless. He puts up one finger at a time for me to count, and I do it, despite my annoyance. *One, two, three, four...*

"There you go," he whispers. "You know the drill, Heartbreaker." He grins, and I hate that my first instinct is to smile. The nickname started in high school, when I learned how to get around my brother's and Ford's tactics of scaring off anyone interested in me.

I was the one who broke boys' hearts. Not the other way around.

Hidden flirting and secret make-out sessions in closets at parties that always led to nothing, leaving each and every horny teenage boy with a broken heart full of hope.

Guys always want what they can't have, and even though, most of the time, I wanted them too, I knew it'd never fly. It only attracted them more.

"Well, that does it, then." Dr. McCarthy is suddenly standing at the end of my bed. "I'll have a nurse draw up the discharge papers, and I'll send the script to the pharmacy. I want access to your glucose levels at our next appointment and then we will go from there."

Dr. McCarthy gives me zero chance for rebuttal.

As soon as he leaves, Ford steps forward and smiles.

"Your chauffeurs are here and at your service, Heartbreaker. And we expect a tip."

I roll my eyes and wonder how expensive it would be to hire my own personal driver instead.

[4]

FORD

THE VELCRO of my bowtie draws my teammates' attention over to me, which I'll admit, I enjoy. Theo stares at me from across the locker room in nothing but a towel.

"What?" I say.

"What the hell are you wearing?"

I pull the white glove onto my hand and wiggle my fingers before leaning down into my locker and pulling the chauffeur's hat out of my bag and placing it on my damp hair.

"For fuck's sake," Emory mumbles, coming to a complete stop. "You're ridiculous."

I grin while running my hands over my black suit. "You don't think Taytum will appreciate it?"

I know for a fact she's going to be beyond irritated with me, which is the only reason I ordered the costume in the first place. In fact, we weren't even out of the hospital yet, and I already had it on the way.

Emory snorts. "I think she's going to punch you in the face."

I grab my bag. "She will threaten it, as always, but she wouldn't dare touch this masterpiece."

The number of threats I've gotten from Taytum over the years is enough to fill every page of a textbook. They no longer faze me, just like it doesn't faze me when guys try to take her into one of the bedrooms at a party and I have to step in and threaten to cut their hands off.

When I pull up to the sorority house, I catch a glimpse into the window, expecting to see Taytum, but instead, I'm met with a cluster of freshies with flushed faces. I chuckle and step out of my car. They duck, as if I didn't just make eye contact with them, and I laugh under my breath while making my way to the porch. The front door opens, and it takes Taytum all of three seconds to slam it in my face.

"Ma'am, I heard you called for a driver!" I shout through the door.

"You think you're hilarious, don't you?" she calls from the other side. There's a hint of humor in her voice, and I hate that I crave the sound of her laugh.

"I know I'm hilarious," I say. "Now, let's go."

"I'm not going with you until you change out of that stupid outfit."

My lip twitches. "Fine."

I strip down to my boxers but keep the black hat on. The cold breeze whisks against my exposed skin, and goosebumps crawl over my chest. I look over to the window and wink at the younger sorority sisters. There's a lot of attention that comes with playing on Bexley U's hockey team, so I'm used to it. Though most of my teammates hate it, I don't. It makes life fun and the parties much more interesting.

The door opens, and Taytum's sugary scent wafts around her, alongside her fury. "Ford!"

I shrug sheepishly. "What?"

"Keep your clothes on! No one wants to see you naked."

Taytum bends down and bundles my chauffeur costume in her hands before shoving it into my chest. I put my hand over hers and hold it there while she pushes it into me harder. "Everyone is enjoying the view." I lean extra close to her and brush my mouth against her ear. "Even you."

She pulls away and storms past me. My laughter follows her swaying hips, and before long, we're on the way to her practice with Taytum sending me a death glare every few seconds from the passenger seat.

"Will you stop?" I finally ask.

"Stop what?" Her arms are crossed over her coat, and the flash of her icy blue eyes matches the beanie she's wearing. She turns away almost as quickly as she turns toward me.

I reach over and flick the fuzzy ball on top of her beanie. "Being negative about all of this. Don't you enjoy spending time with me?"

Taytum closes her eyes and sighs deeply. "I'm not being negative, and no, I do not enjoy spending time with you. Especially when you're driving me to practice without clothes on."

What a liar. Everyone enjoys seeing me without clothes on.

Taytum pulls her phone out and starts texting someone to avoid me. I can't help but ask who it is. "Who ya texting?"

I mimic her the second she opens her mouth. "*None of your business.*"

She flashes me those blue eyes again, and I smile. I can

usually pull a little smirk from her in return, but I come up empty handed. She's on edge today, and that's always a trigger for me because she's either truly upset or she's hiding something. Between me and Emory, we keep close tabs on her. I usually know her next move before she does.

"What's up?" I take the playfulness out of my voice so she knows I'm done messing around. "Talk to me, Heartbreaker."

She scoffs again and turns toward the window. Her chest heaves with an exasperated sigh in her attempt to avoid me, and as soon as we pull up to the auditorium, she hurriedly starts to gather her things to rush out of my car. Practice isn't for another seven minutes, so now I'm fully invested in what's got her so cagey.

When her phone vibrates, both of our eyes fall to it. I'm always one step ahead of her, so I snatch it before she does. I happily chuckle with my victory, but my smile quickly falls when I read the screen.

"What the hell is this all about?" I trap the phone against my chest when she tries to reach for it. Her cheeks match the pink of her lips, but the embarrassment doesn't stop her from climbing over the center console to claw at my hand. I grip the phone so hard it starts to creak beneath my fingers. "Taytum. You can't be serious."

"Do not start with me, Ford Collins." Taytum throws herself back into the seat, and it's high school all over again. She wants to hide behind anger, but there's a million other emotions backing the bite in her voice. My best friend's little sister is the only girl I have ever let myself get close to. I forced myself to move beyond her beautiful features and killer body years ago and learned what's on the inside. I can read her pretty damn well, whether she wants to admit it or not.

I grip the steering wheel while re-reading the messages between her and Claire.

> Claire: What? You've disappeared with plenty of guys at parties.

> Taytum: Disappeared. Yes. Fooled around with? Dated? Nada.

> Claire: Tay, you command a room the moment you walk into it. Your confidence seeps into others. You don't need help dating or having the occasional one-night fling. You could have any guy you want.

> Taytum: I do need help! I've never even been on a real date, and now I have this god awful glucose monitor stuck to my body like an extra limb. No guy wants to deal with that while they fuck me.

> Claire: Oh, come on! That is not true. And what about Tommy?

> Taytum: You mean the guy Emory and Ford paid to take me to prom my senior year? That doesn't count as a date.

I hold back a laugh at the memory. He may or may not have been into guys, but to our advantage, it was unconfirmed at the time, and he was more than happy to step in and take Taytum to prom. I'll admit that it was only because he was trying to prove something to his asshole father, but nonetheless.

> Claire: THEY PAID HIM?

Taytum snatches the phone out of my hand when she notices that I'm distracted, and I bite my tongue to hold in my laughter. "We didn't pay him. You're so dramatic."

Taytum's hot breath fills my entire car. She might as well have fire flying from her mouth like a dragon. I can feel her wrath wrap around my throat like she's seconds from choking me. "I'm dramatic? Are you freaking kidding me?"

"Hey," I try to even my tone. "Calm down. Don't get all worked up and throw your body out of sync. Stress plays a part in raising your blood sugar, in case you didn't know. Your parents will kill me if I'm the reason it spikes."

Taytum throws her hands up in frustration. "Good! Then maybe I can finally get a boyfriend and live my life without you interfering." She pauses dramatically. "Actually, it doesn't matter. No one is going to want to date me with this thing on my skin anyway!" Taytum gestures to her arm that's covered by her coat, and I roll my eyes.

"No one is stopping you from getting a boyfriend."

Taytum snaps her head over to me, but I refuse to look at her because we both know that isn't true.

"Oh, really?" The winter breeze cools the heated car when she pushes open the door with force and steps outside. "Then prove it."

"What do you mean, 'prove it'?" I am not falling for her little tricks.

Taytum leans back into the car with her hand still on the door handle. I've seen this look before, and it usually means she has some wild plan brewing. Her cheeks ripen with heat, and it's the same pinkish hue she has on her face when she tries to run off with some loser at a party, just to spite me. And the little twinkle in her eye is the same bright gleam she had the night she lost her virginity without me knowing. When I found out, the twinkle intensified to a full-on glow.

That was the moment I learned that Taytum loves irritating me just as much as I love irritating her.

"Don't interfere tonight."

My heart skips a beat, and it pisses me off. "What the hell is tonight?" I ask.

Taytum smiles like a devil in red and disappears from my sight.

Not so fast.

I open my door and stand up with one foot still in the car. I watch her skip up the stairs to the auditorium with her dance bag in hand. I reach down and blow the horn to get her attention. She freezes.

"What do you have planned, Heartbreaker?" I shout.

She peeks over her shoulder. "You'll just have to see."

I fully step out of my car, with my costume in hand. I start to get dressed, and her lips purse with annoyance. "You know what, I think I'll stay for your dance practice today."

I really need to go to my study group if I want to ace chemistry, but annoying Taytum further takes precedence every single time. Her glare fuels me like gasoline on a fire, and I can't help but poke her a little more.

She picks up her pace, but it's no use. I know my way around the auditorium. My smirk deepens when I step in line with her to march down the hall. "Tell me what you're up to, and I'll leave."

"No! Go away," she snaps.

"That's not a very nice tone you're using with me."

Taytum stops with her hand on the auditorium door handle. She spins so quickly the fuzzy ball on top of her hat bounces. "You know what's not nice? The fact that you steal my phone, and read my messages, and butt into every part of my life. Or when you swoop in and stop me from having any fun at a party. Or when you and Emory ban together and threaten any guy from talking to me." Taytum turns away in a fury, and strangely enough, I feel wounded. I decide to let her stomp away in anger and slip into the back of the auditorium in silence. When their rehearsal has started, I discreetly text her brother.

> Me: Is there a party tonight or something?

> Emory: Yeah. Rush invited a bunch of people over to gear up for their championship game.

> Me: We're going.

TAYTUM

"What's gotten into you tonight? You're being awfully quiet."

I meet Claire's gaze in the mirror but quickly look away and continue to apply my favorite color lipstick–Fuck Me Pink, which seems fitting.

"Taytum," Claire repeats. "I already yelled at you for hiding your diabetes from me. Don't hide something else."

Her hands land on my shoulders, and she spins me so she can get a good look at my face. She squints and steals the lipstick from my tight grip. "Is this about what we were texting about?"

I sigh and flip back around to run my fingers through my blonde waves before puckering my lips that will likely get zero action tonight. How do you tell someone, even your very compassionate best friend, that you're obsessing over something so irrationally childish? Or is it irrationally childish?

Something Dr. McCarthy said to me struck a chord, and it's been a constant loop in my head.

You've gotta come to terms with this sooner or later.

Sure, he's right. I have diabetes, and it will never go away. It's frustrating that a completely uncontrollable disease is controlling my life to the extent that it is. However, that doesn't mean I can't control the other things in my life that *are* controllable. Like dating and having fun at a party with some guy, locked away in a bedroom, or doing everything humanly possible to act like a normal college student with a stupid monitor on her arm and an overbearing big brother and his sidekick.

Every aspect of my life is closely monitored. Between my parents checking in on my levels, having to report back to Dr. McCarthy, and Ford and Emory obsessing over their teammates wanting to date me, it feels like I hardly have any control.

When you're touched with the kiss of death, it changes your perspective on things. Like letting your older brother determine who's good enough for you.

Spoiler alert: according to him, no one is.

"Just forget it. I was being stupid," I say, stealing my lipstick back. I slide it into the back pocket of my best jeans and grab her hand to pull her out of The Bex's bathroom so we can avoid the conversation, but she puts on the brakes and stops us both.

She raises an eyebrow at me. "I wouldn't be a good friend if I let you walk out of this bathroom like that."

I look at my outfit.

Hot jeans, *check.*

Tight shirt that shows off a sliver of midriff but hides the glucose monitor on my arm, *check.*

Regular shoes instead of my ballet slippers, *check.*

My shoulders slump. "I thought I looked good."

She laughs. "You always look good, and you always have your game face on, which is why I'm confused about what you were telling me earlier. Where's the girl who walks past the entire hockey team with her head held high, bleeding confidence?"

Claire spins me to look at myself in the mirror, and then her face pops up behind my shoulder. "I remember not too long ago when we were in this exact bathroom, and you were making me walk through a cloud of perfume, all while telling me how hot I was. You've always been my number one cheerleader, and you've always been there for me. Now let me do the same for you."

I hesitate for a second, but she's right. If there's anyone I can tell this to, it's her.

"I'm just sick of pleasing everyone."

Claire nods. "I know the feeling. Do I need to remind you of Chad?"

I fake gag. "We do not speak that traitor's name in this precious space."

Claire briefly looks around The Bex's bathroom and laughs softly. Charcoal-colored walls with chalk sayings surround us. There's even a little scripture from yours truly that says, *If someone doesn't like you, it's because they have bad taste.*

"I'm going to go crazy if I don't do something," I admit, feeling myself get worked up. "I feel suffocated! And frustrated!" I pause and suck in a few fast breaths. "Maybe I'm sexually frustrated. I don't know! But I'm sick of bending over backward to please everyone else. I'm wearing the stupid monitor, I'm injecting myself over and over again with insulin, but for fuck's sake, I don't want to die a virgin!"

Claire's face switches from concern to shock to amusement in three seconds flat. "What?!" She laughs. "You won't die a virgin...mainly because you're not a virgin."

"I might as well be! Do you know the last time I had sex or even snuck off with a guy without doing it *just* to piss the guys off?" I'm spiraling. The room spins, and my heart is jittery. I shut my eyes and breathe out through my nose because, for once, this isn't my blood sugar tripping out.

"Take a breath. We've got this." Claire squeezes my hands.

I force my eyes open, and she's smiling.

"Screw pissing Ford and your brother off. We're leaving them out of the equation. You're going to find someone tonight, and you're going to fool around with them, steal back your control and some confidence. You're the hottest girl I know, even with diabetes. If anyone can pull off a glucose monitor, it's you."

I snort out a laugh.

"Stop it. I'm serious." Claire spins me around and makes me look at myself in the mirror. Her heart-shaped face is beside mine, resting on my shoulder. Our wavy hair mixes together, mine the color of the sun and hers as warm as cinnamon. "I don't know when I became your hype girl instead of the other way around, but tonight...we're both getting laid."

I flatten my lips. "That's easy for you to say. You have a boyfriend."

All I have is an overprotective big brother and *Ford*.

"Do you know what having a boyfriend means?" she asks.

I answer right away. "Unlimited sex with the captain of the hockey team?"

Claire's smile grows bigger. "A wingman. We're going to

make it our mission to get you laid. And that doesn't mean finding you someone...because you can do that all on your own. I've never seen someone flirt the way you do."

I smile. It's true. I've had my fair share of flirting.

It's just what comes after that I'm lacking.

"Theo and I will distract Emory long enough so you can sneak away without him following you like a shadow."

"Don't forget about Ford. He's just as bad." If not worse.

Every guy on the hockey team, and mostly everyone who hangs out at the football house, knows that I'm off-limits. Emory has made it his life's mission to decide who's good enough for me, and his threats carry a lot of heat, considering he's one of the best hockey goalies in the nation.

The only difference between now and the past is, all Emory has to do is look in someone's direction, and they'll back off. When he and Ford ruled the halls of our high school, they spread every rumor possible to keep me single forever.

They even went as far as telling everyone I had a rare disorder that would cause me to die if I had an orgasm. When challenged by the captain of the football team, Ford took it upon himself to mock up a fake medical article explaining the disorder and printed it out for "educational purposes." The rumor stood that whoever made me orgasm and killed me would be charged for murder.

They say I should be thankful they've stopped telling people that.

I say I should murder them instead.

"So?" Claire asks. "What do you think?"

I grin. "I think we're both going to get laid tonight."

[6]

FORD

"They say a man who can dance is also good in bed." I send the blonde I'm dancing with a flirty smile. She laughs like a hyena, and I feel my smile slide off my face but decide to overlook the obnoxious giggle and swing her around again. The country song is on full blast, and I wish I had my cowboy hat to drive the point further, but nonetheless, I've been swaying this girl off her feet for the last hour with my sudden Southern accent.

Everyone says it comes out when I've had too much to drink, but I'm not drunk.

I'm tipsy.

There's a difference.

"Quit while you're ahead." Aasher, our co-captain, pulls the drink out of my hand, and I stop mid-twirl. The blonde stumbles, but I catch her around the waist.

"Party foul," I say, hauling her upright. "Give me my drink back."

"We have conditioning tomorrow morning. You show up hungover, and Coach will punish all of us."

"He's right." Theo is standing behind Aasher with his arms crossed. You'd think after he made it official with Claire, he'd be less uptight about the season, but nope. He's even worse.

"Calm down, Daddy," I quip.

Theo's cheeks redden, and his jaw flexes, but then he visibly relaxes when a football player snatches the blonde from my arms.

"She's not a toy," I state.

The hyena-soundalike seems unbothered that she's now dancing with a six-foot-four center, but I still step forward, prepared to give him shit. My mouth opens but closes a second later when I spot Emory moving through the party on a mission.

I know that stance.

His wide shoulders are tight, and his fists are pumped full of blood. If he wasn't wearing a shirt, he'd be showing off every tense muscle along his spine with how rigid he is.

Taytum, Taytum, Taytum.

I knew she was up to something.

"What's going on over here?" I ask, stepping in line with my best friend. The party is lively behind us, but I block it out the second I see Taytum standing beside our captain's girlfriend.

Her hip is popped, and her features are highlighting every ounce of sass. Sometimes I want to take my thumb and smear the pink lipstick off her lips so no one else's eyes are drawn to her mouth.

"Back off, Emory," she snarls.

"Why are you even here?" Emory asks. "Do you really

think it's wise to be at a wild party right now? Go rest or something."

"Wild?" Claire asks innocently. She peeks behind Emory with a furrowed brow and checks out the party. It's a little congested, but it's not at the part of the night where bras are hanging from the ceiling fan or anything.

I elbow him. "I'm with her. This isn't anywhere near wild, bro."

He sends me a glare, and I zip my lips. Not the time for disagreeing. Got it.

I turn toward Taytum. "That's not to say I'm not siding with your brother." Why does she have to look so good? All the time, too. She's always so damn appealing. "You should leave."

"And rest?" she asks, looking at us both like we're completey crazy. "Just because I have diabetes doesn't mean I need to rest, you idiots."

I know that.

Emory does too.

"I'm not leaving, and neither of you are going to inter-fere with my plans for tonight. Got it? I am *sick* of it."

Taytum's gaze skims past her brother, and our eyes meet. There is a subtle raise to her eyebrow, like she's chal-lenging me, and it's clear that this is what she was referring to earlier.

Emory shakes his head. "Not a chance. Do we need to start up our usual tactics again? Because now, more than ever, it's needed. What happens when you're locked away in some room with a loser and your blood sugar drops? Huh?"

Taytum's nostrils flare with anger. "Then it'll freaking alert me on my phone! Remember this little gadget that everyone forced me into wearing?" She goes to move her sleeve, but I step in between her and her brother to try and soften things. I press on Emory's chest. "Let her have some fun."

I lean in closer to Emory and block Taytum from reading my lips. "You know I always keep an eye on her. I never let it go too far." Mainly because the thought of someone touching her sends me straight to the deep end. As if I'd let some guy leave this party with her scent on his fingers...or worse...his *dick*.

Emory growls before turning and stomping through the party. He grabs the redhead that's been eyeing him the entire party and disappears upstairs.

I look at Taytum. "You're welcome."

She rolls her pretty blue eyes and looks at Claire, who is pressed up against Theo. She and Taytum have some sort of silent conversation that we're *obviously* not invited to.

"Let's dance."

I don't wait for Taytum to decline my offer. My hand finds her wrist, and I pull her onto the makeshift dance floor. Her hips are snug in my grip, and she puts her arms around my neck, clawing me lightly with her nails.

"I'm not stupid." She peers at me through her thick eyelashes. "You can play nice all you want, but I know the second I get close to some guy, you'll swoop in with some ridiculous excuse and send him packin'."

I play dumb. "Ridiculous excuse? When have I ever done that?"

Taytum scowls after I spin her around and crush her to my chest. She immediately starts to list my most-used excuses. "Let's see...there was the time you stormed into the room and told me that my dog died. Then, there's the one where you said there's a warrant out for my arrest. Um, you've used the boyfriend one many times." Taytum clears her throat, and I hold back a laugh when she deepens it to sound like me. "*Sorry, man. She has a boyfriend.*" She slips back into herself for a moment. "Who has never even existed!" Then she clears her throat again. "*And he's on his way up here.*"

All I can manage to say is, "I do not sound like that."

Taytum glares at me and tries to turn away. Instead of letting her go, I grip her hips a little tighter and keep her in place.

"Oh, come on. It's funny."

"It's not funny!" she hisses between her perfectly straight teeth. "Do you know what it's like to be me and have this unyielding responsibility to keep everyone happy and stay on top of my sugar and insulin? I'm expected to do what I'm told at all times, no questions asked. God forbid I make a decision for myself. And you and Emory are even worse! You two destroy any little bit of fun I try to have. I'm going to die alone because of you guys. And who knows! It might be sooner than we think."

Taytum started off her little rant with anger backing her words, but it went south *real* quick. She stops moving her feet and shoves my hands off her waist. Her pink, plump bottom lip folds in behind her front teeth, and the gloss of her eyes catches the bright disco light off in the corner of the room.

For once, I'm speechless.

Is she...crying?

In the midst of panic, I'm met with her back as she charges through the party and disappears into the fog of rowdy college students. My first thought is to chase after her, but I stop myself because what am I going to do to make things better? Allow her to drink and fuck up her sugar?

Watch her take off with some guy to lose herself for a little while?

Neither of those options do anything for my sudden irritation.

But seeing her upset doesn't do anything for it either.

[7]

TAYTUM

THE PARTY IS full of hot potential, but as usual, I've run off to be alone. Most of the time, I think everyone assumes I've disappeared into one of the bedrooms with some guy, but nine times out of ten, I'm alone.

There's a knock on the door, and I sigh.

I wonder who that could be.

I turn toward the noise. "Go away, Ford."

There's a raspy chuckle that follows my demand, and I immediately know it's not Ford. "It isn't Ford."

I slip in between the mismatched couches in the room and head toward the voice. The media room is usually off-limits but Rush, who's the captain of the football team and doubles as the rule-maker for these parties, has a soft spot for me and allows me to come in here. But only because his younger sister is in my sorority, and he knows I watch out for her.

I watch out for all the girls, though. We have no room

for mean girls in our sorority—only built-in besties and mentors.

"Rush?" I ask.

I reach for the doorknob but refuse to open it until I know who's on the other side.

"No. Cruz." He says his name like I should know him. After my silence, he adds, "If you open the door, I think you'll recognize me."

Taking the bait, I turn the doorknob, half expecting to see Ford holding someone hostage there to get me to open the door, but I'm wrong, and Cruz is right. I do recognize him. But I pretend like I don't because he obviously has a chip on his shoulder.

"Sorry, I don't know who you are." I move to slam the door, but he stops it with his hand and gives me a look. His lip hitches, and it's the same hot grin he gave me in the hospital days ago.

"You are the most stubborn person I have ever met," he says.

A quick laugh escapes me and causes me to drop my hand. I let him in the room and notice right away that he leaves the door cracked.

"What are you doing at some college party?" I ask.

My arms cross against my chest, but I drop them abruptly when it hits me.

"Oh my god. Did my brother ask you to follow me around?" I throw my hands up in frustration and start to pace the media room. "He did, didn't he? Just in case I faint or my blood sugar gets out of sync, right?" I kick a pillow out of my way and mumble under my breath. "This is getting out of hand. Having some EMT follow me around." I turn. "Was this Dr. McCarthy's idea?"

Cruz grips me by the waist, his fingers pressing into my

bare skin right below my shirt. It's very clear to me that he isn't wearing medical gloves like in the hospital, because my flesh burns beneath his touch. "Calm down. No one asked me to follow you." He chuckles under his breath, and I drop my gaze to his mouth.

"Then what are you doing here?"

He moves his hands after a few long breaths and puts some space between us. "What? An EMT can't just come hang out at a college party?"

I raise an eyebrow because...no.

He laughs quietly, and I'm not going to deny it–Cruz has a very attractive charisma about him. "I'm Rush's brother. I told him I'd stop by for a few and wish him luck for the game this weekend."

"You're Rush's brother?" I ask, watching him take a seat on the leather couch. He looks so different from the other day when he was wheeling me through the hospital. Don't get me wrong, I noticed that he was attractive right away, but there's something thrilling about seeing him in dark jeans, a black hoodie, and messy hair.

He cracks his fingers and eyes me from across the room. "Why are you looking at me like that?"

I blink past my embarrassment. "Well, before now, I thought you were just some rando that showed up at a college party."

He laughs again. "I go to Bexley U."

"You're a student here?"

Cruz nods. "Yeah. I'm finishing my BA in science and then applying for med school."

I open my mouth, but nothing comes out. *That's... impressive?* I walk over and sit on the other side of the couch with just enough space between us for it to be noticeable. "So, you go to Bexley U, and you are an EMT on the side? Plus you're applying for med school?"

He has a cocky smile. "Impressed?"

I snort. *Yes.* "Not even a little bit."

Cruz throws his head back and laughs loudly. "You'd fit right in with my family."

"What does that mean?" I pull my hair off to the side, and Cruz glances at the side of my neck for a second too long. He shifts his eyes away, and a rush of heat kisses my cheeks.

"I don't play football, so naturally, my parents aren't impressed."

I turn toward him. "Wait, what? Are you kidding?"

He looks away. "Change of subject, Stubborn One. What are you doing up here all alone?"

"What are you doing following me?" I counter.

I watch him smile from the side. He leans back and puts his arm on top of the couch. It looks like an invitation, but I'm pretty sure I'm just making things up in my head because I'm so desperate for this to turn into something that it's not.

"Do you want my honest answer?" he asks.

My pulse jumps. "If you say you're here to make sure my glucose is okay, I swear to God..."

He furrows his brow. "I'm off duty. That's not why I followed you."

I eye him carefully. The room grows quiet, and the only thing I can hear is the pounding music below the floor.

"To be honest, I can't stop thinking about you."

My stomach nosedives.

"And then I show up at my brother's house, and there you are. You walked right past me, and I couldn't help it. I had to come talk to you."

What?

I'm tingly, and if I wasn't wearing my glucose monitor, I'd think my sugar was spiking.

"You can't stop thinking about me?" I whisper in disbelief. But then I mentally scold myself. *Of course he can't, you confident, pink-lipstick-wearing baddie.*

A sarcastic puff of breath falls from his mouth, and it almost touches my lips. "No. I can't. The second you sassed me in the ambulance, I was hooked."

"I don't believe you," I admit. "I think you saw me walking through the party and recognized me."

Cruz leans forward and pulls his phone out of his back pocket. He throws it at me, and I catch it with a cat-like reflex.

"Read them."

On the screen is a text conversation with someone named Linc.

> Linc: Go find her. What was her name? Ask Rush if he knows of her. He knows everyone.

> Cruz: Her name is Taytum, but you know I don't have time for a girlfriend. Med school is on the horizon.

> Linc: Who said you have to date her? Bang her and get her out of your system.

> Cruz: I'm not a dick who uses females like you.

Linc: I don't use them. I'm up front and tell them that I'm not looking for a girlfriend. Nine times out of ten, they're down. College girls wanna have fun. They aren't looking for anything serious either.

Cruz: So you mean they're dick hungry?

Linc: Fuck off. We're all just out here having fun. Maybe you should try it.

Cruz: She doesn't seem like a girl who'd be down for that.

Linc: Well then, have fun with your hand.

I click the phone off and hope I'm not wearing my emotions on my sleeve.

"See? Can't stop thinking about you."

Our eyes catch, and I suck my bottom lip into my mouth, trapping it beneath my teeth. *It's now or never.* If I allow myself to think about the risk of Ford or Emory charging in to ruin my night, like always, I'll never get laid again.

Ford is nowhere to be found.

Emory is off doing God knows what.

And this *was* my plan, right? To take back my confidence and make my own decisions?

"What if I am one of those girls?" My question is hardly above a whisper. The room crackles with the tensing of Cruz's jaw, and my stomach fills with courage.

"You're not," his voice is low.

"How do you know?"

Cruz leans forward and rests his elbows on top of his knees. I swear, the more time that passes, the hotter he gets.

It's his voice. It's right in the middle of poised and out of control. There's a slight rasp to it that I'm clinging to for dear life, and the prize is so close I can almost taste it. "'Cause I've asked around."

I decide to pull the trigger. "What would you say if I asked for one night and that was it?"

Cruz slowly sits up right and pushes his legs out in front of him. He pulls the denim on his thighs down a little, and if I didn't know any better, he's feeling just as antsy as I am. My pulse thrums, and it sends a little bit of life through my veins. *This is exciting.* There's something so enticing about doing something with a random guy without being pushed into doing it just to irritate my brother and Ford. There's something more to this moment, because for once, it's for me.

"Then I'd say okay, but–"

"No buts." I quickly stand up on two feet and make my way over to him.

Cruz's eyes burn with rebellion, and I'm more alive than I've ever felt. He raises an eyebrow, as if he's asking me what I'm waiting for, so I move in between his legs and straddle him on the leather couch.

The room spins when he grabs my waist, and then everything goes dark the second our mouths touch.

[8]

FORD

I'm bored.

The whiskey has worn off, and the hyena is back, trying to steal all my attention. I'm allowing it for now, but there's a nagging poke in the back of my head every time I let my mind wander.

There's a perfectly round peach rubbing against my dick, and it's softer than the week-old banana I found in the back of my locker the other day–which explained the rotting food smell that Coach was complaining about.

"Time to go," I say into the hyena's ear.

Unfortunately, she thinks she's coming with me, but there's only one girl I take home from each party, and she's usually kicking and screaming the entire time.

"Hey, Claire!" I shout from across the party. She's sitting on Theo's lap, happy as ever. They both look up, and I instantly pause at the look that flies across Claire's features. I move through the party with ease, dodging the dancing couples. I'm in front of my captain and his girl a few seconds later and ask, "Where is she?"

Claire sucks in her cheeks. "Who?"

Theo snorts behind her back.

"Bryant. Don't mess with me. Where is she?"

The nickname she was given by Theo makes her smile, but she quickly looks away and tries to dodge my question. "I don't know."

I lean to the left and make eye contact with Theo. He sends me a silent warning, and I laugh under my breath.

"Ah, I get it. She told you to keep me from finding her, huh?"

Claire shakes her head and continues to rub her fingers over Theo's knuckles.

My chest is tight, and I'm starting to sweat. Emory is going to kill me if she's getting rammed somewhere in this damn party, and Taytum is going to kill me when she finds out I lied to Claire to find her, but a guy has to do what a guy has to do.

"Well, her glucose monitor just dinged, and I want to make sure she takes her insulin. So where is she?"

Claire sits up a little taller and pushes her brown hair behind her ear. "How do you know that?"

I think fast on my feet, because I'm me. "Because I downloaded the app to my phone too." It's a blatant lie, but it's a good idea.

Her lips part. "Does *she* know that?"

The music switches to an upbeat song, and I glance around the party to see if I can catch a glimpse of her sunshiny hair. I'd call her, but I know she won't answer.

"Claire, where is she? I'm ready to go home, and I'm not leaving without her, especially if her sugar is out of sync."

Claire starts to nibble on her lip. "Claire, come on. For once, I'm being serious. Where is she?" It hurts to lie to her like this, but what she doesn't know won't hurt her.

"*For once,* being the key words," Theo jokes.

Claire pulls out her phone and shoots Taytum a text. "I really don't know, but I'll text her." She shows me the screen, and although Taytum might text her back and let her know which room she's hiding in, I'm not waiting.

I turn and walk over to the stairs and jog up them one by one. I nod to a couple of teammates, and they're lucky they're within my eyesight and not trying to pull one over on Emory by fucking his sister.

"Taytummmm," I sing, striding down the long hall. Most of the doors are shut with couples trapped behind them, but I know that Taytum is either in the media room, or she's climbed through Rush's window to sit on the roof and peer up at the stars—one of the many things she does that scares the shit out of me—which is precisely why she does it.

I slowly push on Rush's door, hearing the creak echo throughout the room. The window is shut.

Come on, Taytum.

I spot the media room across the hall, and the door is cracked.

Ready or not, Taytum. Come out, come out, wherever you are.

My phone vibrates, and I pull it out of my pocket.

> Emory: You got Taytum? Can you drive her home?

> Me: Yeah, I'll get her home. We're leaving in a second.

Whether she likes it or not.

I shove my phone back into my pocket and skip across the floor. My hand is on the door, ready to push it wider, but I freeze in place when I hear noises that better not be coming from her. I peek through the crack like a peeping Tom, and my mouth parts. I catch her blonde locks cascading down in between her stupidly hot top and some guy's head.

My brow furrows, and my mouth runs dry. *How dare she?*

I shake my head.

It's the same reaction every time I find her with someone. It's not often, but when I stumble into a room and she's being touched by some guy, it feels like they're taking something away that belongs to me. It's utterly insane, but I've never been able to control the debilitating fear of losing her, even though she isn't mine.

Not in that way, at least.

But right now, I can't help but think she is.

I press on the door slowly and clamp my jaw. There's a play-by-play inside my head of me rushing into the room, pulling her off this guy's lap, and punching his lights out. But instead, I make my movements unknown. There's no creaking of the door hinges, and my footsteps are stealthy.

Taytum is moving over him sensually as his hands roam over every perfect part of her body. There's fire in my veins, and the longer I watch him touch her curves, the hotter I burn. His mouth pulls from hers, and I raise an eyebrow, eager to hear what he has to say to her to get in her pants.

"You're fucking perfect," he whispers.

He's right. She is.

But he's still on my shit list.

Taytum is staring down at him, and unbeknownst to her, I'm standing right inside the threshold, watching with my arms crossed. My veins are bursting with something I refuse to name, and when he reaches up to pull her shirt off, I take a step forward.

Taytum straightens with unease, and I know exactly why.

"She doesn't want her shirt off," I snip.

And...there goes my cover.

Taytum's hot gasp flies through the room, but I can't stand to look at her flushed cheeks because I'm afraid it'll only piss me off more. If she knows I'm annoyed, she won't stop for anything.

"Ford! For fuck's sake. Leave!"

"Bro, whoa. It's called privacy." The shitbag looks familiar, but I can't pinpoint where I know him from. He peers back at the open door, but his hands are still on Taytum's waist, and I can't pull my glare away.

"It's time to go, Heartbreaker." I refuse to look her in the eye.

"I am not leaving." She is seething, and fuck if it doesn't turn me on a little.

"Who is this? Please don't tell me you have a boyfriend."

Taytum scoffs and throws her arms across her rising chest. "No. He's my brother."

The guy looks between the two of us, and I smirk. "I am *not* her brother."

Taytum drops her arms and places them on his shoulders. She scoots closer to him, and my chest constricts.

Is she trying to play games with me?

Because she'll lose.

"Rush said you were single, but I'm beginning to feel like I stepped into something I shouldn't have."

Well, he isn't an idiot. I'll give him that.

"He isn't my boyfriend," Taytum reiterates. "He's my brother's best friend, and they're both determined to ruin every bit of fun that I try to have."

I laugh. "You call *him* fun?"

Truth be told, there's nothing wrong with the guy. I've known worse, and he's obviously not a complete douche if he isn't mouthing off to me for interrupting his one night of bliss with Taytum, but still, he can fuck right off.

I step forward. "Let's go."

Taytum's chin tilts, and that's when I finally give in and meet her eye. It's a sucker punch right to my jaw. The apples of her cheeks are flushed with heat, and the pink lipstick is wiped clean from her swollen lips. There's a subtle gloss to her blue eyes, and I wonder what she'd look like after a good fuck.

Stop it.

"Let's go," I say again but this time with a little more of an edge to it.

Taytum shakes out her blonde hair, and I watch as the waves roll over her shoulders. She peers down at the guy with her doe-like eyes, a silent plea for him to keep going instead of listening to me.

The second her hips start moving over him, I see red.

I stomp over to her, lift her up by the waist, and haul her over my shoulder.

"I don't know who you are, but she's off-limits," I snap.

The guy stands up, quietly laughs, and walks out the door—all while Taytum is hitting my lower back and kicking her feet into my hard stomach.

"Thank God for these abs of steel, or that would actually hurt," I joke.

"I fucking hate you, Ford!"

"No, you don't," I counter, flexing my abs again. The number of times I've heard that exact line from her is astronomical, and yet, I've never seen her smile at anyone else the way she does at me.

Taytum hits me a few more times but eventually gives up. I prepare myself for a verbal scolding, per usual, but she says nothing.

In fact...is she breathing?

I quickly pull her upright and frantically look at her face to make sure she hasn't passed out. The second our eyes make contact, I lose my breath. Tears flood her eyes, and when one breaks the dam and tips over her thick eyelashes, I stop dead in my tracks. I drop my gaze to her quivering lip.

Shit.

I press her face into my chest, and my fingers disappear into the thick waves of her hair. "Hey, hey, hey. Stop."

Please.

Taytum shakes in my arms, and if she doesn't stop crying, I might start shaking too.

I can't take it.

I can't stand to see anyone cry.

I can't stand to see her cry.

My nose burns, and my throat closes. I grip her harder, hoping it'll give her enough support to pull it together so I don't have a fucking panic attack and add to the chaos.

My mind is reeling, so I think of the rink, the little black puck, the worn handle of my stick, and the cool ice beneath my skates. I shut my eyes and go to the one constant in my life that has never changed. *Hockey.*

I picture the last game I played and remember the number of assists I had. I think of everything about the game so I can hide from the trauma that's creeping toward me from hearing her cry. I block out the sterile scent of the hospital that I know isn't really there and pretend I'm in the middle of the rink, celebrating with my team, instead of in a room, watching the doctor's failed attempt at bringing my mother back.

My hand grips Taytum's head a little tighter, and when she pulls back and peers at me with watery eyes, I know I'll do anything to make her stop crying.

"I don't want to die alone," she whispers, licking her swollen lips.

Her hiccup cuts through her cries, and I swallow. *What?*

"You're not going to. You have me," I say.

"That's not what I mean!" She's getting worked up again, and I try to ground myself.

My hands find her cheeks, and I wipe away the moisture soaking her soft skin when I sit us on the couch. "I'm sick of pleasing everyone. The pressure is suffocating, Ford." She turns away and holds back the rest of her ambitions before snapping her soul-wrecking blue eyes to mine. "Don't you get it? I'm just *so* tired. I don't want to feel apologetic for experiencing college and dating, or losing myself to some guy in a random room at a party when I'm already apologetic for this." She points to the monitor that I know is under her shirt. "I can't control this, and I can't control everyone worrying about me." There's a hitch in her voice, and I hate it.

"Stop being so perfect, and maybe we'll stop worrying that we're going to lose you," I crack, trying to lighten the mood. My eyes bounce between hers, and I say something a little too emotional. "If I could take your diabetes away, I would." It's a staggering truth, but it's out there in the open now. "But we can't control that."

Her head pops up, and I'm not sure I like the look festering in her glossy eyes. "You're right. That's why you're going to help me."

My heart beats a little too fast, especially with her on my lap. "Help you with what?"

The hope blossoms, and her tears start to dry. She doesn't know it, but I could be swayed to do anything with her looking at me like she is right now. "You're going to help me date."

No.

No way.

Nope.

Taytum sits up, and I'm too shocked by her straddling me to muster up my refusal. She flips her blonde hair over her shoulder, and her desires begin to fall from her mouth like a waterfall. I'm drowning by the end.

I want to talk to a guy without you and Emory sending him a death glare.

I want to go on dates.

I want to have one-night stands.

I want to feel as confident as I make myself seem.

I want to fall in love.

Each of her wants is a knife in my stomach, but the last one twists in real good. The thought of her falling in love and getting her heart broken will send me and Emory to prison. The thought of her falling in love and him loving her back? That'll kill me.

"You owe me, Ford."

I snap to attention.

"You've ruined every date I've ever had. Guys look at

me like I'm a game instead of a potential girlfriend, and that's your fault."

I swallow because she's right. I've always been on a one-track mindset that was planted by Emory years ago. Taytum has been off-limits to everyone, and if I couldn't have her, no one could.

I sigh. "Fine."

She perks up, and I think about other guys touching her to keep my dick from getting hard beneath her shifting in my lap. "You'll help me? You'll take care of Emory? And you'll stop interfering?"

I nod.

Taytum rolls her eyes. "Say it."

The look I give her causes her to raise her eyebrow with attitude. "Fine," I grit. "I will hide your little rendezvous from Emory, and I won't interfere..."

"Like you did tonight," she adds.

I growl with annoyance. "Like I did tonight."

She looks pleased with her little victory before losing her smile and tapping her chin with her finger. "And..."

I drop my hands and grab her waist to steady her. "Whatever you're going to add...no."

"I need you to teach me how to date and..."

My heart skips a beat. "And what?"

She looks away bashfully, so I put my thumb on her cheek and bring her eyes back to me. Her thick lashes flutter against her pink cheeks. "Teach me how to be one of those girls that has one-night stands."

No way.

"Please, Ford."

I wish she'd stop looking at me like she is, but the hope in her gaze makes me feel like I can help her hang the moon.

"Okay, Heartbreaker," I say. "I'll help you."

She smiles, and my world spins.

I grab her hand, and for once, she doesn't pull away.

I'm not exactly thrilled about what I just agreed to, but at least she stopped crying.

A win is a win.

[9]

"ONE, TWO, THREE." The vitamin D supplements drop into my pill sorter one by one with a little clink. This is something I've been doing since being diagnosed with type 1 diabetes, all because a nurse once mentioned to me that Vitamin D has been shown to improve insulin sensitivity, but it still makes me feel like I'm eighty-four instead of twenty-two. I shake the pill bottle and pour a few more vitamins out into the palm of my hand and drop them in before closing the lid and pushing it to the far corner of my nightstand.

A pill a day–that's what stands in between me and no longer having diabetes.

I laugh under my breath with the manifestation. It's unrealistic, but a girl can hope.

I turn toward the door when I hear girly squealing downstairs. I already know that some hot jock has shown up on our doorstep to take one of the girls out, because it's the college-girl chorus. The shrill squeal is what every single freshman does when they come into contact with someone other than Joe Schmo from their little ol' hometown.

It's exhausting trying to teach the younger sorority sisters how to be safe and not trust every guy who pursues them just because he has a hot smirk and a devilish glint in his eye.

"Ladies, ladies, *ladies*. I'll sign autographs later."

There are more girly giggles, and I snort at Ford's smooth voice. I roll my eyes so hard it hurts. My back is to him when my door slides over my fluffy carpet, and for the first time in a very long time, my stomach flips with nerves.

I cried in front of him.

Me. Taytum Elizabeth Olson, the composed ballet-dancing college student with an airy attitude who has always seemed collected on the outside, cried.

I never cry, and even though it was in front of Ford—someone who has seen me at my worst—I'm still embarrassed by it.

Even days later.

"You gonna pretend I'm not standing behind you?" Ford asks.

My lips want to curve, but I do exactly as he says. I pretend he isn't there. I grab my copy of *A History of Romantic Literature* and sit on my bed. I flip open to the chapter on Sylvia Plath, but my finger freezes on the corner of the page when Ford begins to recite her entire biography from memory.

He acts like an airhead most of the time and strives to make everyone in the room laugh, but he's smarter than most guys his age. The one thing about Ford is that he never wants to disappoint anyone, so he always goes above and beyond to excel at everything he does.

I disappoint people constantly–mainly my parents and Dr. McCarthy.

"Am I dazzling you with my intelligence?" he asks after finishing her biography.

I flip the page and continue to pretend he doesn't exist, which makes him laugh out loud.

"Are you seriously going to ignore me? You know very well that I can make you look at me. I know how to press your buttons, Taytum."

He sure does.

I sigh, continuing to look at the same sentence on the page that I've reread five times, and keep my voice neutral. "That depends. Are you here to stay true to your word, or are you going to act like the other night didn't happen?"

My bed dips, and his jean-clad leg is an inch from mine. I glance at him, and he's resting against my pillow with his hands behind his head. "The other night...?"

My face is on fire. *I hate him.* I slam the book shut and begin to stand up. I'm a second away from walking to ballet practice instead of letting him drive me.

"Nuh-uh." Ford moves quickly. He pops up and traps me in between his legs like a pair of scissors. Our eyes meet, and I wiggle angrily with an attempted escape. "Keep it up. I love a girl who fights."

"Ford." I try to unclamp his legs but stop when I realize how stupid I must look. Ford's cheeks are hollow from sucking them in to stop his laugh, and it makes his jaw sharper than ever.

"Will you relax? I was kidding. You know I always stay true to my word."

I snort sarcastically and push his legs away. He lets me go and throws my heart-shaped pillow into the air only to catch it a second later without looking.

"You don't always stay true to your word." I stand up and grab my ballet bag before moving closer to my door. If I don't put space between us, I may throw my book at his head.

The pillow falls to the floor, right out of Ford's hands, and he stares directly at me. "Yes, I do."

"You do not," I counter.

I remember the very moment he broke his word, like it was yesterday. "Remember when you promised me you wouldn't tell my parents about that one night you found me crying in my bathroom with a ripped shir–"

"Don't." I look away when I hear the brash tone he uses. "You know I had to tell them."

"Just like you'll have to tell Emory about every date I go on or every one-night stand I plan to have? Or what if one of your teammates pursues me and wants to keep it a secret from Emory? You gonna keep your word then? Or..." I smile deviously and bring up my next topic. "What if Cruz shows back up at Rush's and we're in a room together again? Are you going to break the door down and make up some excuse to force him leave? Are you going to tell him that I'm off-limits again?"

I'm out of breath by the end of my rant, and my hands have made their way to my hips. Ford stood up at one point, and his feet are now planted firmly over my pink rug. My eyebrow hitches as I wait for his answer. I've already prepared one hundred responses by the time he says, "No."

Surprise renders me speechless. "No?" I'm hesitant but for good reason.

I trust Ford with my life, but I don't trust him with his ability to keep something from my brother or to sit back and watch me disappear with another guy. I've been burned far too many times.

Ford strides over to me with his usual confidence. "I heard you the other night, and I understand where you are coming from." He shrugs innocently, and I'm left confused. "I said I'd keep your little adventures a secret, and I will. I also said I'd help you...figure it out."

I blink once, then twice, and then a third time before I blurt out the first thing that comes to mind. "Why?"

There's a harsh silence that follows my question, and the more Ford bounces his blue eyes between mine, the more skeptical I become. But then he looks away and flexes his tight jaw, and it clicks.

"You feel bad for me," I whisper.

Ford quickly rebuts, "No." He rolls his eyes before snatching my ballet bag from my hand. "Well, yes, but not in the way you're thinking." The zipper echoes throughout the room, and he grabs my emergency sugar kit. He opens it up and checks the contents before shoving it back into the bag. "I feel guilty, alright?"

I try to take my ballet bag from him, but he slaps away my hand. "You feel guilty?" I repeat.

He nods. "You were right. I have ruined almost every date you've ever had, and it's a dick thing to do. You're no longer fifteen, surrounded by a bunch of little fuckboys who don't know a pussy from a papaya." There's a look in his eye that I don't recognize, but it vanishes before I comment on it.

Ford heads for the door, but instead of following after him, I stand in the middle of my room and cross my arms. "Did you just compare my pussy to a papaya?"

He turns and looks over his shoulder. He grins, and this time, I can't help but let my mouth curve. "I sure did. I bet you taste better, though."

A clipped laugh leaves me, and I quickly try to brush

past him, all while pulling on the straps of my bag. His grip is tight, so it doesn't let up. Instead, he jerks it, and I slam into his chest. "You gotta promise me something if I'm going to do this for you."

His cologne engulfs me, and my mouth runs dry.

"Don't let some guy break your heart," he whispers.

My bedroom feels infinitely smaller with the sobering look in his eye.

I give him a half-smile. "As if I'd let some guy get close enough."

My back? Maybe. My heart? Never.

Our heavy moment is fleeting. Ford drapes his arm over my shoulders, and we walk to the stairs together. "Good girl," he whispers in my ear. "Why do you think I've been calling you Heartbreaker all these years, babe? I'm glad to see it has stuck."

My stomach tumbles down the stairs before us. I keep my steps steady, but I'm so starved for a guy's attention that Ford calling me *babe* sends me into a tizzy.

His arm drops when we reach downstairs. Naturally, he stops to flirt with my sorority sisters before we head to his car and climb inside.

"Seatbelt." I roll my eyes again but do as he says. Once the seatbelt clicks, Ford takes off toward the auditorium.

"Have Claire drop you off at The Bex after practice. And before you try to walk there or refuse a ride, she's aware that Dr. McCarthy doesn't want you to drive."

He knows me too well.

"Why The Bex?"

"You and I have some things to iron out, so The Bex, me and you, seven-thirty sharp." The car comes to a stop, and we're suddenly out of time.

"What things?" I ask, reaching for my bag.

"If I'm going to help you with your little exploration, we're going to need to set some rules in place."

"Rules?" *Great.*

Ford unlocks the car door and lets go of my hand.

"What kind of rules?"

He winks at me. "See you in a bit."

I open the door and step out. Ford doesn't drive away until I'm safely inside.

Even though I'm reluctant to hear these so-called rules, I'm sort of looking forward to meeting him at The Bex.

For once, Ford might be on my side.

See ya later, celibacy.

FORD

I sit in silence while Emory scarfs down a cheeseburger and fries from across the table. I've hidden something from him twice now, both times regarding Taytum, and after she and I have our team meeting, I'm going to be hiding a whole lot more.

"Why did you want to come here if you aren't going to eat?" Emory wipes his mouth on the back of his hand.

I glance to my untouched plate and pull a handful of fries into my hand. I stuff them in my mouth and flip my hands. "Better?" I ask through a mouthful of mushy potatoes.

His eyebrows knit together, and although he has darker features than his sister, they look identical at the moment. They both send me the same look often–as if they're sick of my antics.

"Y'all ready for the game tomorrow?"

I glance at Rush, Bexley U's star football player, as he

sits down in the booth behind Emory, waiting for our answer.

It's been a thrilling season. There was drama on the team at the beginning of the year from both our captain and co-captain, but now, it's time for us to come together to win the Frozen Four. And, you know, secure our own spots playing pro, like Theo did. As long as we keep our heads down and continue on our winning streak, it'll put the majority of us on the path to securing our futures.

"We're ready," I answer, watching him scoot over so a few more guys can slide into his booth. "You got a bye week?"

"Yeah, we play Wilder U next week, though. They're *almost* as good as us." He shrugs. "If I were to join their team, they'd be unstoppable."

Emory snickers. "And here I thought hockey players were cocky..."

The waitress comes over and starts to take their orders, but she stops mid-sentence, and I turn to see her wrap Claire in a big hug. Taytum is standing beside her, buried in her phone, likely ignoring me and Emory on purpose.

I scoot over. "Well, come on. This food isn't going to eat itself."

Taytum glances up from her phone, and her eyes widen at my plate with a mound of french fries. She immediately sits and reaches for one.

"Don't even think about it," Emory seethes.

I can feel her anger, even though we aren't touching.

One fry isn't going to affect her blood sugar *that* much, yet Emory scolds her anyway. He asks her to list off all the carbs she's had today before pointing out better menu options. In the middle of his itemizing, she quickly looks at me, and her eyebrows draw together, as if she's proving a point to me. She doesn't need to, though. After she pointed her frustrations out to me the other night—in a rather dramatic way—I'm fully aware of the problem.

I clear my throat and nod to the booth behind Emory. "You know that guy?"

Emory spins, and I quickly snag a couple of fries and turn to Taytum. I put my hand on the back of her neck and stuff them inside her mouth. A smothered laugh leaves her before she smashes her lips together to hide the evidence.

When her brother turns back around, he shifts his attention between the two of us, but Taytum looks back to her phone and chews her fries subtly.

"The dark-haired guy?" he asks.

I nod, because there is no wrong answer at this point. I made the whole thing up as a distraction.

"That's Rush's brother," Emory says.

Taytum's head pops up so fast I feel a breeze. The smallest amount of possessiveness plants itself into the pit of my stomach, and I watch the exact moment Rush's brother makes eye contact with her. His eyes light up, and Taytum's cheeks turn pink.

I put my hand on her leg and dig my fingers into her thigh to bring her back down. If Emory gets wind of what I walked in on the other night, he'll be irate and do something much stupider than me picking her up and telling him she is off-limits.

That's part of the reason I'm always the one to step in when Taytum plays her little games. I'm much more level-headed than her older brother.

Emory moves his attention to Taytum, and I move mine to Rush's brother.

I hear Emory as he talks to Taytum. "You okay? You

look flushed or something." I stare right ahead. Cruz's gaze moves to mine, and I shake my head. *Don't.*

"Tay?"

I turn to Taytum, and her neck is becoming splotchy. She swallows the last bit of fries I shoved in her mouth, and I tap her leg a few times.

Chill.

A breath leaves her, and she pushes my hand off her leg. "I'm fine." She rolls her eyes at her brother. "Jeez."

Emory snorts. "Whatever. You ready, bro?"

I gesture to my food. "I'm not even close to being done."

"Well, I'm out. We've got a game tomorrow, and don't even try to pull that bullshit tonight about pre-game rituals. I've got my own rituals to do."

Taytum pretends to puke because we all know what his rituals consist of. Emory pairs his smirk with a wiggle of his eyebrows.

"You got her?" He tips his chin to his sister.

"Always." I take my elbow and ram it gently into Taytum's ribs. She smacks my arm away and scoffs.

"Later," he says before leaning down to Taytum. "Oh, and stop eye-fucking the guy behind me."

Taytum's mouth pops open, and I laugh under my breath. Her cheeks turn an even darker shade of red. When he's gone, she snaps over to me. "Did you tell him?"

I'm quick to prove a point. "Is he still alive?"

She rolls her pretty eyes. "Good point."

I nudge her with my knee. "Go sit where Emory was sitting."

"Why? Don't want to sit next to me?" she teases.

I grab another fry, but instead of stuffing it in my mouth, I stuff it in hers. I smirk when her eyes widen. "That's to get you to shut up." She glares at me while chew-

PUCK BLOCK / 69

ing. "And I want you over there so you quit eye-fucking Cruz."

"This isn't going to work," she murmurs. Regardless, she slides away from me and into the opposite side of the booth. "I can't even look at a guy without you acting like a caveman."

I wag my finger at her after placing my water down on the table. She steals it and sucks the rest of it through the straw. Her throat bobs up and down with a slow swallow as she waits for my rebuttal, but I hesitate.

Because, *is* this going to work?

A very recent and vivid memory appears in my head of her with tears in her eyes, desperate for my help. "It's going to work, but you've gotta sign this first."

I lift a hip, pull out a piece of paper, and slide it across the table. My hand stays on it when Rush and his brother pile out of their booth. I keep my gaze glued to Cruz as he slowly walks past and glances at Taytum. When she peers up at him and bats her eyelashes, I kick her under the table.

She gasps. "Oww!"

"Eyes on me, and pay attention."

Her eyebrows knit together, and I almost snap my fingers at her when she peers past my head and watches him leave The Bex.

"You done?" I seem impatient, but really, I'm just irritated that she's showing interest in someone other than me at the moment.

Taytum sighs and shoves my hand off the paper. She flips it over, scans it for a second, then laughs under her breath. "Are you kidding me? Did you get this idea from Theo?"

I tap my temple and shoot her a crooked smile. "I've got a good memory. I saw the little list Claire gave him when they became roommates. It had you written all over it. I thought it was only fair to set some of our own rules."

She concentrates on the list.

FORD'S RULES:
1. NO FUCKING HOCKEY PLAYERS
2. NO SEXTING HOCKEY PLAYERS
3. NO FLIRTING WITH HOCKEY PLAYERS
4. FORD GETS FULL APPROVAL OVER WHO TAYTUM CHOOSES TO PURSURE AND WHEN

The paper crumples in Taytum's grip, and when she looks up at me, I have to force myself to keep it together.

Okay, fine. They're a little extreme, but they're also necessary.

I tap on the paper. "If you want to do this behind Emory's back, then you're gonna have to follow these rules."

Taytum tucks some hair behind her ear and reads the list once more before getting up to head over to her best friend. Claire is at the bar, chatting with some of her co-workers, and I can't help but watch Taytum's swinging hips for the entire walk. Claire gives her a pen, and then she's marching back over to me.

We keep eye contact the entire time, and when she's done scribbling on the paper, she pushes it back to me and curls her mouth.

FORD'S RULES:
1. NO FUCKING HOCKEY PLAYERS - *DIDN'T WANT TO IN THE FIRST PLACE.*
2. NO SEXTING HOCKEY PLAYERS - *FINE.*
3. NO FLIRTING WITH HOCKEY PLAYERS - *WE'LL SEE.*

4. ~~Ford gets full approval over who Taytum chooses to pursue and when~~

"Then I'm not helping you." I'm as matter-of-fact as they come. "That last one is the most important rule on the list."

Taytum sits up a little taller. "I'm not letting you pick my boyfriends for me. That's practically the same as it is now!"

I shrug. "Well, I'm not willing to let some guy fuck you and never talk to you again."

She slaps the table but lowers her voice when she realizes people are looking at us. "What if that's what I want?"

I shake my head. "It's not."

She's annoyingly cute when she pouts. Her lip juts forward, and her arms cross even tighter against her chest. "And how many one-night stands have *you* had, Ford Alexander?"

My name rolls off her tongue with distaste—yet, I still enjoy the sound of it. "That's different."

"No, it's not," Claire adds as she sits down beside her best friend.

"No, no, no," I start, wagging my finger, "I'm not about to go up against both of you. Go on and get." I point behind me to the door, and it's no surprise that she doesn't listen.

"Stop being crazy, Ford. She just wants to be a normal college student."

I purse my lips. "You mean like you? Fake dating the hockey captain? Because *that's* normal."

Claire's mouth opens wide. "Faking dating him was *your* idea!"

Oh, right.

Taytum grabs the paper after Claire makes me feel stupid and rips it in two. They both laugh, and I scowl.

"Your rules are stupid," she says.

My immaturity gets the best of me, and instead of having some witty comeback, all I can think to say is, "Well...you're stupid."

Taytum laughs out loud at my lack of creativity, which causes me to chuckle.

Claire pops out of the booth and taps the table with her fingers. "Well, good luck, you two."

Then, it's just Taytum and me, all alone and at an impasse.

I lean back, spread my legs out under the table, and knee her to get her attention. She's nibbling on her bottom lip, and I'm reminded again that, although she appears so damn confident with her perfect looks and assured struts around campus, she's actually inexperienced and a little self-conscious after her diagnosis. A little sad too.

Fuck.

"Okay, fine," I snap. "Scratch the last rule...but the others still stand. No hockey players, because this is already crossing a line. If Emory knows I'm in on this or covering for you..."

Her eyes light up at my acceptance, and she nods with excitement.

Taytum could have any guy she comes into contact with, and it's partly my fault that she can't see that. Stepping in line with Emory and taking on the role of protective older brother was the easiest route for me to take when we were younger. If I wasn't allowed to pursue her, no one was.

It's going to be difficult to pull myself out of that role, but I'm going to keep my word.

I'm going to back off—*a little.*

I'm going to give her some breathing room.

That doesn't mean I have to like it, though.

"Emory won't find out," she assures me. "It's not like I'm going to let some guy fuck me in front of him."

Something hot slashes the back of my neck with thoughts of her beneath some guy.

"Come on," I say, after putting money down on the table for the bill. "I have a hot date tomorrow with my hockey stick and a little black puck."

The tiniest dimple pops out on Taytum's cheek, and I drape my arm over her shoulders. When we make it to my car, she peers up at me, and I see the real her—the vulnerable one without a hint of anger or irritation.

"Thanks, Ford."

I open her door, and she climbs inside my car. "For what?"

She smiles softly, and it's like looking at a ray of sunshine. "For listening to me. And for understanding."

The feeling I get when she looks at me like that is enough to make me panic. I slam the door in her face and curse under my breath.

Taytum is going to end up putting me in my grave.

[11]

TAYTUM

THE CROWD IS ON FIRE, and booze is spilling all over the place from everyone jumping up and down. A smile reaches my lips when I watch the black-and-white jerseys come together on the ice with their sticks raised high.

Claire is jumping up and down beside me, and I laugh at her excitement. Theo, who just scored the goal, points at her, and even I can feel the warmth. Our hands clasp, and we raise them in the air. I shift my attention to the one Bexley U player who is skating laps around the ice, encouraging the fans to roar louder, before he nearly tackles Theo with excitement.

Ford is skilled beyond belief on the ice–as are most of the Bexley U players–but he doesn't get a lot of recognition because he's never the one shooting the goals. His assists, though? Those are insane, and it's something Theo brags about every time he has an interview. In fact, Ford is close to breaking the school's record. My smile grows deeper when he takes Ford's gloved hand and raises it in the air for the crowd to cheer his name too.

Ford eats up the attention.

He bows like a ballerina, and I can't help but laugh.

There's one minute left in the game, and Bexley U has it in the bag. I pull out my phone and video chat with my parents so they can catch the end celebration.

My mom's face is the first to appear, and although I told them I'd call them when the game was almost over so they could catch the live action, her first reaction is to worry.

"Is everything okay?"

I sigh. "I'm fine, Mom. Enjoy the game."

I flip the camera around at the perfect time, because Emory blocks a puck. The crowd loses it again, and there are multiple fans high-fiving one another for the block. A few moments later, the buzzer sounds, and the game is over.

The team comes together on the ice, and I hear my dad talking about the scouts that are at the game, watching the guys. They'll be off to the pros later this year—there is no doubt about it. Unfortunately, I'll be stuck here, still testing my sugar and injecting insulin.

That is, if my parents don't try to guilt me into moving home so I can be closer, since Emory and Ford will be off somewhere else. There's a flicker of sadness at the thought of them leaving, but that is ridiculous because, since high school, I've wished for nothing else but for them to give me space. Now that it's about to become a reality, though, I notice the tiniest bit of emptiness.

I shake my head at the thought.

That's exactly why I need to start dating and tapping into that independent light that's been dimmed for years. Otherwise, I'll be lost when they leave.

"You ready?" Claire pulls on my hand.

I nod and tell my parents to hold on while we follow a few of the other girlfriends of players on the team toward the locker rooms. We meet the guys there after every game and head to the after-party together, where Claire ends up leaving with Theo, and I get hauled out by my brother or Ford.

It's loads of fun.

"Sweetheart?" I put my attention back on my phone.

"Sorry, Mom. We're walking to the locker room. Want me to just tell Emory to call you later? It may be his turn to give an interview."

She nods and sends me a soft smile. "Sure. But before you go..."

Here it is.

"How were your sugar levels today? Are they starting to level?"

"They were fine. They seem to be leveling now that I'm able to keep better track of it with the monitor," I lie and also leave out the part where I accidentally forgot my phone in my bedroom while I was in the common room studying, and my sugar levels rose a little too high. It's a great feature to have your levels on your phone–except when you leave your phone in another room.

My dad sighs from nearby, and I see his hand squeeze my mom's shoulder. A muscle in her jaw ticks, and I furrow my brow at their silent encounter. "Okay, good. We love you. Be safe."

I say my goodbyes and hang up, but I'm left with the taste of concern that quickly vanishes when the guys begin to pile out of the locker room. Theo pulls Claire in for a hug, and I stand by, admiring them. There's a gang of puck bunnies behind us that glance at him before remembering that he's taken, and then they move on to the next set of hockey players, which just so happens to be Ford, Emory, and Berkley. Aasher, the co-captain, moves right past them and gives Theo a nod before going down the hall to leave, likely to find Riley.

"We going to the party after The Bex?" Theo asks Claire.

She looks at me, and I know it's her way of asking if I want her to go.

"You know I'm fine going alone. I have the girls from the house that I can take with me."

"I'll go with you," Ford says, sliding up beside me. I lean forward, seeing there's a girl tagging along beside him, and I'm instantly annoyed.

"No thanks."

He peers down at me and raises an eyebrow. "So you're not going to the party?"

I laugh. "Oh, I'm going." My chin raises, and I straighten my shoulders. "Just not with you." Theo and Claire laugh, and we start to walk down the hall, but I stop when I feel Ford's breath tickle my ear. "I thought you wanted my help, Heartbreaker."

My heart skips. "All I need from you tonight is to back off. I'll take care of the rest."

The girl pinned to his side shoots me a dirty look, and I smile.

"I'll see ya there," I say to Ford before winking at the puck bunny. He chuckles quietly and reaches for her hand.

When I slide up beside Claire, I ask her if I can borrow her black top from the other night.

Theo answers for her, "Yes, and keep it."

Claire looks over at him. "What? Why?"

He snorts. "Because it's a hot top, and every guy pictures you beneath him when you wear it."

I smile. "Perfect."

▭

Me: Theo was right.

Claire: About the top? Let me see!

I step back from my mirror and snap a picture before sending it to Claire. It's a little more revealing than I usually go for, but my glucose monitor is hardly visible through the mesh lining. It's snug in all the right spots, and if you look hard enough, you can see my lacy bra through the fabric. My ripped jeans show off some of my thigh, and the black strappy heels pull the outfit together.

My head tips back, and my blonde hair falls down my back. I swallow my vitamin and head for the door where Sadie and Liv are waiting. We sit in the back of the Uber while on the way to the party, and although they're only a year younger than me, I run over the *Party Girl Rules* that every sister has to memorize in their first year of the sorority.

The idea of these rules started when one of our sisters was sexually assaulted at a party a couple of years back–by a hockey player, nonetheless. That's the entire reason why the hockey team doesn't have their own house on campus. The coach put an end to that real quick.

"Use the buddy system," Sadie says, glancing at Liv.

Liv holds up her finger when she repeats another rule. "Never take a drink from someone random."

"And...?" I ask.

"Never leave your drink unattended."

I nod in between them and squeeze both of their hands. "Can I trust you two to get home safely without me?"

Sadie laughs softly. "We're not the youngest in the house, you know that, right?"

The car comes to a stop, and the Uber driver, an older male who has been quiet the entire ride, speaks up. "It doesn't matter how old you are. People make stupid choices all the time."

"Touche," I say, siding with him.

I peek up at him in the rearview mirror, and he smiles. "I have a daughter, and I have to say, she'd be lucky to have a friend like you."

I smile. "Thank you. Have a good night."

He nods and says, "Be safe." Before pulling away.

The door to the football house is wide open when the three of us skip up the stairs. Even though it's freezing outside, it's so congested inside that it feels hot and muggy when we enter the party. I ping-pong my gaze around the room and brace myself for the scathing look I know I'll get from Emory, but then I feel a hand snake around my waist.

I know it's Ford without looking.

"He's not here," he whispers in my ear. "You're off the hook."

Butterflies rush to my belly. I get a whiff of his crisp cologne when I turn slightly. His blue eyes grip me, and although he's sporting his charming grin, his shoulders are tense.

"Enjoy your night of freedom, Taytum."

Ford's throat bobs, and he lingers on my face for a

breath before turning and storming the dance floor. He steals a drink from an innocent bystander and tips it back before dropping the cup to the floor. I watch in silence as he runs his gaze down my outfit and then back to my face. He shakes his head slightly, but to my surprise, he turns away.

And suddenly, I'm left to my own devices.

[12]

FORD

I'm NOT sure what Taytum is waiting for.

I'm also not sure why I can't just turn my back and pretend she doesn't exist for the night. I've done it before, so I know it can be done. Except, this time, I've blatantly told her I won't interfere, and I'm pretty certain it's messing with me.

There's been a safety net around Taytum for years between her brother and me, but now that she's torn some bigger holes in the net, she's able to swim away and up the stairs into some guy's arms if she wants to.

Berkley moves beside me on the dance floor with his hands on some girl's waist. "You got any whiskey?"

I crook a feigned smile at him. "I always have whiskey." I pause. "But you don't want it. I've seen the way you drink after we win a game."

His brows furrow. "What's that supposed to mean?"

I chuckle. "You'll have whiskey dick if you drink my whiskey."

My flask is nearly empty anyway, and I don't like to share.

The girl in his hands turns. She pats his chest with her red fingernails. "We wouldn't want that, now would we?"

Her smile is flirty, and Berkley drags her off the dance floor right away to head for a bedroom. I turn and look for Taytum after pulling my half-empty flask out of my pocket. Everyone around us is having a good time, and I usually would be too, but how can I when she's surrounded by a ton of guys who are vying for her attention, yet she's still looking like a little wallflower.

"I'll be back," I say to the blondie that's been dancing with me for the last twenty minutes. I move through the party after draining my flask. I'm the only one on the team that drinks something as strong as whiskey, but I didn't grow up like most of my teammates–whiskey was the only thing Aunt Jo kept in the house.

As soon as I center myself in Taytum's ring of brave admirers, they all scatter like marbles. I laugh under my breath and lean against the same wall that's been holding her up for most of the party.

"Are you kidding me?" She huffs.

I turn my head and peer down at her. "I thought you weren't going to cock block me tonight!"

I snort. "I block pucks, not cocks."

With the way Taytum's nose wrinkles, I know she's about to snap back. "Well, I'm about to cock block you. I'll tell that girl you have herpes."

A loud laugh leaves me, and some drunken college girls look back and show off their glossy eyes. "I do not have herpes."

Taytum moves in front of me, and the girls all turn

around. I raise an eyebrow but continue to lean against the wall with my arms crossed in a relaxed manner.

"Stop cock blocking me," she sasses.

Her pretty eyes dart away, and I watch her carefully. I've seen Taytum command a room with a single wink before, but right now, she's stiffer than she was the night she found me with two of her friends in her childhood bedroom.

Not my best moment, I'll admit.

"Alright, that's it." I grab her hand and pull her through the party until I find a deserted corner. "What's going on with you? I thought you wanted your pick of the litter without me or Emory interfering." I gesture to the party. "And I distinctly remember you telling me, no less than a couple of hours ago, that you didn't need my help."

Even though Taytum and I are tucked back into a corner with nothing but the cheap disco light I gifted to the football house flashing over us, I can see the red tint on her cheeks. I take the back of my hand and press it to her warm face. "Talk to me, Heartbreaker."

Taytum shoves my hand away, but her voice is fragile. "I...I don't know how to do this." She turns to hide, and I instantly feel like shit. "How am I supposed to just go up to some guy and... Damn it, Ford. You and Emory ruined me! I know how to flirt and skim the line, but...then what?"

Doesn't she understand that all she has to do is throw those beautiful blue eyes in some guy's direction, and he'll buckle at the knees? He'll do anything she says.

I reach up and grab her chin gently, pulling her face to mine. The truth comes out a little more sincere than I mean for it to. "Just be you."

The light catches her watery eyes. "That's just it," she says. "I don't even know who I am anymore." She bounces her attention across my face. "I've been so focused on defying you and

Emory for the last several years, and now I'm stuck with trying to please everyone, and I'm so worried about this dumb thing..." She flicks her elbow, and my eyes fall to the lump on her arm. "I don't even know how to make my own decisions anymore."

I try to lighten the mood with a quippy joke. "You mean, you don't know how to make your own decisions when you aren't trying to actively piss Emory and me off?"

Taytum's lip twitches, and I know I've got her attention again. My hand tightens on her chin, and she peeks at me through her dark lashes. "How about this? Just go out there and take what you want. Someone will give it to you willingly."

You know, like every guy at this party.

Hockey player or not.

She rolls her eyes. "But how and who?"

I gawk at the rowdy party before pulling my attention to her again. I drop my hands and smirk. "Watch and learn."

Taytum's brows knit together, and I turn to walk over to the blonde that hasn't been able to keep her eyes off me since showing up two hours ago.

"You're back?" she peeps.

I place my hands on her hips, and my fingers slip beneath her shirt just enough to feel her warmth against them. I pull her in close, and a sweet gasp flies from her mouth with surprise. "Let's dance."

I take her arms, put them around my neck, and place my hands back to their rightful spot. I move her hips in the way that I want with the button of her tight jeans rubbing against me. When I glance at Taytum, she's in the same spot that I left her in, with her eyes glued to my every move.

I push things a little further. I spin my partner around and pull her in to close the gap between us. Her ass is rubbing against my dick to the beat of the music, and her head tips back into my chest.

"You played a good game tonight," she whispers while looping her arm up and over her head. She grips the ends of my hair, and I grin.

"I know." I wink before stealing a glance at Taytum. Our eyes meet from across the party, and she's nibbling on her bottom lip. I raise my eyebrows and mouth the word, *See?*

She doesn't look convinced. But if I can stand here and touch another girl in front of her, then surely she can get out on this dance floor and grab some guy by the hand. I've stood back and watched her flirt endlessly until I'm fuming so much I can't take it anymore, so what exactly is stopping her now?

My stomach twists the longer she stares at what my hands are doing. There's a hitch in my pulse when I notice her breathing is a little more erratic than usual, and there's something wickedly dangerous brewing in my blood at the thought of Taytum being turned on.

I act quickly and shift my attention. I gently push the puck bunny to the far wall, catty-corner from my little audience, and back up her against it. My knee wiggles in between her jean-clad legs, and I slowly run my hand up her thigh. The tingling in my fingertips draws attention to her curves, but I know it's a desperate attempt to pull myself together instead of focusing on Taytum's dazed expression.

Except, the moment I steal a glance, I burn.

The girl I grew up with, the only one I have ever confided in, the only one who has ever called me out on my bullshit and seen me at my very worst, is staring at me with fuck-me eyes and plump, parted lips, like she's about to touch herself at the show I'm putting on for her.

It's not true.

It can't be.

But damn. Just the thought of it pushes me a *little* bit further.

TAYTUM

THUMP, thump, thump.

My pulse is flying. I feel it everywhere. My neck, my wrist, my thigh...in between my legs.

I'd rather relive the moment when I walked in on my brother getting a sexual favor from the captain of the cheer team my freshman year of high school than ever admit that Ford's little lesson has me completely turned on.

My cheeks are flushed, and my legs are wobbly. The floor beneath me moves, and everyone else disappears the longer I stare.

He told me to take what I want, but after standing across the party, watching him touch some girl with hot seduction, I find myself fully entranced and wanting *him* to touch me.

I press the back of my hand against my warm forehead. The wall holds me up as I continue to stare at Ford's talented hand round the curve of a perfectly perky breast. I follow his movements like a magnet. His show has me in a chokehold, and I hate the warmth in between my legs, because Ford is the very last person I could ever toe the line with.

His hand quickly snaps to the blonde's chin, and he grips it with a bone-chilling possession. My eyes widen, and I'm at a standstill. Her attention is fully grasped, and suddenly, mine is too, because he flicks his hooded eyes to me for the briefest of seconds before kissing her so deeply I can't breathe.

The kiss is hot. Ford's mouth moves over hers so seductively that it belongs in a porno. I'm suddenly involved in a provocative espionage, yet I refuse to look away. Ford is taking what he wants, and when his plaything's leg creeps up, and she traps him to her, I know she's giving herself up willingly.

They make-out for what feels like an eternity, and I fumble to breathe when he finally breaks the kiss. My lips part with shallow breaths, and I'm sweating. I finally force myself to look away, because if Ford sees the look on my face, he'll be able to read my thoughts and I'm not willing to admit what I'm thinking to him. In fact, I'm not even going to admit them to myself.

Instead, I frantically search the party for someone to push my dirty thoughts onto. I pass on the hockey players, because that's a no-go, and linger on someone I've never seen before. His dark hair catches a shine from the light, and he sees me staring right away.

Ford's voice is in my head, feeding me encouragement, but I wish I could block him out. He's paying no attention to me. Instead, his face is buried in the puck bunny's neck, and it annoys me so much that I find myself walking toward the unfamiliar guy with steel-blue eyes.

"Hey." He flicks his chin at me when I make my way over.

Flirting is second nature to me, so I don't overthink it. I do exactly what Ford told me to do, I act like myself. "Hi," I greet him with a sugary voice and smile. His eyes drop right to my mouth. "I haven't seen you here before."

The guy shrugs and then tips back his beer. There's a little bit of foam on his mouth, but he is quick to jolt his tongue out from behind his lips to lick it clean.

"You could say that I'm new." His voice is hot too.

I bite my lip and eye him closely. "Let me guess. You play..." After leaning back and checking him out, I laugh lightly. "Football for sure."

His mouth tips into a grin. "You're right, but I'm curious as to how you know that."

I shrug. "I grew up around athletes. I can spot them pretty easily."

He throws his beer bottle in the trash and looks at my face for a few seconds too long. "You're Taytum."

I shoot him a sideways glance. "How do you–"

"And your brother is the goalie of Bexley U's hockey team, yeah?"

Here we go.

Disappointment flares, and I want to spin around, look at Ford, and shout from across the party, "*See what you two have done!*"

My shoulders drop, and I'm about to walk out of the party with my tail tucked in between my legs, but then the guy tsks his tongue and steals my attention. "Don't look discouraged. Your brother isn't going to stop me from asking you to dance."

Disbelief takes me hostage, and the shock must be evident on my face, because his eyebrows knit together with confusion. In an attempt to hide my stupor, words fumble out of my mouth that take us both by surprise. "I don't want to dance. I want to go upstairs."

My subconscious is shaking her head in the back of my mind because I'm about to disappear with a guy I don't know, but in my defense, I know almost everyone at this party, and they have all been warned by my brother or Ford that I'm completely off-limits, so the choices aren't vast by any means.

He quickly grabs me by the wrist and starts to lead me upstairs. I want to look back at Ford in the worst way, but I don't, because this has nothing to do with him.

"I'm Jasper, by the way."

I stiffen for a brief second when he tells me his name, but I can't pinpoint the reason why. I loosen my tense shoulders, letting Jasper pull me to the very last door at the end of the hallway and brush away my nerves. My subconscious is likely trying to trick me into turning my back on Jasper because, deep down, I know I'm on my own by having Ford's word that he won't barge in and ruin my night.

That is, if he keeps his word.

"Jasper," I repeat, still feeling a little dose of familiarity when I repeat his name.

He shuts the door behind us, and before we even share another word, he pushes me up against it and starts touching every part of my body that he can get his hands on. My head hits the wood, and my hair falls down my back when he tugs on the long strands.

My neck is his for the taking, and when his mouth hovers above my racing pulse, I grab onto his torso to steady myself against him.

"Fuck, you're way hotter than any girl here," he mutters.

Jasper's lips move from the hollow part of my collarbone, and he pulls back to stare at me for a second. There's a
strange look in his eyes, and my heart starts to beat faster. I
lean forward to kiss him but pause when his hand finds its
way to my throat. He isn't squeezing hard, but it still makes
me sputter.

"I'm going to fuck you," he states, squeezing a little
tighter.

I freeze when his other hand starts to pull at my shirt. I
grip his wrist and pull because there's still a very self-
conscious part of me that doesn't want anyone to see my
monitor. "No," I murmur. "My shirt stays on."

"The fuck it does."

My eyebrows knit together, and anger replaces my
nerves. "Excuse me?" I bite back.

I'm repeating his name in my head over and over again,
like my brain is trying to figure out where the familiarity is
coming from in the midst of anger. *Jasper, Jasper, Jasper...*

He chuckles, and I'll give it to him—he has a smooth
laugh, and his dangerously dark features are enticing, to say
the least. But I am not the type of girl who likes to be bossed
around. Ford and Emory can attest to that.

Jasper takes my wrists and pulls them up above my
head, slamming them onto the door. I'm not sure if he thinks
I'm into the little game he's playing, but he's about to learn
that I trust very few people in my life, and he isn't one of
them.

"I want to see your tits, so I'm going to take your shirt
off. You got that, pretty eyes?"

My *pretty eyes* flare with his tone, and he chuckles
again. My rebuttal cuts through a sarcastic laugh. "No,
you're not, Jaspe–"

I gasp.

I was wrong.

I do know him.

His grip on my wrists tightens when I try to pull them away.

"I know who you are," I say, baring my teeth. "And if you think you'll get away with fucking me like you fucked Aspen, you have another thing coming."

Jasper's lip rises into a half-smile, and I tug on my wrists again. This time, he lets me go and takes a step away.

For the first time, I'm grateful for growing up with a hothead brother like Emory, because thanks to him, I not only know how to break up a fight, but I know how to start one too.

I brace myself for the pain and steady my stance. My fingernails dig into my palm, and I wind my arm back with enough force to bring it forward quickly, landing right on Jasper's nose.

He bends at the waist and calls me a bitch, but I hardly hear him because I'm already out the door and halfway down the hall.

[14]

FORD

THE MOMENT TAYTUM is out of my sight is the very moment I become sober. I'd down more of my whiskey if I had any left, but the flask in my back pocket is empty, and unfortunately, the sloppy kissing isn't nearly enough to make me feel drunk either.

Damn it.

I pull away from the kiss and crook a smile at Wanda... or Wilma? Willow. Her name is Willow. "I'll be right back."

I'll be surprised if she's in the same spot I leave her in, since I've been back and forth all night, but if I don't make contact with Taytum and confirm that she's okay, I won't be able to pay much attention to Willow anyway.

I scan each and every face as I make my way through the party, subtly looking for her throughout the sea of blonde females. Once I reach the stairs, I place my hands on my hips in defeat and stare up at the steps leading to the upper landing. My chest is tight with anxiety, and guilt is knocking on my back door.

Leave her be.

I shake my head and let out a low grumble before backing up into someone.

"My bad, bro," I say, taking in the sight of a guy who looks less than pleased that I've run into him. He has a little bit of dried blood underneath his nose, and I immediately search the party to see who decided to take part in a fight.

Rush doesn't allow much conflict in the football house. Everyone knows that. So either this guy got one past Rush, or Rush hasn't found out yet.

"You got a little..." I point to my nose, and his bloody nostrils flare. I laugh under my breath when I look past the guy and see that Rush is right behind him. "You might want to brace yourself for another hit."

His eyebrows dig down into a crevice, and I take a step back when Rush's hand makes contact with the Rocky Balboa wannabe. "What the fuck are you doing here, Jasper?"

I grab the beer out of Berkley's hand when he saunters up beside me. All we need is some popcorn, and we'd be set.

Rush bundles Jasper's shirt in his tight fist. "I thought I told you to stay the fuck away from my house."

Jasper appears to be humored by our BU football captain's temper, and it's obvious that he's only here to piss Rush off.

"Who'd you fuck with this time?" Rush asks, pulling on Jasper's shirt again. He's wearing a Wilder U shirt, and I assume there's a little rival going on between the two. "Looks like she did a number on you."

A girl hit him?

I turn my head and peer up the stairs before turning back and staring at Jasper's bloody nose. My shoulders tighten, the beer can in my hand crumpling slightly with my assumption.

"The goalie's sister. Thought I'd pick a fight with another athlete for a change."

My beer can falls to the floor, and I step forward. My chest screams a lethal dose of violence, and even though I'm like Rush in the sense that it takes a lot to get under my skin, Taytum is my number one trigger.

A hand grips my shoulder, and I crack my neck.

Rush moves in front of me and shoves Jasper toward the door. "If I see you again, I'll make a conscious decision to do more than give you a bloody nose. You got it?"

Jasper laughs. "See you on the field, big guy."

Not so fast.

I slide past Rush and storm the guy. My forearm is against his windpipe, and his sick smile feeds my hunger like I have a craving for pain.

Someone pulls me back and shoves me inside the front door before slamming it shut. "Do you know who he is?"

I scoff. "Dead meat?"

Rush shakes his head. "His father is the dean for Wilder U, and he has strings. Don't fuck with him. Trust me."

I know there is probably more to the story, but I don't care to ask questions. I sigh and shake out my tense muscles. Rush stalks off, and I turn around to see Berkley and Efrain smiling like clowns at me.

"What?" I snap.

An underclassman from nearby snorts. "Same ol' shit. Taytum is trying to get railed, and Ford has to step in and save her."

There's a reddish tint clouding my vision when I take a step to the left and eye the pipsqueak who thinks I won't actually drop him to his ass in three seconds flat.

"Come here and try saying that to my face."

"Ford, relax." Berkely gets in between us, and I know I'm acting completely out of character.

"It's the truth, though." I ignore the girly voice coming from the puck bunny who adds her two cents that no one asked for.

The underclassman opens his mouth, likely to add more to his death wish. "I mean, come on, man. If you're not going to make a move, let someone else have her. No hard feelings, but Taytum is..."

I block out the rest of his sentence because I know what's good for me.

The crowd parts as I storm through the house. If Taytum isn't in the middle of this debacle, it's because she's off hiding somewhere.

I skip every other step as I jog up the stairs and open each bedroom door. I see two pairs of tits in the first room, a dick in the third, and the stench of sex hits me in the face on the last.

The media room is empty, and after sweet-talking a few girls, I'm first in line for the bathroom, only to be let down when Taytum doesn't open the door to step out into the hallway.

Damnit!

I make it to the athletic dorms on foot in record time and knock on room 213 while ignoring the scrunchie hanging on the doorknob, indicating what's happening on the other side. I snatch the blue fuzzy hair contraption and fling it right at Theo's face when he appears with Claire.

"What?" he snaps before bending down and snatching the hair tie off the floor. Claire's hair is messy, and she's wearing his shirt, but I choose to ignore the scene I've walked into and ask where Taytum is.

"Last I knew, she was at the party." Claire reaches for her phone, and I wait anxiously. She tucks her hair behind her ear and quickly types something.

"Well," I press. "Where is she?"

Theo holds the door open and looks between us impatiently.

She shakes her head and pads over on bare feet to show me the picture on the screen. I pinch the bridge of my nose at the sight of Taytum's bright-red knuckles and blue bruise forming.

"She said she thinks it's broken. What the hell did she do?"

"Did she finally punch you?" Theo looks at my face a little more intently, but I catch his smirk.

"You're not funny," I say, although it wouldn't be that farfetched. "And no, she didn't punch me." Frustration starts to fill me. "I leave her be for one fucking night, and she punches some guy and possibly breaks her hand."

The tiniest slip of a laugh leaves Taytum's best friend, and she puts her hand over her mouth to hide it. Theo chuckles, and I flip them both off before storming down the hallway. I open my phone and type aggressively.

> I thought I taught you how to throw a punch.

She doesn't text back, which is really no surprise.

[15]

I TRACE the line of stars above me and blow a puff of air out of my mouth, only to watch my breath disappear into the cool night. The roof is slanted enough to give me an adrenaline rush but still safe so I don't fall to my death.

After wiggling my fingers a few more times and cursing the pain radiating to my wrist, I place it back on my lower belly and close my eyes, only to open them a second later when I hear a footstep against the shingles.

"I hate when you come out here," he says.

"Leave me alone, Ford."

He is the last person I want to see right now. I'm already frustrated enough from what happened tonight. I definitely don't need his teasing jokes to add to it. But as always, he ignores me and plops down on the roof anyway.

"Here."

I peek an eye open, and he's holding a bag of frozen peas out for me to take. When I make no move to grab them, he takes my hurt hand in his warm grip and studies the swelling with an intent to diagnose me. After a few seconds, he places my hand on his lap and presses the cold bag of peas on top and says, "I'm gonna start calling you Nose-breaker instead of Heartbreaker."

I let a soft laugh leave me by accident.

"What happened?" he asks. "One second, I'm demonstrating how to seduce someone, and the next, I'm looking at some guy with a bloody nose talking about how the goalie's sister punched him."

I turn my head to stare at his strong profile. Ford's jaw is cut like a piece of stone, and there isn't a single flaw on him. When he smiles, he's everyone's favorite guy in the room. When he's serious, he looks like a perfectly sculpted statue. He's always been painfully flawless, so much so that, when I was younger, I would stare at him from across the dinner table just to try and find at least one flaw.

Years later, I still haven't found one.

"I'm surprised you noticed anything at all with your face glued to the lips of that puck bunny."

Ford's eyes fall to mine, and the air crackles. "Jealous?"

I'm quick to tell my lie. "Not even a little bit."

He grins down at me and shakes his head. I turn away and continue to stare at the stars because I'm afraid he'll know I'm lying.

"Well, are you going to tell me what happened, or do I need to finish what you started?"

"Nothing happened," I say.

Ford grips me by the arm and pulls me upright from my lying position. My thick hair flies out of my face, and when our eyes meet, I know he's being serious. I suck in my cheeks and force out a play by play for him, because if I don't, I know he'll run off and tell my brother—or worse, go back on his word and refuse to help me in the dating department.

"He deserved the punch, then." Ford removes the peas to study my hand some more, and I wait with my lip tucked in between my teeth. "Well, good news is that I don't think it's broken."

"And what's the bad news?" I ask.

He looks me dead in the face. "Bad news is that you didn't get laid."

A sudden laugh erupts from me, and Ford flashes me his perfect smile. "Oh, and by the way..." He looks out into the darkness. "You suck at picking guys."

I huff. "If my hand wasn't in pain, I'd punch you."

He turns toward me. "You'd never."

I lean in close. "You know I would."

Neither of us move. Our faces are inches apart, like we're ten years old again and having a staring contest in the back of my parents' minivan. He gulps, and I suck in a breath. When he opens his mouth, I drop my gaze, but my phone beeps before words leave his lips.

He flicks his chin to my open window. "Up you go. Time for insulin."

My eyebrows furrow. "Who said I need insulin?"

He's half in my bedroom with one leg still on the roof. "Because I know what that ding on your phone means."

I follow after him. "How could you possibly know that? You've never even heard it."

Ford is already washing his hands when I walk into the bright bathroom. He quickly wipes his wet hands on the pink towel before throwing it down onto the counter. "I just do."

I eye him suspiciously and watch as he handles my insulin pen, putting it to the correct dose after looking at the sugar reading on my phone. I should be more shocked that he does everything correctly, but Ford is adept in everything he puts his mind to. He doesn't do anything halfway. If he needs to adopt a new skill, he becomes an expert.

A swallow works itself down my throat when he meets my gaze in the mirror, and before I know it, he's pulling me closer by the fabric of my shirt. He lifts it up and winces at my irritated skin from the injections.

"Let's do the thigh." Ford's voice is low and tender, but I swear there's a breathlessness to it that wasn't there before.

I look down and watch him trace my red skin around my usual injection site with the pad of his thumb before pushing the button of my jeans through its hole and unzipping them slowly. There's a crease in between his eyebrows when he pulls my jeans down past my hips. I hold my breath when he grabs my thigh with his warm palm, and he probably thinks it's because I'm bracing myself for the injection, but that isn't the reason why. A shiver shakes down my spine, and I exhale, catching his hooded blue eyes briefly when he peers up at me while on his knees.

Whoa.

The scent of alcohol wafts around us, and I ignore the pulling in my lower belly when I feel his hand snake up my thigh and wrap around my butt to hold me steady. My cheeks flame when I realize his palm is on my bare ass, because *of course* I wore my most scandalous thong to the frat party where I thought I'd get laid.

He swallows loudly. "Nice choice of panties."

I tilt my head to look at the ceiling because I'm both embarrassed and turned on.

"Though, I don't know if I'd consider this scrap of fabric panties." I snap my attention to him when I hear the roughness in his tone.

I scowl and decide to press his buttons because that's clearly what he's doing to me. "Jasper didn't seem to mind them."

Ford chooses that exact moment to dose me with my insulin. His fingers dig into my butt to steady me, and I watch his mouth silently count to ten before he removes the pen and flicks his steely blue eyes to mine.

"Breathe," he whispers.

Goosebumps cover my flesh when his finger trails my thigh, circling the spot that has the tiniest bit of blood seeping. I breathe out of my mouth a few times, matching Ford's steady breathing. Our eyes catch, and my heart flips. Instead of looking away, I keep my gaze on him and whisper, "Thanks."

His eyes drop to my mouth a second later, and I'm frozen. The air in the bathroom is suddenly heavy with something unfamiliar, but before I can decipher what it is, my bedroom door flies open, and Ford and I fly apart like shrapnel.

I pull my pants up and turn around, putting my back to Ford.

Emory's voice carries into the bathroom. "Taytum!"

"What?" I snap after flicking my eyes to the mirror and catching Ford's stoic expression.

"Did you punch some guy tonight?!" he asks, stepping into the bathroom.

His tight shoulders and disapproving scowl are nothing new, so the only response he gets is an eye roll. I push past him and leave both guys in my wake before flopping onto my bed. I grab my English notes and pop in my Airpods to tune out Emory's questions and Ford's attempt to calm things.

I read his lips word for word. It's the same reassurance

as all the other times, but we both know it's a lie because for once, Ford kept his word and didn't interfere.

Professor Petit eyes me from across the stage, and I have to try my hardest not to sigh dramatically after doing an arabesque. I turn my back to her blank expression and try to push the annoyance away. Now that I've fainted at practice, she watches me far more than before.

I wish it were because of my skill, but it's not.

It's a precaution.

Sweat trickles down the side of my face, and I know if I just untie the purple wrap top and practice in my regular leo, I won't be so hot, but it's bad enough that the other dancers are already on edge that I'm going to faint in the middle of a show. I don't want them to roll their eyes at the robot device on my arm, too.

Kate has already made a note to mention, rather loudly, that I need to wear a long-sleeve costume for our upcoming show because everyone in the audience will be distracted by the "thing" on my arm.

Speaking of the *thing*. A familiar beep comes from my bag off to the side, and I know it's my sugar reading. It strikes a nerve—for more reasons than one as of late. Claire looks at me from across the stage, and I send her a reassuring nod. *I'll get it in a second.*

I shake out my limbs and clear my head. I press up onto the ball of my foot and throw my back leg out behind me, trying to lengthen my arabesque as far and as gracefully as I can. The stretch rips down my torso and then I quickly drop my leg back down.

There. That felt better.

"Taytum Elizabeth."

My head whips toward the familiar smoothness of Ford's voice, and my pulse quickens.

What is he doing here?

His one eyebrow is raised beneath the hood of his Bexley U hoodie from the front row, and his jaw tenses the second he knows I see him.

"Excuse me, do I know you?" I ask, acting confused.

I put my back to Ford and slowly make my way over to Claire, pretending he isn't there. She laughs under her breath when I pretend to engage in a full-on conversation with her, but I feel his glare against the back of my head like he's forcefully tugging on my hair.

Claire's eyes widened. "He's climbing on stage."

"He better not be," I seethe.

"Are you forgetting something?" His breath is warm against the back of my neck, and all it would take is one step back, and I'd likely run into his chest.

I peer behind my shoulder. "The stage is for dancers only."

Ford grins mischievously, and I spin around quickly to put my hands on his arms. "That was not an invitation for you to start showing off your dance skills."

"Afraid I'll be better than you?" he asks, lowering his voice.

I sigh. "What are you doing here? Professor Petit is going to scold you in a few seconds if you don't get off this stage."

She won't, because she loves Ford. But I threaten it anyway.

Ford unpeels my fingers from his arms and crosses them against his chest. "Your meter went off."

Yeah, I know. There is a perfectly valid reason as to why I'm not rushing off to inject myself, but that isn't something he needs to be privy to.

"I know," I say.

His eyebrows crawl to his hairline. "Well?"

I fumble with my explanation. "I was just practicing one more–"

He cuts me off. "Your arabesques are amazing. You don't need to practice them or prove yourself to anyone on this stage. Now go check your sugar level and do what you're supposed to do."

My lips clamp shut. I sigh with frustration and attempt to irritate him. "You may be the only hockey player that knows what an arabesque is."

It doesn't work. He steps closer to me. "And you may be the only female at Bexley U that doesn't know how to get a date."

I gasp. A smirk slowly curves onto his face, and I'm pretty sure every ballet dancer in our vicinity is fanning themselves at the sight of it. I go to smack him lightly, but he catches my sore wrist in his grip and holds it steady.

"Don't you worry," he says through a smile. "I've got a plan. I said I'd teach you how to date, and I'm sticking to my word."

"A plan?" *Great.* "Every single time you've ever said you've had a plan, it ended badly."

Ford doesn't let go of my wrist. "That's not true. Give me one example."

I put a finger up with the first one that comes to mind. "The time you said you had a plan to replace my dad's tequila that we drank, and you put water in it, which turned to ice..."

Ford's lips flatten. "How was I supposed to know that liquor didn't freeze? I was twelve."

A laugh bubbles in my throat, but I hold it in.

"Plus, I distinctly remember Emory and I taking the fall for it so you wouldn't get in trouble."

My smile fades because he's right. When I think back on the other examples I was going to list, I shut them down one by one because with every plan Ford has ever had that hasn't gone right, there was another plan brewing so he could protect me from getting in trouble.

He finally lets my wrist go, and I sigh.

"Fine. What's the plan?"

Ford starts to make his way over to my ballet bag, and I follow him reluctantly. "First, take care of this." He has my insulin pen in his hand and shoots me a sideways glance. "And then I'll fill you in, lil' lady."

I stare at him as he backs away toward the end of the stage. "Lil' lady?"

He winks. "It's all part of the plan. Now giddy up."

I try to figure out what he's up to, but he gracefully jumps off the stage and seemingly tips an invisible hat in my direction before taking his seat to watch the rest of our practice.

[16]

FORD

I send Taytum a reassuring smile when we enter her room. She's looking at me with little hints of skepticism, and when I reach forward to pull her hair out of her bun, she quickly jolts backward and tries to stop me.

"What are you doing?" she rushes out.

"Will you stop?" I ask through a chuckle. "Don't you trust me?"

I flick her bottom lip the second it pops out with her pout. She's used to my endless flirting, just like I'm used to her attitude.

Her voice follows me as I walk into her closet and scan the overflowing racks of clothes. I have no idea how one person can have so many articles of clothing, but toward the end of the rack, I find exactly what I'm looking for. I toss out the outfit along with her cowgirl boots and try my hardest to shove away the memory of the last time she wore them.

Taytum + slutty cowgirl Halloween costume = hell.

I clear my head and throat as I walk out of her closet. She's holding up her best pair of skinny jeans–the pair that puts any peach to shame–and the little top that I know looks good on her.

"Your outfit for tonight." I take a seat on her bed. "Now get dressed."

I bite the inside of my cheek to hide my smile. I know my tone will irritate her because Taytum *hates* being bossed around, especially by me.

"What does this have to do with me and dating? I thought you said you had a plan to help me." My mouth opens to explain, but Taytum squeezes her eyes shut and stops me by holding her hand up. "I swear, if you say something like you're 'showing me the *ropes*' or 'teaching me how to *ride* a horse,' I will throw one of these boots at your head. I am not dressing up in a cowgirl outfit just for a pun, Ford."

I laugh out loud and kind of hate that I didn't think of using those jokes myself. "I'm taking you out. So, get dressed, and I'll fill you in on the rest of the plan when we get there."

She stares at me, and I stare right back. I know how stubborn she can be, so instead of wasting any more time, I pop up from her bed with her girly scent following my every movement, and I rip her shirt off in a single whoosh.

"Ford!"

I move back when Taytum tries to slap my chest. I quickly bend down and grab the shirt I threw at her moments ago off the floor prepared to pull it down over her head before I fumble at the sight.

Pretend it's a bathing suit, Ford. It's just a bathing suit.

Taytum's light-pink bra has suddenly grown hands, and they're wrapping around my throat. I choke at the sight of her perfect creamy mounds and the way they spill over the thin lace to the point that I can't breathe. I discreetly clear my throat, and with some well-honed self-restraint, I pull myself together enough and shove the top over her head to hide her perfect body from my untrustworthy thoughts.

I start to button the first few buttons of the little cropped shirt but stop when I notice that she's gone eerily silent. Her eyes dart to her left arm, and anger fills me when I realize her focus.

"Knock it off," I demand.

Her blue eyes flare with anger when she peers at me, but I'm angrier than she is for acting self-conscious in front of me. My hands fall to her hips, and I spin her quickly to walk us up to her mirror. "Never do that again."

I'm surprised at how gruff my voice is and even more surprised when Taytum doesn't snap back with some kind of rebuttal at my tone. I snag her stare in the mirror before I shift my attention and look at our reflection.

She's half-dressed, and her long, messy hair is hanging over her shoulders, hiding those perky breasts that I couldn't stop staring at a second ago. I'm towering behind her with my hands on her hips, and I *hate* that, for a split second, I picture her as mine instead of my best friend's little sister who I'm forced to keep in a tightly tied little box that has the word *danger* printed on the front.

I snake my hand across her body and place it beneath the glucose monitor. "Stop acting like this is a flaw instead of a perfect addition to this killer body, Taytum."

I nearly twitch from the compliment I give her but it's the truth, and she clearly needs to hear it.

"Perfect addition?" She continues to stare at her arm, and I want to growl, just to make her look at me. "It's...the furthest thing from sexy. Can you imagine some guy taking off my shirt and the first thing he sees is this?"

"*This*"—I circle the device with my finger—"keeps you alive," I remind her. "So, to me, it's a fucking gift."

Taytum says nothing, and the longer we stand in the mirror with nothing but our heartbeats to fill the space, the more I feel obligated to prove to her that she's perfect—which isn't in my plans for this evening—or *ever*.

"Spin."

Taytum doesn't budge, which isn't surprising.

I forcefully turn her, and my fingers slip into her tight leggings. In a single whoosh, I shove them down her smooth legs, ending at her ankles, and rip them from her cute little feet.

My teeth clank together when I turn and grab her ripped skinny jeans that make every guy salivate, and I beg myself not to drop my eyes to her panties when I turn back around, but I'm not that self-disciplined.

Matching bra and panties. Fuck me.

I hold out her jeans, and she snatches them with frustration. As soon as she buttons them, I move her to the bed and make her sit. I slip the cowgirl boots onto her feet, and I'm honestly a little surprised when she doesn't kick me. Her high-pitched yelp makes me chuckle when I pull her to her feet. "You ready?"

She throws her hands up before they land on her hips. "I don't know! Am I?"

"Oh, you're ready." I wink at her, and we head for the door.

To make myself feel better for the dirty little thoughts coursing through my head at the sight of her in nothing but a bra and a pair of panties, I glance behind my shoulder at her. "Give me some space, will ya? I don't want your hot sorority sisters to get the wrong idea and think we're together or anything."

Taytum's eye roll is the first of many for tonight, I'm sure.

[17]

TAYTUM

THE NEON SIGN that flashes *The Rodeo Bar* every few seconds is probably tempting to every girl my age, in *any* other situation except the one I'm currently in. Ford opens my door, and I peer up at him through my thick lashes that I coated with mascara on the drive over and immediately laugh.

"Are you kidding me?" I ask through a laugh, all while ignoring his outstretched hand.

My cowgirl boots crunch against the gravel as I erase the short distance between us. I tip my chin and meet his lazy smile, but even with my boots giving me an advantage, Ford is at least a head taller than me.

His cowboy hat is at least *two* heads taller than me.

"What?" How he keeps a straight face, I'll never know.

My father always said Ford had the best poker face, and at this moment, I agree.

Another laugh falls out of my mouth, and before I know

it, I'm placing my hand on his crisp white tee to steady myself as my shoulders shake with laughter.

"Excuse me, *ma'am*..." Ford has a Southern drawl to his voice that typically makes an appearance when he's been drinking, but I know for a fact he's sober, because otherwise, he wouldn't be able to stay in character. "Is something funny?"

I snort, and there's the tiniest dimple digging into his cheek.

"Come on." I flip my blonde hair over my shoulder to get a glimpse of the business behind me. "What is all this?"

Ford gestures to the bar sign flashing. "It's our stage."

I bite my lip with confusion, but Ford grips my hand and tugs me to the front of the bar before I can ask any questions. Blue lights illuminate his tight t-shirt, and I can't help but stare at him for a second too long. Who would've thought that a hockey player in leather boots, blue jeans, a perfectly clean white t-shirt–hugging his biceps–and a cowboy hat could look so *hot*?

I briefly touch my forehead with the back of my hand when shame heats my skin. Even though he's dressed up as a cowboy like it's Halloween, he's still *Ford*. He's still the guy who sabotaged every date I've ever been on and the one who helped my brother spread rumors around our high school so no one would ask me out. He's also the same broody hockey player that has interrupted every kiss I've ever encountered in the last several years.

"After you, pretty lady."

My lips quiver and beg to smile at his feigned Southern accent. His hand lands on my lower back, and I'm instantly aware of his touch as he pushes me farther inside the establishment. After giving it a once-over, I meet his eye, and he's smiling sheepishly.

"How the hell did you find this place?" I ask in awe.

It's dark and moody inside with another neon sign placed above the bar. The walls are lined in bricks that are made to look like it's a dilapidated building, but the wooden beams and shiny dance floor look sturdy enough—especially with a ring of people line-dancing over top of it.

Ford nods at a few people here and there as we continue to walk toward the bar. Chills coat my arms when his warm breath skims my ear. "You know I always do my research. I thought it would be good to get out of Bexley U for the night so I could hand you the reins." Ford wiggles his eyebrows and knocks his shoulder into mine. "You get it? *Reins.*"

I try not to smile. "I knew you'd have at least one pun with me dressed like this."

He chuckles and leads me to the bar. "You fit right in dressed like that. We both do." After I sit down in a seat, Ford tips his cowboy hat to me and then turns to leave.

I panic and grip his arm. "Wait! Where are you going? You're just going to leave me here?"

Ford peels my tight grasp from his bicep. "Excuse me, do I know you?"

My mouth drops open at the same time my boots touch the sticky floor. "Are you seriously quoting me from earlier? Is this payback?"

The shadows along Ford's flexing jaw catch my eye before he quips his lip. "Stay in character! We're here for you to practice, Taytum. Why do you think I brought you so far away from Bexley U?"

I raise my voice when a crew of loud college girls pulls up to the bar and asks for shots. "Practice what?"

"Scoring a date, babe." He leans in closer, and I get a whiff of his cologne. "With me." The music switches to an ear-splitting country song, and Ford pulls me in close to whisper-yell into my ear. "Tonight, you're not Taytum. You're..." He thinks for a second. "Belle?"

"Belle? Like a Southern belle?" He can't be serious.

He shrugs, and I purse my lips. "Fine, then who are you?"

My stomach dips when he shoots me his best grin. I know the girls behind me are staring at him, and he drives the point further when he crosses his arms against his chest and flexes his biceps. "I'll be anyone you want me to be."

His tone is beyond sexy, and it does something scary to me. Warmth flows to my cheeks, and my thighs clench. *No way.* I quickly shake my head. "I'm not practicing with you."

Ford and I share silence, and there really isn't anyone more stubborn than me when it comes to him. Our little bubble is becoming tighter as more customers pile at the bar, and it's hard to breathe the longer he holds my stare.

Ford is the first to sigh, seemingly giving up. "In that case..." He turns and taps the bar with his knuckle. Right away, the female bartender pops on over. She was practically salivating the moment we walked in. "Whiskey. Neat."

"Yes, sir."

I roll my eyes at the drag in her tone.

Ford leans back onto the bar and gestures to the dance floor. "Well, take your pick, then, *Belle.* I'll be here if ya need me."

I look away from his strong profile and skim the dance floor a few times before he leans into my space with his whiskey breath. "I know how you like to challenge me, so let's see who can score first."

I stomp my boot onto the floor. "That is not fair. You're

one of Bexley U's most sought-out playboys. You can have anyone here, and you know it."

"Not true." I go to argue, but he looks away and says, "I can't have you."

My heart does a weird flip. I take my hand and press the heel of my palm into my chest for a brief second before rushing out onto the dance floor to run from whatever that statement just did to my insides.

I can't have you.

I know he's only saying things to get a rise out of me, but it totally worked. I survey the dance floor like a floozy predator and bounce back and forth between several guys. My stomach fills with nerves, but I can't figure out why. My jaw tightens with frustration. I turn to look at Ford for help, but I'm suddenly struck in the chest with a heavy punch. He's already surrounded by wannabe cowgirls wearing daisy dukes and crop tops.

A rush of adrenaline pushes me to latch onto the nearest guy, and I'm quick to turn up the charm. My spine tingles when his hand wraps around my waist, and I pray he doesn't mention my glucose monitor.

"Hey," he says, pulling me in closer. I turn and press against the front of his jeans. "I already know you're not from Wilder U."

My hair falls down my back when I tilt my chin to look at him. "How do you know that?"

"Because I would have noticed you." His fingertips trace the skin above my jeans. "Trust me."

I bat my eyelashes and smile before snagging the near-empty drink from his hand and downing it in a single gulp. Alcohol is on my no-go list, but Dr. McCarthy told me that one won't cause too much of an issue once I get my insulin dosage stabilized. There's a spark of excitement that follows the burn, and with every one of his touches, I feel a little more confident. When I spin around and put my arms around his neck with the change of song, my confidence wobbles a little. I'm grounded by Ford's lingering gaze, and my cheeks flame—like I'm in trouble. *Did he see me finish off the drink?*

The flirty gleam in his blue eyes hardens with something dangerous, and I gulp. His neck moves with a slow swallow, and I stop functioning when he grabs the nearest girl by the hand and drags her to the dance floor.

Right beside *me*.

[18]

FORD

I SHOULD HAVE NAMED her something other than Belle, because with the way Taytum is moving her hips against some dude, she is the *furthest* thing from a Southern belle.

It's typical of her to go against me in every scenario, so I knew she'd throw a fit when I offered to be her test dummy, but I didn't expect to feel this cagey over watching her dance with some random guy, considering I mentally prepared myself for this. I can't deny the strong urge to get in between them, though, and it has nothing to do with her brother's protective streak rubbing off on me.

The song changes, and I should be paying attention to the two chicks dancing in front of me and how their tempo is nothing short of sexy, but I'm too busy staring at the sweat forming on Taytum's hairline. My mouth runs dry when the guy leans down and says something inaudible in her ear, and I have to turn away to keep myself from doing something stupid.

This is for her.

I brought Taytum here, without the watchful eyes of our peers, so she could embrace her freedom. It was supposed to be about liberation. It is supposed to loosen her up, yet I want to reach my hands out and trap her body to mine.

I take the brunette's hand, and I spin her around, only to stumble and let her go at the last second. Taytum's mouth is being ravished by the guy she's dancing with, and I can't breathe.

My heart falls to the floor, and my blood runs hot. The girl I let go of recovers from our stumble and starts dancing again, but I impulsively send her flying into Taytum and her *boyfriend*. They break apart instantly, and she sends me a glare, but I can't help but drop my eyes and give her mouth a once-over.

The pink lipstick I watched her smear on her lips on the way to the bar is gone, and I'm annoyed. I want to wipe the remnants of her off his mouth with my fist.

Fuck. Stop.

My jaw locks, but I try my best to pull my shit together. "Howdy," I say to Taytum, acting like I don't know her. "Sorry about that."

Her swollen lips fall into a scowl.

"What's your name?" I ask, refusing to let go of her attention.

Taytum clears her throat. The guy she was dancing with keeps a hold of the brunette I practically threw at them, and I hope he takes her and gives me Taytum in exchange. "Belle."

I raise a brow, and we stare at each other for a few seconds before her shoulders drop slightly, and a sweet sigh flies from her mouth. "What's your name?" she asks.

Oh, are we playing the game now? I hold my hand out

and step in front of another guy who has lined up to dance with her. I repeat my earlier line, but this time, the humor is gone. "Anyone you want me to be."

Taytum tries to hold back a smile, but she fails. When her hand lands in mine, everything suddenly feels *right*.

I spin her around and chase her girly laughter. I pull her in close, and she rubs against the front of me, and just like every other time I've danced with her over the years, I regret it instantly.

Taytum reaches up, and I lower my head so she can grab my hat. She puts it on her head, and we dance for so long we're both sweating and out of breath. I do a quick scan of the room and make sure there aren't any wandering eyes that belong at Bexley U and spin her to face me. I take her arms and put them over my shoulders like we're high-schoolers again, dancing at prom.

"Come closer, Belle." I grin when she erases the space between us. My mouth is *right* beside her ear when I tip my chin lower. "Good work. But now what?"

Her voice is a rasp as she says, "What do you mean?"

"What's your next step?" I snake my arm around her lower back. The small space between us crackles, and I wonder if she feels it too. "You've danced long and hard with me after I stole you away...so now what? What do you do next? This is practice, remember? So, what's your next step if you were trying to score me?"

I feel her smile against the crook of my neck. I get a whiff of her shampoo, and my abs tighten. *Shit.* "Why did you do that?"

I pull away to get some distance between us. "Do what?"

"Why did you steal me away? I thought you weren't going to interfere."

A rough swallow works itself down my throat as I try to come up with a good excuse. "You don't seem mad about it."

She scoffs lightly to conceal the truth, but it doesn't work. All I can think about is how cute she looks in my cowboy hat.

"Were you *jealous*, Ford?" She's teasing me, and typically, I'd tease her back, but her flirty smile and glittering blue eyes do something wild to me.

"I wouldn't say I feel jealous when I see you with another guy," I answer truthfully because I know how it feels to be jealous, but I've moved past jealousy when it comes to her. I feel something much more dangerous.

My arm tightens against her lower back as I creep my other hand up her body and cup her warm cheek. There's fire in my veins with our close proximity. There's no one around that can bring me back to reality and remind me that she's Emory's little sister and the daughter of two people that I owe most of my life to. Taytum is gasoline to me, and I've never burned the way I burn with her.

"Then what would you say you feel? Because that was totally something an ex-boyfriend would do. Not my brother's best friend who swore he would help me get laid."

I grip her face a little tighter, and her blonde hair gets trapped beneath my fingers. The word flows out of my mouth without restraint. "Possessive."

The air shifts around us. Taytum jolts in my grip from my truth, and the little grin that she was wearing a few seconds ago disappears when she registers what I just said.

"I feel *so* fucking possessive when it comes to you."

Fuck. Shut up.

I'm not drunk, but I'm speaking the truth like I am.

"Possessive..." She toys around with the word a few times, and I hate myself for letting it slip.

"It's hard to let someone kiss these lips." I lift my thumb and rub the soft skin. My hand has a mind of its own, and I'm trying to lock my muscles so I stop giving away all my dirty little secrets, but Taytum is pulling them out of me one by one with the unexpected surprise I can see swimming behind her baby blues.

Shit. I have to fix this.

"Stop looking at me like that, *Belle*." I wink and hope, for both of our sakes, that she buys my act of pretending I'm in character and that this is all a little game.

Taytum blinks a couple times, and I see the realization click.

"Are you still playing the game?" I ask.

She looks away, and I wait with a breath trapped in my chest. There is a part of me that wants to take back everything I just said if she, even for a second, thinks that it's true, but the other part of me wants her to keep playing the game just so we can take it a step further.

"Walker."

I pause. "What?"

"You said you'll be anyone I want you to be, so your name is Walker." Taytum's warm fingers snap onto my wrist, and she pulls my arm snug around her slim waist. She pushes us back together like that's where we belong. "I'm Belle. And you're Walker."

Relief settles onto my shoulders, and although the plan was in the back of my head the entire night, the moment I saw her in those boots, I knew I was going to regret this night come tomorrow morning.

But still, I run with it.

"Okay, Belle." My voice is strained, and my hands itch to touch parts of her body that I refuse to let myself fantasize about. "Then, what's next? You have me. What are you going to do with me?"

Taytum parts her lips. I zero in on her bow-shaped mouth and nearly buckle at the knees when she smiles.

"A friend once told me to take what I want, so that's what I'm going to do."

TAYTUM

I'll never admit it out loud, but for a split second, I forgot the real reason Ford brought me to a bar several towns over from Bexley U. We're here to hone my dating skills, because if I were to be graded on it, I'd get an F.

However, if I were to be graded on my naiveness, I'd get an A.

Frustration backs my every move like I have a point to prove. But I have nothing to prove to anyone except myself.

For a second, I let myself get worked up by the one guy who is the reason I'm in this predicament in the first place. I'm not stupid enough to think he and I could ever be anything, and yet...there was a fleeting moment where I'd hoped he was telling the truth.

Ugh.

I pull Ford across the dance floor, and instead of being the flirtatious college girl that I usually am, filling the air with my airy laughter, I do exactly what he told me to do the other night. I take what I want.

Ignoring the sign on the door that says *Out of Order*, I push it open and shut it tightly once we're inside. It's one of two bathrooms, and it's exactly what you'd expect a bar bathroom to look like—especially one that isn't in use. Dim lighting, a musky scent that's barely disguised with Lysol, and hand-carved notes all over the walls. There are even a few red lipstick stains on the mirror from girls blotting their mouths after reapplying.

Ford looks around before staring at me from across the small space. "What's your plan now?" His voice is seedy, and it throws me off balance. My stomach takes a nosedive, and I have to force myself to feel the frustration I felt a few moments ago that set me on my mission.

He stays still when I slowly walk across the sticky floor to erase the space separating us. I take the cowboy hat off my head and place it on the doorknob before stepping back in front of him and pressing up against his chest. Our body heat mingles, and I reach up on my tiptoes to push my shaky hand through his sandy hair. At the last second, I grip the strands and pull his face down to mine.

I catch the faint groan coming from the back of his throat, and although I want him to kiss me, he goes for my neck instead. There's a delicious squeeze against my hips from his strong grip, and every nerve ending in my body sparks when his lips brush against my delicate skin.

I gasp like I've never been touched before, and it's followed by a line of chills racing down my spine. We're so close that not even a breath could fit in the space between us. Ford's lips skim over me as he trails kisses past my collarbone. I crane my neck to give him more access, and my vision becomes hazy when his warm breath mingles in front of my ear.

"Is this what you want?" he asks. "For me to kiss you and touch you all over?"

God, yes.

I shake in his grip. Ford presses against the door when I move closer to him, and my fingers tingle when I feel that he's just as turned on as I am.

I pull away just enough to make eye contact with him and finally answer, "Yes."

His jaw tenses, and his heavy hands squeeze me around the waist again. "Say it, then. The sooner you learn to take what you want, the sooner you'll be on your way to those one-night stands you crave so much."

He says it with a bitter tone, but I don't let it deter me. I'm too eager to feel his mouth on mine and too infatuated with the idea of my brother's best friend teaching me how it feels to be kissed by someone as experienced as him without the fear of someone pulling me away.

"Kiss me." Our mouths are almost touching, and I'm on fire. If he asked me to get on my knees and beg, I probably would.

Ford's fingers dig into my hair when he cups my face roughly. He's breathing heavily against my mouth, and the only thing it does is put me into a frenzy. "And after I kiss you? Then what? Because I'm afraid I won't be able to stop."

I swallow. "Whatever you want."

"Fuck."

I'm tangled with lust, and his clenched eyes make the pulse between my legs beat harder. I breathe out a lustful sigh, and Ford's eyes open right away. I jump from the sudden heat in his gaze, and then his mouth is on mine, and everything just *stops.*

His lips linger for a split second, like he knows he

shouldn't be doing this, but then his hand races up my body, and he traps me by the neck. Just when I think he's going to pull away, he goes in for more, and his hot tongue laps against mine like he can't get enough. He kisses me over and over again, plunging in further and exploring every inch of my mouth before he pulls back unexpectedly and squeezes my face with one hand.

"Did..." He clamps his mouth shut and abruptly pulls his gaze from mine. "Did you drink?"

Uh-oh.

I remain quiet—mainly because I can't catch my breath from our kiss. I've never felt that way from a single kiss before. Ford took my thoughts, jumbled them, and now I can't even form a sentence.

"Taytum." My name is a harsh sound squeezing from between his gritted teeth.

I want to go back to being Belle.

The disappointment I feel knowing that we're back to being *us* is ground shaking. I try to fling his hand off my face, but he squeezes my cheeks harder, keeping me in place.

"Answer me." The playful Ford, the one who insisted we play this little game, is gone.

"I had *one* tiny drink. A sip."

"Goddamnit, Taytum! You can't drink with diabetes! When did you even have a drink?" Ford groans and drops his hand. He quickly turns his back to me, and guilt washes away the last of my blissfulness. I know he thinks that I'm being irresponsible by having a drink, even if it wasn't much, but that's not true. I am well aware of my actions and the reasons behind them, and it's not something I'm willing to explain to him.

"Calm down, Ford. And if you weren't so entranced

with the daisy dukes running around this bar, you would have seen me take a sip from that guy."

Ford hurriedly turns around, and we're both glaring at each other. I cross my arms over my heavy breasts, cursing him for turning me on so much.

What a terrible idea.

"Let's go," Ford snaps.

"No," I snap right back.

He stops right beside me, and there's a twisted feeling digging into my lower belly that tells me to smile, just to push his buttons. When he turns his head to look at me, his glare is heated, and I can't decide if he's angry, turned on, or both. "I will put you over my shoulder and carry you out of this bar. Do not test me right now." He half laughs, but I recognize his sarcasm. *"Especially* now."

I open my mouth to refuse, but he stops me with the narrowing of his eyes. It isn't often that Ford lets his guard fall and shows the true feelings behind his grin, but right now, he isn't trying to hide.

"In fact..." he talks down to me like I'm a child. "I'll call your parents right *fucking* now and tell them that you've been drinking."

I gasp. *He wouldn't.* My forehead furrows, and he raises an eyebrow as a challenge.

"I can make my own decisions, and if I want to take a sip of beer from a guy, I will! Stop treating me like a fucking child."

"I would if you stopped acting like a *fucking* child." Ford swarms me, and I'm pressed against the bathroom door in two seconds flat. He moves too quickly for me to react and grabs onto my arm right below my monitor. "In case you've forgotten, this thing is helping keep you alive." Our eyes clash, and I can't speak because I know I've struck a chord. "I'll be damned if you do something to jeopardize your own health. I won't lose you to your own stupidity." He drops my arm in a huff and steps away. "Now *go*."

The bathroom door flies open from his hasty movement, and he holds it open for me. When I pass by him, I drop the act because I know exactly what chord I struck, even if he doesn't say it aloud.

[20]

FORD

I press further into the wall and bend my knees to work out my stiff muscles. Taytum has one of the best bedrooms in her sorority house, and I'm pretty positive her floor is more comfortable than my bed that the school supplied to every dorm room, but still, I've hardly gotten any rest.

Looking over at Taytum for the one hundredth time since getting back from the bar, I can't help but trace the outline of her lips with shame. I'm suddenly thirteen again, training my brain not to get a boner at the sight of her. I'm happy to announce that after several hours of being in her bedroom, I've finally stopped thinking about how fucking hot it was to kiss her in that stupid bar bathroom. Even if I'm still angry with her, my heart can't help but skip a beat when I remember the madness I felt when kissing her.

I rub my hand down my face and think about everything *after* the kiss. The panic that came from an obvious trigger of the past lays heavy in my gut, and I feel partly guilty for not keeping it under wraps in front of her.

Taytum is the only one who has ever seen me have a panic attack, but I promised myself, long ago, that I'd never lose it like that in front of anyone ever again. Naturally, she'd be the one to bring it out of me, because if Taytum is involved, everything is intensified. *Everything.*

Her phone dings, and I wait to see if she'll stir in her sleep. We haven't spoken since I put her in my car and drove back to Bexley U last night. She has no idea that I crept back into her room after dropping her off, because my anxiety couldn't handle it.

To my surprise, she stays asleep even though the sun has begun to rise and is casting an angelic glow over her. I sigh and stretch my legs out in front of myself as I reach for her phone to check the alert. I swipe away the text from her group chat because I already crept on it through the night, and it was practically a foreign language to me as they were talking about makeup.

I open the glucose tracker app that's linked to her monitor. The little ding was an alert for a high glucose reading, but it isn't any higher than normal at this time. I won't admit to her that she was right, and the one sip of alcohol she drank last night didn't affect her sugar too much, but it's hard for me to trust her when she'd been in the hospital more times this past year than ever before.

When it comes to Taytum, I can't even trust myself.

Clearly.

I yawn and reach up to massage my sore neck. My own phone buzzes, and I quickly pull it out of my pocket to see Theo's text about a spur-of-the-moment practice this morning before our game.

I mumble under my breath. "Shit."

There goes my naptime.

I click my phone off, slip it into my pocket, and busy

myself in the bathroom to get her insulin pen ready. I walk over to her bedside table and put her prepped pen there, along with an alcohol swab. After I change her alarm tone to the most annoying one and set it to go off in a few minutes, I go to exit out of her insulin app before pausing with my finger hovering over the X.

It's a controlling thing to do, but I take out my phone, and download the same app.

Taytum's login information hasn't changed since we were teenagers–it only took Emory and me three tries to guess her password the one time we went in and broke up with her boyfriend of three days on her socials without her knowing.

Not our best moment, but whatever.

Relief replaces the last remnants of anger that I've kept a hold of when I have her blood sugar readings right at my fingertips.

She'll be irate if she knows I have access to the app. She specifically told her parents *and* Emory that it was unneeded because she was an adult, but it's as much for me as it is for her.

Maybe now, I won't have to stay in her room all night to make sure she's not going into a diabetic coma and potentially play like shit at my game from lack of sleep.

After scribbling on a torn piece of her notebook paper, and signing it *Walker,* I place it on her forehead. Then, I walk out her bedroom door and head straight for practice with a little chip on my shoulder.

My skates glide over the ice as smoothly as they always have, but I'm unfocused, exhausted, and every time I look at Emory, all I can think about is how I had my tongue halfway down his sister's throat the night before.

Whether we were role-playing or not, I'm fucked up over it.

"What is with you?" Ice flies up behind Theo when he skates over to me. He slaps the side of my helmet, and the only thing it does is make my head pound harder.

I try to clear my vision. "Nothing, nothing. I'm good. Swear."

"Then start fucking defending. It's the best of seven, and I don't want to gamble with it. This isn't practice."

Practice.

One simple word, and I'm thinking about Taytum again.

I won't even let myself look into the crowd to see if she's here, because I'm afraid I'll lock eyes with her and get a boner on the ice. A boner when you're wearing a cup is my own version of hell.

"You look like shit," Emory chimes after skating past to head to his home, also known as the net. "You're playing like shit too."

I follow after him and attempt to play it cool in a desperate measure to erase the shame from last night. I'd like to erase the very vivid memory too. "At least I don't smell like shit," I quip.

Our teammates laugh before the rest of us skate to meet at the net for an encouraging chat from our captains, who I refer to as Dad One and Dad Two. Coach, who is off on the sidelines with a beet-red face, is Gramps.

Though, he doesn't know we call him that behind his back.

It's even funnier now because Aasher is shagging his daughter, so the joke of him being called Gramps is a real zinger in the locker room.

"Alright, who are we?" Theo slaps his stick on the ice.

We follow suit and slap ours at the same time while chanting, "*The Wolves!*"

"It's the best of seven, but fuck that. We're gonna sweep the ice in the first four games and be on our way. Got it?"

We slap our sticks again in agreement.

"It's 2-1, them. We have one period left to secure the W. So let's fucking go."

The sounds of the sticks echo off the ice, and we all break to get into position. Aasher does a lap and gets the crowd fired up, then he and Theo both look up into the stands with their sticks raised for a cheesy salute to their girls.

By reaction, my eyes follow. I immediately land on Taytum, who is planted dead center between them.

She didn't. Taytum's sweet smile wakes me right up. Then, she yells, "Yee-haw!" and takes *my* cowboy hat off her head and tips it in my direction.

I turn around to conceal my grin.

It's not the reaction I was hoping for. What I need is to be angry with her or, at the very least, for her to be off with some guy so I can stop secretly hoping she's saving herself for me like she's a reward for after we win this game.

Because she isn't mine, and she never will be.

TAYTUM

"OVER TO THE RIGHT," Claire says through a stretch.

We're both balancing on top of the red leather barstools, and although we're limber from years of ballet, we're still having a hard time hanging the banner over top of the bar.

"Why are *we* doing this?" I ask, reaching up higher on my tiptoes. "Shouldn't those mammoth-sized hockey players do this instead?"

Claire hooks her side of the banner and squeals with excitement just before almost toppling over onto the bar.

"Damnit, Claire! Get down." Theo rushes over and scoops her up mid-fall, holding her to his chest. His brown hair is still damp from his post-game shower, and he's peering down at her disapprovingly.

"Oh, relax. I'm fine!" She pats his chest, and I laugh under my breath.

I'm still stretching on a barstool before I decide to just climb on top of the bar for a second to hook the left side. As soon as I have it hooked, I brush my hands together and nod at our handiwork.

"You gonna pay me for hanging this?" I point to the black sign while looking at Claire's boss.

She snorts. "I'll give you free fries."

I gesture to the sign again before putting my hands on my hips. "Everyone gets free fries tonight!"

Her eyes scan the sign, and she reads it out loud. "Hockey night. Free fries when the Wolves win." She shrugs and acts surprised by the sign she made. "Darn. You're right."

I huff out a laugh. "Plus, I can't even have fries. But it's *fine*. I'm happy to help."

Angie's eyebrows furrow. "What? Why?"

I look away uncomfortably. "I have diabetes. I have to watch my carb intake."

Angie stares up at me from down below. The Bex is starting to fill up with rowdy fans. I know the rest of the team is going to show up soon. "What? Since when?"

Claire comes over and places her head on her boss's shoulder. "It's a new diagnosis. Remember when I told you that a customer fainted a little while back, and the EMTs had to come?"

Angie looks at me with shock for a quick second before sending me a comforting smile. She's just one of those women that has a natural motherly touch. She's warm and kind to not just Claire, but me too. "You know, my father had diabetes. He had some ICU admissions at one point, so you make sure you take care of yourself, Taytum."

I force a smile.

"That's what she has me for," Claire adds.

"Okay, now get down from there before I get the health department called on me."

I laugh and start to climb down from the bar just as Claire heads back to the booth. The bell over the door chimes, and I lock onto Ford walking in beside my brother. They're both freshly put together with fully dried hair, unlike Theo who had rushed over here to be with Claire.

Snow falls off the tip of Ford's nose, and he shakes off the lingering flakes on top of his wide shoulders. My stomach fills with nerves, and it's so unexpected I almost fall. I wince when I hit my glucose monitor on the barstool. I quickly cover it with my hand.

Shit, that hurt.

My brother rushes over. "What the hell were you doing on top of the bar? Are you okay?"

I turn away. "I'm fine." I slowly lift my sleeve to make sure the device is still attached, and although there's some redness around the site, it's still attached, and there aren't any alarms going off, so I'm good.

I pull my sleeve back down then turn and jump when I see Ford standing beside my brother with his strong brow furrowed as he stares at my arm.

"Will you two relax?" I brush past them, mainly to avoid Ford.

It was all fun and games when I was Belle and he was Walker, but that time is over.

I clear my throat when I scoot into the booth beside Claire. Theo pulls her onto his lap to make room for me, and since it's par for the course, Ford and Emory make their way to the other side, right in front of me.

Ford shows Emory something on his phone, and I watch my brother's shoulders drop. They fist bump, and I watch them closely. Our table fills up quickly with some more hockey players and puck bunnies, along with some of my sorority sisters, and then several heaping plates of French fries are placed in the middle.

Everyone reaches forward to take bites in between talking about the game and the after-party at Rush's. Angie comes back to our table and places a plate in front of me—and no one else. "Here." I stare at a personal pizza that's topped with leafy green vegetables. "It's thin crust, so hardly any carbs. I used to make it for my dad."

We share a quick smile, but hers disappears before she slaps Ford's hand with her waitressing notepad. "Hands off."

"Angie," he chides. "I am your best customer. Come on!"

She tips her chin toward me. "Well, I like her better, and she's prettier than you."

Ford throws his hands up but finishes with a nod. "I'll accept that."

I pull my plate in closer and stick my tongue out at Ford. He zeroes in on my mouth, and I swear, time stops. We're both frozen, whereas everyone else is carrying on with their fry grabbing and conversations. A swallow rolls down his neck with a little flare of his eye, and it's obvious that we're both thinking about what happened last night.

I cross my legs under the table, push away the thought of his hands roaming all over my body and the way he took me captive with the world's hottest kiss, and go back to eating my pizza.

"You going to Rush's?" Claire asks.

"No," Emory answers for me, and I glare at him from across the table. Ford is buried in his phone beside him, which is unusual. Emory looks to Ford's phone for a second too long and then moves his attention back to me. "She's going to go home."

"Why are you like this?" I ask the same question I've been asking him since the moment I grew boobs. He has yet to answer me.

Emory looks at my arm. "Have you checked your monitor since you hit it?"

I look around the table, thankful no one is really paying attention. "Yes..." Emory and Ford catch eyes, and I scrutinize their shared look.

"Okay..." I push myself back into the booth. "What are y'all up to?"

I refuse to let last night deter me from staring across the table at Ford. If one of them is going to break, it'll be him. "Ford?"

His jaw flexes, and he glances away.

"I hate you both." I nudge Claire with my elbow and climb out of the booth. The crowd parts, and I can't even be bothered with saying goodbye to anyone because I'm too in my head about Emory's and Ford's side glances.

They're up to something, or they're keeping something from me.

My phone buzzes, and I expect it to be Claire, but I groan the second I see the name Walker.

> Walker: If you don't come back, I'm eating your pizza.

I send him a middle-finger emoji and change his name back to Ford.

> Ford: Get back in here.

> Me: I'm going home.

> Ford: You're walking? After dark? Wearing those tight jeans? Not a chance.

> Me: I'll come back in when you tell me what you and Emory are keeping from me.

I nibble on my lower lip and wait for his response.

> Ford: He found out about last night.

I drop my phone like it's on fire. My heart falls to the snowy ground and lands right beside my phone. I turn and peer through the foggy Bex window. *There's no way.* Emory would kill Ford, even if Ford told him it meant nothing.

After sweeping my phone off the ground, I quickly type a message.

> Me: Tell me the truth, or I'll make sure Emory actually does find out about last night.

Excitement pulls me backward, and my hand is on The Bex's door as a pleased grin curves onto my face. I walk into the bustling restaurant and slowly make it to our table. Ford peeks at me from above his phone with a scowl on his face, and I'm back to feeling like myself almost instantaneously.

It's always rewarding getting a rise out of him.

I slide into the booth, all while keeping Ford's attention. I shift to Emory when Claire leans in to whisper in my ear, "Are you okay?"

I nod.

She whispers again, "The air is tense. What's going on?"

"I'll fill you in later, but play along," I whisper back.

"What are you two whispering about?" Theo asks, pulling Claire closer to him.

"Oh, just this new bar I found last night."

Emory snaps to attention. "What?"

I feign excitement. "Yeah! It's a few towns over in between here and Wilder U. It's western themed. It was a great excuse to wear my cowgirl boots."

Nola pouts. "You went without me? I want to go."

I smile at my sorority sister. "I'll take you. We'll invite the rest of the girls too."

Ford is rapidly texting, and I know I'll feel another vibration against my leg in a moment.

"Wait," Emory says. "Who did you go there with?"

I shrug sheepishly. "Just this guy named Walker. He was a *great* kisser."

Ford chokes on his water and kicks me at the same time. Emory ignores him and asks me who Walker is, but I can't stop watching Ford squirm. My phone vibrates for the third time in the last thirty seconds, and I finally put him out of his misery and read the messages.

> Ford: You won't tell him because you know I won't help you anymore.

> Ford: I have something that I think will help, but first you need to fix your monitor.

> Ford: Will you knock it off?

> Ford: Seriously, Taytum?

> Ford: And thanks, but I already knew I was a great kisser.

A tiny smile falls to my mouth, and I want to push his

buttons even more, but there's a notification at the top of my screen from my glucose tracker. *Damnit.*

"Come on." Ford nudges his head to the door.

"Go," Emory agrees, dropping the interrogation about me going to the bar with some guy. *Wait, what?*

I play stupid, because there is obviously something going on that I'm unaware of that they *are* aware of. "Go where?" I ask.

"Go fix your monitor. It needs to be re-synced."

"How do you–" I snap a glare at Ford and quickly run through the last few seconds of them sharing looks and looking down at Ford's phone. "You didn't!"

I quickly reach across the table for Ford's phone, but he's quicker than me. His fast reflexes drive me wild, and when he dips out of the booth, I'm following after him faster than I can even shout his name.

Snow pelts me in the face with the door chime following my chase. I don't get a chance to rush after Ford's footsteps because he grabs onto my waist in a swift manner and pulls me to the side of the building out of sight. My back is against the bricks, and my hands are trapped by my sides.

"Exerting yourself when you could be in a diabetic crisis isn't smart, Taytum." Ford clicks his tongue a few times, and I'd bite it if I could. "Re-sync your monitor."

I tug on my arms. "Did you seriously download and login on the app? How do you even know my password? When did you do that?"

His mouth is so insanely hot now that I know how it feels against mine. I hate that his grin twists my insides with desire instead of irritation. "I know everything about you. It isn't hard to guess your password, and I did it when you were sleeping."

A sarcastic laugh fills the space between us. "You stayed in my room all night, didn't you?" I ask.

Ford looks away, almost like he feels bad. There's a teeny-tiny slip in my anger with the thought. He can be overprotective, irritating, and borderline obsessive, but *God,* he can be so thoughtful too.

"That's why you weren't playing your best tonight, isn't it? You stayed up all night to watch me."

And here I thought it was because he couldn't stop thinking about our kiss—silly me to think I was running circles in his mind like he was in mine.

Ford pins me with a look, and there's something unreadable trapped behind the blue hue. "Partly."

The snowflakes that fall in between us do nothing to cool my flushed skin. Before, there was a playful hint in his tone, but now, there's something else. Something heavy and so damn enticing.

"And the other part?" I blink at the sound of my raspy voice. My chest rises and falls too quickly, and I pray he doesn't notice. I'm focused on his tight grip against my wrists and the small space separating us. It's too similar to last night in the bar bathroom when his hands drifted over my curves like he couldn't have stopped himself from touching me even if he wanted to.

Ford angles his head to the dark sky, and his jaw is sharper than a knife. "Don't make me say it."

My lips part when he peers down at me.

"Because once I say it out loud, I can't take it back."

I'm following his movements like my life depends on it, and when he peels his fingers from my wrist, he snakes his arm around my lower back, and instinctively, I arch. My chest brushes against his, and we lock eyes.

The snow makes everything quiet.

Silence surrounds us.

My heart races when Ford bounces his eyes back and forth between mine, and I've never felt so desirable from a single look.

The chime on the door carries to where we are, and Ford flies from my body quicker than I can take a breath. He looks like I've slapped him, and I feel like he's slapped me.

Shit. What are we doing?

Ford's hollow cheeks fill with air, and he grips the back of his neck. "After you fix your monitor, I'll show you what else I've downloaded on my phone to help you find a date..." His sentence trails, and I barely hear him when he says, "Or someone to fuck."

He takes another step backward and adds to his sentence. "Someone who isn't me."

I blush but can't fathom a response because he's right. Maybe if I can find someone to curb my insane pining, then I can stop wishing my brother's best friend would put me out of my misery and do the deed himself.

[22]

FORD

"A DOUBLE DATE?" Taytum shakes her head. "No. No way. You already get to see the guys who swipe right, and now you want to come along on a date with me...for what?" she shrieks. "You want to watch me get railed by one of them too?"

I choke on air at the visual, and I can't decide if I'm angry at the thought or turned on. Maybe both? Which, honestly, is just as bad.

Taytum climbs back onto the stage in her stupid little leotard that does nothing to help my wild thoughts. Our kiss awoke something in me, and I'm afraid the only way it's going to fall dormant again is if *she's* the one to shut it down. Which is precisely why I need her to be more active on the dating app I set her up on. She needs to be swept off her feet by some guy who isn't me, and I need to sit back and watch so I can be put in my place. As each day passes, our subtle touches are becoming less playful and more tempting.

I know she feels the chemistry just as profoundly as I do, because her pupils dilate every single time we touch. It's messing with my head.

"What's up?" Theo takes a seat beside me, and I click out of the dating app on my phone. He sends me a sideways glance when he looks from the screen and then back to my face. "Having trouble finding a girl you haven't fucked yet?"

"As if I wouldn't double dip," I say.

He chuckles. "Then why are you on Bex Hex?"

Bex Hex is the school's dating app that some college dropout created and now makes millions from. It's in the opening bio before you set up your profile, along with some inspirational shit, like how he was a nerd and couldn't score a girl until he started online dating.

Now, I imagine he's having pussy for breakfast, lunch, and dinner because of how deep his pockets go.

Good for him, though.

"I'm not," I answer.

Theo eyes me suspiciously, and I turn back to the stage to watch Taytum.

"Ah," he laughs under his breath. "Gotta do a background check on every guy who's trying to get with Em's sister?"

Something like that.

"Does he know she's on a dating app?"

I'm quick to answer, "No. And don't tell him."

Theo scoffs. "I'm not getting anywhere near that drama."

The music starts, and most of the ballerinas are on the stage, working on their opening act for next month's showcase. The number of rehearsals I've sat through are endless, yet I never mind tagging along when Taytum is dancing.

She is a ray of sunshine up there. I effortlessly follow

her leaps and twirls, and the rest of the dancers fall into a blur. Taytum's blonde hair is pinned in a bun, but there are a few curly tendrils hanging around her face. My breath hitches when she pops up from a split leap to smile brightly at Claire, who takes the next eight count.

"They were both born to dance, huh?" Theo muses, clearly in a trance while Claire moves across the stage.

I nod, and we watch the rest of the dance in silence. As soon as the music cuts off, the air shifts, and I know Theo is staring at me.

"Take a picture. It'll last longer."

He ignores my immature joke and sighs. "*You're* Walker, aren't you?"

My spine straightens.

Ever so slowly, I twist and peer at him through a squint. He's smirking, and I don't like that the roles have reversed between us. A warning is going to come out of his mouth next, but he doesn't have to say it because I already know, so I beat him to the punch. "It's under control."

Actually, I am fully fucking out of control when it comes to Taytum, but Theo doesn't need to know that, and neither does she.

He laughs so loudly Professor Petit gives us a dirty look over her shoulder. Theo lowers his voice. "Yeah, just like I had it under control with Claire."

I shake my head. "That's different. You two were fake dating. Of course you'd fall for her. You were together all the time, touching...kissing...*fucking*."

Theo's grin deepens. "The only difference between me and Claire faking our relationship is that we did it in public. You can fall for Taytum even if it's behind closed doors." He leans back, and his chair squeaks. "Trust me. I fell for Claire in the quiet moments when no one was watching."

I want to tell him to fuck off, just like he used to tell me whenever I'd tease him about falling for her, but instead, I open up the dating app under her profile and message every guy that has swiped right.

Taytum is going to go on a date with someone, and I'm going to have to swallow the bitter pill.

———

I reread the conversation between Taytum and a guy named Jack. Except, her name isn't Taytum on the app. It's Belle. Because even if Emory isn't on Bex Hex, some of the hockey players are, and he'll be the first person they turn to if they find her on there.

It's partly why I cut her face off when uploading her profile picture.

The other part is because my selfishness didn't want anyone to see her face.

I flip through the various messages that Taytum has been engaged in for the past few days. How can someone who flirts endlessly with me be so naive to all the signs these guys are giving to her? It's like she isn't even trying.

I spot her across the hall as the entire hockey team, plus some others that live in the athletic dorm, gather for the football watch party. Bexley U's football team is up against a hard opponent for the college football championship, and we're all cheering them on. Taytum jumps up and cheers beside one of her sorority sisters. Her shirt rides up a little too far—the same shirt that Emory rolled his eyes at from the snug fit—and shows off the purple bruise a few inches from her belly button.

I know it's from her insulin injections, and my first instinct is to take her off to the side, rub the sore spot, and then spend all night relearning how to do the injections so they don't hurt.

I spin around, irritated that the more days that stack in front of our kiss, the more I think about her. I mean, she's always been in the back of my head, but feeling those lips against mine sent her into my bloodstream.

My teeth grind against one another. I try to focus on the flatscreen one of the soccer players set up at the end of the hall, but I'm too antsy. I follow Rush on the TV when he does a fake play, but as soon as I hear Taytum's girly laughter from behind, I open the app, log out of her profile, and make another.

Fake name. *Check.*

Fake bio. *Check.*

Discreet profile pic. *Check.*

I search the name Belle and smile deviously when her profile pops up. I swipe right, and to my surprise, it only takes a few minutes for her to accept the chat.

Emory is paying me no attention at all with his eyes on the game, so I decide to play my own game.

I'll be on the losing side by the end of the night, but after I'm through with her, Taytum will surely score.

Hopefully, it'll snap me back into shape, and I'll score too.

But definitely not with her.

TAYTUM

I SEARCH for my brother in the crowded hall to confirm that his eyes are elsewhere before clicking on the little heart icon in the corner of Bex Hex.

Admittedly, I thought Ford's plan of putting me on a dating app was another one of his idiotic ideas to find me a boyfriend that couldn't be swayed by my brother's influence, but after getting numerous right swipes, it was sort of a confidence boost.

Of course, all the guys are boring, and not a single one of them has made my heart skip, but it's still beneficial to get some practice conversation in.

I read the message from the latest swipe.

> Favorite color, favorite food, favorite sport to watch... 3, 2, 1, and go.

I'm instantly intrigued because at least he's not automatically asking for boob pics.

> Purple, coffee... oh wait, that's not a meal, and hockey.

I click my phone off and go back to watching the game until I feel another message come in.

Oh, he's fast.

The other guys take days to respond, and sometimes they don't respond at all if I refuse to send nudes.

> Coffee is absolutely a meal. I'm with you on that.

I smile and type.

> I like you already.

I take a few steps away from my sorority sisters and lean against the wall. I place my attention on the game, and to the naked eye, it looks like I'm watching intently, but instead, I'm waiting for another message.

> Let's get coffee sometime, then.

> Someone is eager.

I'm not mad about it, but the conversation is definitely different from the rest. Most of the guys use Bex Hex for booty calls, but this guy seems...different. He doesn't text back right away, and I start to second-guess myself.

> Is coffee code for sex or something?

> I don't joke about coffee.

I quietly laugh.

> A man after my own heart.

> Why exactly are you on this app, Taytum?

My heart jumps to my throat, and I hurriedly click my phone screen off. *What the hell?* I press the device to my chest and panic. I laser in on my brother, but he's in the middle of a conversation with some girl I don't recognize, and Ford is lazily leaning against the wall, watching the football game.

I slowly peel my phone away from my chest and stare at the message, when another comes in.

> You could walk up to any guy in this crowded hall, and they'd fall to their knees for you.

My jaw slacks for a split second before I clamp it shut. I survey the hallway and scrutinize each and every male. There are a few that make eye contact with me, but none of them have a phone in their hand.

I'll give it to him. I'm definitely intrigued now.

> Are you some sort of stalker?

I don't get a chance to search the crowd for someone typing on their phone because his message comes in too quick.

> That depends. Does that sort of thing turn you on, or does it scare you?

Okay, who is this guy?

I relax into the wall again, right beside Claire's closed door with a fuzzy scrunchie hanging off the doorknob.

> It depends on what you look like I guess.

I bite the inside of my cheek and wait eagerly for his message.

> I know your type.

How could he possibly know my type when I don't even know my type?

> Oh? Please tell me what my type is. Then maybe I wouldn't be on this app.

I roll my eyes after I hit send.

> Do that again. I love it when you roll your eyes.

My neck cracks from how quickly I snap to attention. I scan the crowd again, and it doesn't take long for my beating heart to tell me that I'm more excited than I am irritated.

> Who are you?

> When you find me, you'll know.

I exit out of the conversation and look at his name. *Runner?* Is that a nickname? Or a last name? A lot of athletes go by their last name, so that would make sense. I'm about to search the student directory, when he messages again.

> Stop trying to figure it out and play the game with me.

I grin.

> You don't want to play a game with me. I always win.

> I'd love to see you score.

My fingers pause over the screen because I can't decide if it's meant to be a sexual innuendo or if I'm just that messed up from the other night when Ford got me all twisted. I'm desperate for anything at this point–even dirty messages on a dating app from some guy that's potentially a stalker.

For the love of God.

I'm pathetic. I can't even get myself back to normal with my own imagination and fingers. Unfortunately, Ford always pops into my head right before I'm about to orgasm, and then I end up denying myself the one pleasure I can get.

Another message comes through.

> And yes, I meant it in the way you're thinking.

Bexley U scores a touchdown on the screen, and everyone cheers around me. I seem to be the only one within eyesight that has their phone in their hand, so I move a little farther into the chaos for a better vantage point.

> Your cheeks turned pink when you read that message.

Oh my god. *Who the hell–* Another message comes through.

> Does that mean you want to score tonight, Taytum?

I've wanted to score since I was kissed by Ford.

> You do. You're biting your lower lip like you're thinking about something inappropriate.

Oh my god. I type quickly.

> Who are you?

My stomach fills with butterflies, and I'm starting to sweat.

> Now what fun would that be if I told you?

He's right. It's more exhilarating this way. It would be even more exhilarating if Ford was reading these messages and foaming at the mouth with jealousy. But he's the one who wants me on here to find a guy who isn't him, so I push that thought right out of my head.

> What are you thinking about? You've got that look in your eye...like you're about to do something that your big brother wouldn't approve of.

My eyebrow flicks.

> He doesn't approve of anything I do, so I have to do everything in secret.

Like kissing his best friend in a dirty bar bathroom.

I bite my lip again and wait for a response. I take a look around the crowd and linger on a few guys who have their phones out, but when they put them away, I don't have a message, so I internally pout.

> Tell me what you do in secret...

I lock onto the back of Ford's head, because he's now one of those secrets. There's a little turn of my belly when I see a girl standing beside him with her hand on his bicep, laughing at something he said.

My breath hitches, and I'm instantly irritated at the bite of jealousy I feel.

I type hard and fast, as if playing this little game with a stranger is going to erase my body's reaction to him.

> When I'm alone?

I start to get antsy when he doesn't message me right away. When I feel the vibration against my palm, I almost drop the phone.

> Yes.

> I want to know what you do when no one is around.

> Late at night.

> Behind closed doors.

With every message that comes in, my skin flushes hotter. I gather my hair at the nape of my neck and pull it to the side to get some air flowing.

> Oh, it must be pretty good if you're starting to sweat.

I refuse to look around the hallway again, and I absolutely will *not* look in Ford's direction to see if that girl is still beside him, because deep down, I know I shouldn't care.

> It is good, and I definitely sweat.

> Where do you touch first?

Why is this so hot? And why am I letting some random guy on a dating app turn me on? My mouth runs dry, and I break my one rule and look at Ford again. My heart slips when I find the same girl beside him.

I have no right to be jealous or, even worse...hurt. Yet, I am.

My fingers fly over the screen.

> My thighs

My pulse picks up pace, and I'm determined to find my mystery guy before the night ends.

> If it were me, I'd touch you there too. I'd trail a finger up each smooth leg until landing at the brim of those lacy panties I know you're wearing.

My jeans suddenly feel too tight as I imagine the relief I'd feel if I shimmied out of them and were able to do the thing he just described.

> Then what?

I ask, desperate for his answer.

His message is quick, and butterflies fly to my throat.

> I'd peel them off your body and spread you wide.

I exhale and lazily scan the sea of students again because I have to know who he is.

> Is that what you do next? Shove your panties past your hips and spread yourself wide so you can get yourself off?

Jesus. A delicious heat brews between my legs, and I'm suddenly thirsty.

> Wouldn't you like to know...

I tease.

I nibble on my bottom lip and try to cool myself off with a quick puff of air from my mouth. My panties are wet, and if I listen hard enough, I bet I can hear the throb between my legs.

> I'd love to know.

> I'd love to suck on that lip that you can't seem to stop biting too.

I'm panting at the thought of this mysterious guy touching me. It's the first guy I've had even an inkling of an attraction to, besides Ford, and I don't even know what he looks like.

> Are you nice and turned on, Taytum?

Thank God I'm leaning against the wall, because my knees are weak, and my chest screams for air.

> Look at you over there. All hot and bothered in the middle of a crowded room.

I type quickly.

> Are you going to do something about it?

I immediately look up when I hit send.

He's *obviously* watching me, and I'm going to find out who it is.

I pass over the guys who are sitting with their girlfriends and the ones who are in a deep conversation about the football game playing on the screen. There's an intense game of beer pong at the end of the hallway that I ignore, so I swing my gaze to the other side of the hall, and my stomach bottoms out.

My heart thumps so hard I hear it in my ears. I'm engulfed in flames when I latch onto a set of familiar blue eyes a few feet from my brother.

We stay locked in a deep stare, and I type my message without looking.

> Do you enjoy tormenting me?

I wish I could disguise what I'm feeling as anger, but my body disagrees on every front.

Ford slowly looks down at his phone, ignoring the girl beside him, and types something.

I feel the vibration against my palm and finally pull my eyes away from him.

> No, but I do enjoy turning you on.

My fingers fly over the screen.

> I hate you.

I turn my back and stomp down the hallway to the back set of stairs. I don't say goodbye to my brother or to any of my sorority sisters. I'm too worked up to think straight, let alone speak in a coherent manner.

How dare Ford message me under a fake profile, turn me on, and then drop a bomb like that?

What kind of game is he playing?

And why do I enjoy playing it?

I push open the door and rush down the stairs. I crave to feel the wintry air on my heated face, because maybe it'll be enough of a shock to cool me down.

Instead, I get another type of shock. The kind I feel in my bones.

Leaning against the door that stands between me and the snowy weather is my opponent.

Unfortunately for him, he's about to lose at his own game.

[24]

FORD

I could ravish her.

Wide-eyed with pink-tinted cheeks, Taytum stops on the last step with those baby blues that suck me in with one look.

"Where're you going?" I quip.

I shove my hands inside my pockets to lock them away because I don't trust myself not to grab her waist, spin her around, and whisper more dirty things into her ear.

That is not part of the plan, and it's vital that I stay on course.

"I'm leaving!" Taytum is on the edge of insanity, and I fucking love it.

I shake my head. "No, you're not."

She straightens her spine when she descends down the last step. I almost want to tell her to stay put because I can't afford for her to get any closer to me, but instead, I remain in my casual stance with one shoulder leaning against the wall and my hands in my pockets. "You're going to turn around, go back upstairs, and score." A heavy sigh fills the tight space, and it seems like I'm frustrated with her, but I'm not. I'm frustrated with my semi-hard dick. "You're supposed to take what you want, remember? And I'm supposed to be helping you score a few one-night stands and a potential date or two."

Her arms fly across her chest, and it's a temptation like no other. My eyes fall to her perfect tits, and my throat closes.

"What I want is to punch you in the face," she snaps.

I chuckle. "That's not what you want to do to me."

Abort. Abort. Abort.

My restraints are loosening, and the seed of anger in Taytum's glare is nothing but a lure. I push off the wall and stalk over to her, ignoring the warning bells going off in the back of my head. I'm not surprised when she doesn't move, but I really wish she had.

I take the back of my hand and slowly brush my knuckles against her warm cheek when she tips her head to stare up at me. "I got you all worked up, Tay. So, what are you going to do about it?"

The pad of my finger tingles when I trace the curve of her lips. A raspy chuckle leaves me when she tries to bite it, and a second later, her back is up against the wall. The red exit sign paints the small space with a reddish hue, and the only thing I can think is how badly I want to unbutton her jeans, slip my hand in between her legs, and feel how much I've turned her on.

"You going to fix the problem I gave you? Or are you going to puss out like you keep doing with all those other guys you're messaging?"

She swallows, and I tilt my head like a predator. I feel

wild with her trapped in my arms with no one around to stop me.

I lean in closer, and Taytum's blonde hair brushes against my hand on her waist when she tips her head against the wall. Her rib cage expands a second too fast, and the only thing I'm doing is making things worse, yet I can't stop.

"It's almost like you're scared. I thought you wanted freedom, yet you won't take it."

Taytum's sweet breath hits my face, and my mouth waters.

My dick is so hard it hurts, but I know better than to brush it against her. One single touch and my limit will be reached.

"Well, considering that every time in the past when I've run off with some guy, you or Emory show up like a fucking nightmare, yeah, maybe I am a little afraid. I don't like to be left high and dry." Her little jaw tenses, and I grip her chin to make her loosen it.

"You have my word. Emory has already disappeared with some puck bunny, and I promise you I won't interfere." I pull my gaze away and stare at the door. "Why do you think I sent all those messages? I'm trying to help you. I told you I'd help you date, have one-night stands, whatever. This is me keeping my word and pushing you out of your comfort zone."

It's total bullshit.

I'm pushing her out of her comfort zone so it'll stop me from keeping her for myself.

Taytum's fingers trace every one of my knuckles on the hand that's holding her steady. I tighten my grip and watch her lips form words that are dangerous to my ears. "And what if, right now, I want you?"

I have to physically pull myself away. The images in my head of what I want to do to her are going to send me straight to the grave, and if she doesn't get out of my sight, I'm going to do something I'll regret.

"No." My tone is harsh. "Go find someone else."

A short gasp cuts from her mouth, and it's sharp enough to make me bleed.

"Fine!"

I can't fathom turning around to watch her stomp up the stairs, so I wait until I hear the door open and close before spinning and slapping the part of the wall I trapped her against.

Something would have happened if I kept her hidden away in this little nook with no witnesses, and I'd likely regret it. But standing here alone while she's upstairs flirting with some guy who probably doesn't deserve her is something I may regret even more.

I take a few more deep breaths and decide that it's been a reasonable amount of time since she left, so I climb the same steps she stomped up and return to the party. The hall has cleared significantly, and it looks like Bexley U is on top with hardly any time left in the last quarter.

Theo and Claire have emerged from their room, and she's leaning against his chest while they watch Rush take a blow after throwing a pass downfield.

I try to keep my attention on the game, but I can't help myself. I do a quick search-and-rescue for Taytum. I turned her down, and it wounded her, which means she's most definitely going to act out. She's probably with someone I detest. Knowing her, she's probably fucking him in my room.

"Where have you been?" Theo asks, throwing me his knuckles.

I hit them a little too hard, and both he and Claire look at me suspiciously. Theo studies me, and he likely knows where I've been, but I brush him off and stare at the screen before pulling out my phone and deleting all the messages between Taytum and me.

If there's no evidence, it didn't happen, right?

"Do you know where Taytum is?" Claire asks.

She's on her tiptoes, looking past the group of girls wanting my attention, but I can't even pretend to be interested in them.

"Nope."

Theo clears his throat, and I shoot him a lethal glare. Claire steps right in front of me, and I'm forced to shift my attention to her small frame. "Yes?" I ask, dragging the word out.

"What happened?" Her hand falls to her hip with the same amount of attitude her best friend possesses.

"Nothing happened." It's the truth, but it feels like a lie. "Emory is distracted, and she asked me to stay away, so I'm giving her freedom."

"Is that so?" There's a hint of skepticism behind Claire's question, but all I do is nod and go back to watching the game. She sighs, shakes her head, and then strides over to Theo again. Before long, the game is over, and everyone is clearing out of the hall.

My cheek is raw from chewing on it, and I've checked my phone at least five times in the last minute. I turn it on silent for my own mental sake and shove it in my pocket. I force myself back to my room, ignoring the girls hoping to get my attention, and plan to stay there all night.

It wasn't supposed to be this difficult to distance myself from Taytum. I've done it for years, pretending she wasn't sleeping two doors down from me in high school and acting like she didn't exist when we were in a crowded room when all I really wanted to do was look in her direction. I used to force myself to grab the girl off to the side instead of grabbing her, but right now, I feel tormented.

I open the door to my dorm with my head hung low.

As soon as I'm inside the threshold, I stop dead in my tracks.

She fucking didn't.

It's scary how well I know her.

Taytum's shirt lays at my feet, and I kick it halfway across the room. I pull my eyes away from the bundled cotton and land on her half naked body on top of my bed.

The ground shakes.

Her flimsy bra strap is pulled down her shoulder, and the guy she ended up with is sucking on her neck like a fucking vampire.

Words are nonexistent. All I can do is stare.

I take in the scene with an alarming calmness. A lethal dose of anger flies though my blood stream that's quickly followed by desire. A little moan falls off her lips, and it's the sexiest thing I have ever heard.

I have never been so jealous in my life.

Taytum knows I'm standing here. I know she can feel it when I enter a room, just like I can when she does. She's putting on a show for me because she's still playing the game, but I want to call it quits.

My throat bobs when I watch her straddle him. She wraps her smooth legs around his waist, and his dirty hands fall to her hips like she's his to touch. His face goes to her breasts, and I know what he's going to do next, because it's what every guy would do. He wants to taste her, suck on her nipples, and make them pucker against his tongue.

That's it.

Now I'm going to have to set my dorm room on fire, get thrown out of Bexley U, and never make it to the pros. But at least I won't have to stand here and die a slow death as some guy touches what's mine.

The moment Taytum peeks at me through the thick strands of her hair, I glare. At first glance, she appears deceitful. She's so proud of herself, and the saying *Payback is a bitch* is ringing true at the moment. But then, something changes. She blinks those thick, dark lashes a few times, and her brow furrows. Her porn-star hip movements stop, and the guy—probably some stupid underclassman who fell for her lure—asks her why she stopped.

"Out!" I bark.

The guy practically throws Taytum, and I'm about to throw him. Fortunately, I'm too concerned with Taytum's glazed daze to worry about if he lives or dies.

I rush over to my bed and run my hand down her face.

Her skin is clammy, and her breathing is erratic. I quickly scoop her into my arms and press my fingers to her pulse. *Shit.*

"Taytum, when was the last time you've eaten?" I'm on the edge of insanity. Fear grips me, and my pulse matches hers. I pull my phone out of my pocket, and nausea races toward me.

Her eyes drift, and I shake her. She blinks a few times, and I can tell she can't focus.

"Fuck, Tay. Your sugar is low. Did you take too much insulin?"

"Yes. I mean, no. I...I'm fine." *No, you're not.* "I know what I'm doing."

I place her on the bed and rush over to my gym bag. With a shaky hand, I undo the emergency snack kit that Emory and I both purchased as soon as she was diagnosed and pull out the bottle of glucose tablets. I open the bottle so quickly half of them fall to the floor, but I swoop up a couple into my palm and pull her into my lap.

"Open your mouth."

She does as I say, and I pop the pink tablets into her mouth and close her jaw. Her head sways to the side, and we're both sweating. I brush her hair away from her sticky forehead, and she closes her eyes.

"I've got you," I whisper.

We stay in the same position for almost twenty minutes before she nods against my chest. I run my hand down her arm and watch goosebumps rise. "Better?"

"I'm okay," she croaks.

Her eyes are shut, and she turns further to her side. I shimmy down onto my bed, and she exhales slowly when my arm comes around to trap her. I cup her head to my chest when she drapes a leg over mine.

I have no idea what just happened or why her sugar was so low, but instead of asking, I let her rest with the promise of bringing it up later.

Right after I punish her for trying to fuck some guy in my bed.

[25]

TAYTUM

I HEAR the click and feel the tiny pinch half a second later. My eyes clench when someone squeezes my finger, but I decide to keep my eyes closed because I already know it's Ford. I try to drift back to sleep because if I never make eye contact with him, then I won't have to acknowledge what happened earlier in the evening.

My head dips when he exhales, and his heartbeat grows steadier against my ear, telling me that my blood sugar reading is okay.

I want to ask why he's taking it manually when I'm wearing a monitor on my arm that everyone insisted on, but I choose the avoidance route instead.

After at least twenty minutes of keeping my eyes closed and making sure his pulse stays steady, I peek one eye open and see that it's completely dark in his room. The hallway noise has quieted, and the random guy I pulled into Ford's room before anyone could see is long gone.

I replay the night over and over again, hating that I can

still feel the effects of Ford's dirty messages and how good it felt to tease him...until things took a nosedive.

My blood sugar dropped quickly, and truthfully, I'm lucky that Ford walked in when he did, because I was unprepared—which was careless of me, considering I knew that it would drop eventually.

It's a shame I didn't get to finish my rendezvous because of the events that came after. I should be used to the feeling of disappointment, but the longer I lie on top of Ford, the more my body is reminded of what I didn't get.

I shift and pray he's fallen asleep. I breathe evenly through my nose and try to straighten my thoughts, but I keep ending up in the same place: *Ford*. His tongue in my mouth, his hands on my curves, the flare of jealousy in his eyes when he saw me on top of his bed. I shift gears and force myself to think about the handsy sophomore and his hot kissing, but that only makes things worse.

"Taytum."

I freeze and pretend to be asleep.

"Are you okay?" Ford asks. "You keep squirming. I checked your blood sugar. You're pretty level right now."

I nod softly against his chest. I unhook my leg from around him, but his hand comes down on top of it, and he pushes it back down.

"What's wrong? Don't lie to me if you feel sick," he demands.

"I don't," I whisper. "I feel fine."

It's a half truth. I'm one big giant knot that needs untying, but it has nothing to do with my blood sugar, so in that sense, I *am* fine.

A few moments of silence pass, and I'm right back to where I was before—turned on and itching to be alone.

"Stop moving, and tell me what's wrong," he urges.

"I'm fine, really." I slowly sit up, but Ford forces me to my back. There's likely a scowl on his face as he peers down through the dark, but all I can see is the outline of his messy hair and broad shoulders. "*Taytum.*"

I copy his low tone. "*Ford.*"

His grip against my upper arms tightens. "What is it? I know when something is wrong."

I quietly scoff, but he's right. He always knows.

Ford's breath brushes against my chest, and I just remembered that I'm in my bra. *Great.*

"I don't trust you," he admits.

My eyebrows furrow. "Says the guy who made a fake profile just to message me all sorts of dirty things." I pull on my arms, but he doesn't let up. "I don't trust you either."

"You tried to fuck some guy in my bed." His words are clipped with anger, and my cheeks feel hot.

I try to turn away, but Ford blocks me, so I'm left with only my words. "Well, that's your fault. You turned me on and then told me to go find someone else."

"Isn't that what you wanted all along? To find some guy and have a few one-night stands here and there? To go on dates without me interfering and without Emory bursting through the door?" Ford flops to his back, and my arms suddenly feel cold without his touch. "And to clarify, I didn't tell you to fuck them on my bed."

"Well, I still didn't get what I wanted, so there's that!" I'm brimming with irritation, and I'm still turned on, which is only pissing me off further.

"That isn't my fault!" he argues. "I walked into *my* bedroom. It wasn't like I was purposefully interrupting your little fuck sesh." Ford is angry, and that doesn't happen often.

I sit up abruptly. "Yeah, well, I didn't get off! There!

Are you happy? I finally got pushed far enough with your little tactics that I broke down and pulled some guy in here, and I still didn't get what I wanted!" My shoulders drop in defeat, but I'm frantic on the inside. "Now you know what's wrong with me. I'm turned on and full of irritation. It's not a nice combo." My body flushes with heat. "Thank you for showing up and giving me some glucose tablets and for making sure my blood sugar is okay, but I'm leaving now, because I cannot lie comfortably in this bed with you after how my night started *and* how it ended."

I hook a leg over his and try to scramble off his bed for my shirt, but I'm hauled to my back. Breath whooshes out of my lungs and past my lips quickly. I try to scan the dark room for an escape because there is nothing good that can come from me staying in his bed.

"I'm not leaving you alone after you nearly fainted." My lips open to fling out a rebuttal, but Ford puts his hand over my mouth to silence me. "If you're in need of a release that bad, then go for it. But you're stuck with me for the rest of the night, Tay."

I want to scream and kick my legs, but I remain unmoving and silent.

When he feels it's safe, he slowly removes his hand from my mouth and lies down on his side of the bed.

Between clenched teeth, I forcefully say, "Fine," but still attempt to climb over him. His hand snaps to my hips before I can even explain myself. "Relax! I'm not leaving. I'm sleeping on the other bed. Away from you."

He says nothing. His hand leaves my waist, and I pad over to the other side of the room on quiet feet. I tear open a dresser drawer and steal one of his shirts. The sound of my jeans hitting the floor echoes in the silent room, and my bra goes next. I know he can't see much, so I don't bother covering up when I pull his large t-shirt over my head. Then, I climb into the bed opposite of his and am thankful he no longer has a roommate so I don't have to torture myself by lying in his bed.

"Are you going to make sure to listen to blood sugar alerts? Or do I need to continue to check for you?"

His condescending tone sets me on fire, but I keep my response nice and steady. "I can check my own blood sugar."

A beat of silence passes.

"Are you going to get yourself off, or do I need to do that for you too?"

My jaw slacks at the audacity. "Actually, I was wondering if you could go find that guy that was in here before to see if he can come finish the job."

"Over my dead fucking body," he mutters. "How's this? Just go to sleep."

I roll my eyes. "I think I'll just wait for you to fall asleep, and then I'll get myself off."

A few seconds pass before he pretends to sleep, and his fake snoring fills the room. My lips wobble as I try not to break the tension with a giggle but fail miserably, and we're both quietly laughing.

Ford's ability to make me laugh when I'm angry with him is unmatched. It's the reason why I haven't killed him yet.

I pick up a pillow and throw it at him from across the room. "You're annoying."

"Goodnight, Heartbreaker."

I sigh, turn to my side, and try my hardest to go to sleep.

[26]

FORD

I WOULDN'T BE SURPRISED if we are still awake when the sun starts to rise. It's torture lying in my bed and having to listen to her quick shifting and dramatic sighs.

With every second that disappears into the night, the tenser the room becomes. We're trapped in a bomb, and if I don't fall asleep soon, it's bound to explode.

Visions of her on my bed with her bra half-hanging off her arm gives my spine a thrill, and her ragged breathing across the room is baiting me like no other.

I fiddle with my phone in my palm and stare at the Bex Hex app in the far corner.

It's bait too.

And it's one I take.

My fingers hover over the screen, and although the room is illuminated slightly by my screen, I still can't see much of her through the darkness. I have no issues coming up with a visual in my head, though.

> Go to sleep.

I grin when I hear her phone vibrate. There's a second glow on the ceiling from her screen, but I refuse to look at her.

> I would, but there's an annoying presence in the room that's keeping me awake.

I snort. She's so incredibly irritating, but I love bantering with her.

> You think I'm the one keeping you awake? It's so tense in here that I can't breathe.

Her fingers type aggressively. I see her turn to her side out of my peripheral vision, but I stay on my back to avoid facing her.

> Well, let me go home, and then you'll sleep just fine.

> Not a chance.

> I would rather stay in this room with you and continue being tortured from the sexual tension than let you go off on your own and potentially fall into a diabetic coma. So no. You're staying in here until we have a little chat about earlier.

She sighs, and I wish I could catch it with my mouth. My stomach pulls at the thought and...*fuck*.

> There's nothing to talk about.

> Like hell there isn't.

Her phone screen shuts off, and my jaw clicks. I type another message.

> You think you can avoid me? I'll get out of bed right now, pull those covers off your bare legs, and torment you until you agree to talk about that little comment you let slip. Did you purposefully take too much insulin? Why would you do that?

There's an angry force driving my fingers to type harder and faster. Taytum knows more than anyone why I'm triggered by her irresponsible actions. It's like she's gambling with her health, and I can't understand why she would do that to herself.

Or why she would do that to me.

My nostrils flare with irritation when I read her next message.

> Tormenting me won't work because there's nothing to talk about.

She's testing me, and I'm not in the mood for games.

I slowly place my phone down on my bedside table. I can practically feel the disappointment from across the room. Taytum likes arguing with me as much as I like arguing with her, but I'm about to put my best friend's little sister in her place.

Despite growing up together and having an obvious soft spot for her, her little stunt tonight–both of them–is beyond enough to provoke me.

I let a few minutes of silence pass before I hear another sigh, and that's when I quietly rise from the bed and stalk across the room.

"You think I can't force you into talking?" I ask, staring down at her darkened form on the bed. She turns toward the wall and puts her back to me.

What a little brat.

"I think I can hold out a lot longer than you think," she whispers over her shoulder. "Don't forget, I've lived with your tormenting antics for years."

My lips curve as I walk right into the deep end. I rip the blanket from her legs and climb onto the bed.

"What are you doing, Ford?" The way my name falls from her lips is enticing. She can act annoyed, but I know, deep down, she isn't.

"You're right..." I slip an arm under her pillow while the other arm falls to the curve of her torso. "You have lived with my tormenting antics over the years..." I move my mouth to her ear and whisper, "But never like this."

Touching her is euphoric. My heart swells, and my dick tingles when I pull her t-shirt up high enough to expose her hip. There's a throb in my temple from clenching my jaw so hard, and I want to sink my teeth into her skin after I slip my fingers underneath the very top of her panties. *God.* I love the way she feels against my palm.

"Ford." My name squeezes out in between her raspy, shallow breaths.

"Rethinking how long you can hold out until you agree to talk?" I tease.

She shakes her head quickly but pushes her ass against me. My eyes widen, and I drop my head to her shoulder to brace myself. I continue rubbing my finger against her skin until I feel goosebumps rise to her flesh, and then I push her a little further. I take my middle finger and swipe it just low enough to drive her wild. There's heat pulsing from in between her legs, and it makes me feral.

I know how wrong this is, but I crave to know what she's hiding between her legs. I want to feel her on my fingers and lick them clean so I can finally stop wondering how good she tastes.

Fuck.

Taytum's feverish breathing is the only sound I hear besides my racing heart. I inhale deeply, smelling her sweet shampoo, and attempt to hold myself back.

Don't give in.

I brush a finger over her clit, and she shivers. Something inside of me breaks when I pull back, and I almost bite my own tongue off.

"You think I'm going to give in that easily and touch you?" My words are strained, and that's exactly how I feel on the inside. "I will tease you until you're begging me to let you have that orgasm you're desperate for..." Taytum flips to her back, but I'm quick to pull my hand out of her panties so I don't *accidentally* slip a finger inside her.

What a grave mistake that would be.

"I don't need you," she snaps.

I act fast and quickly pull up on her panties. The rip of the lacy material echoes throughout the room, and she gasps. "Looks like you don't need these panties, either." I bundle the scrap of fabric in my hand and chuck them to the floor.

"Ford."

My heart flatlines because my name is more of a moan coming from her mouth.

I might die if I don't touch her.

But she'll die if she doesn't get her shit together and stop fucking with her insulin, which is why I refuse to let her win this little game.

"Hmm?" My finger trails down one thigh slowly and

back up until I move to the other one. I brush her clit with my knuckle on the way, and she whimpers.

"Stop it."

A chuckle leaves me. "Ready to talk about it?"

"No." The moon has moved to the corner of the window, and if I wait just a couple more minutes, the glow will land right on her, and I'll get the perfect view.

She's playing dirty, though. Her sexy little whimpers and heavy breathing are highly addictive, but I've been keeping myself from her for years, so I know I can hold off until she breaks. I was born for this.

"Okay," I whisper. "But just remember that you asked for it." I remove my hand from her leg, brush over her clit once more for funsies, and grip her by the neck. I feel her throat bob beneath my palm, and when she turns her face to mine, I claim it.

The kiss is just as intense as it was the other night. Only, this time, I don't hold back. I move my mouth against hers, and my tongue plunges inside further with each brush against hers. I'm blinded by how overwhelming it is to kiss her, and I wonder how I'll ever be able to move on from it.

Taytum breaks away after I nip her lip. "Fi–fine."

My world stops spinning. I blink a few times to ground myself. "What was that?"

"You win. I'll talk...just put me out of my misery."

Her shaky fingers land on my wrist, and she pulls it from the grip I have on her neck. I let her lead it over her soft skin to land between her legs.

I'm going to hell.

It's hard to force the question out, because I'm afraid of her answer, but I do it anyway. "So, you *do* need me to get you off?"

I wait nervously for her answer, fully prepared for her

to come to her senses and push me away, but instead, she nods. I shift in surprise, and the bright glow from the window shines along her face, showing me how desperate she is. Her long eyelashes flutter with a vulnerability that I rarely see, but doesn't she know that I'd give her my life if she asked for it?

"I can't do it."

"Can't do what?" I ask.

She glances away. "Every time I try to get off, I can't finish, and it's all your fault." Her bottom lip juts forward. "You messed me up the other night, and now all I can think about is you."

Ah, hell.

"I really wish you wouldn't have said that."

Her teeth sink into her bottom lip. "Why?"

"Because now I'm about to fucking devour you."

TAYTUM

THE LONGER FORD toys with me, the greedier I become. It isn't long before I'm desperate for his touch and crave to have some sort of release. We both know that, come morning, we will likely never be allowed in a room alone together again, but right now, my brother could be banging on the door, and I'd still beg Ford to touch me.

He peels my fingers from the grip I have on his wrist and pushes both of my arms up above my head. The oversized t-shirt I'm wearing is pushed up high enough that Ford can probably see the bottom of my breasts, and I want to arch my back further just so he can get a full view. I don't just want him to get me off; I want him to do exactly what he threatened.

I want him to devour me.

I want him to touch every single part of me, even if I know we'll both regret it later.

"Keep your hands there," he demands. "If you need me to get you off, I don't want your help."

I inhale sharply, but for once, I do as he says. The backs of my arms press into the pillow that my head rests on, and I curve toward him when he climbs on top of me. He shoves my shirt up higher, and the cool air brushes over my sensitive nipples before they're suddenly covered in warmth. He pinches one with his hand while his mouth sucks on the other, and I whimper softly. He shifts and does the same thing to the opposite side, and I hold my breath.

"Breathe, Tay," he whispers before placing a soft kiss in between my breasts.

The way his hands grip my body sends me into a frenzy. I'm twisted and knotted in every way possible.

Ford hovers above me, and I stare at his sexy smirk. "Let's see how many times I can get you off, shall we?" His raspy chuckle vibrates against me. "Surely it won't be anywhere near the number of times I've imagined it, though."

I flutter when he rubs against my clit. I'm already spiraling, and part of me feels like I should be embarrassed at how turned on I am, but I can't seem to find it in me to care. There's a deep need rooted inside of me that wants to make him proud by how many times I get off for him.

Wait, what?

Ford repeats the action over and over again, continuing to rub against the most sensitive part of my body. I shut my eyes when he glides the same finger inside, and I swear the room sways.

"Fucking hell," he hisses.

I open my eyes, and he's sitting back on his ankles, staring directly at his finger inside of me. His hot gaze flits to every one of my curves, and when we make eye contact, the knot that needed to be untied becomes frayed at the ends. The room grows dark, and I chase the high with him staring down at me like I'm the most desirable thing he's ever laid eyes on.

As soon as I make it over the peak, Ford's mouth brushes against my ear. "That's one. Now give me another."

How? How could I after that?

I've never had back-to-back orgasms. Can I even do that?

"I don't know if I—"

He interrupts me, "You can."

All of a sudden, Ford pops up with that natural-born agility he has and his feet plant on the floor. I don't have time to wonder what he's doing, because I'm quickly pulled to the edge of the bed, and he's kneeling in between my legs.

His face is masked by the dark room, but I swear I see his eyes brighten.

"Open," he coaches, pushing my legs apart.

They spread willingly, and I place my hands behind me to brace myself, but there is no preparation when it comes to Ford. I can see why every girl he's ever been with comes crawling back for more.

I count the kisses he trails up my inner thigh, and his lips are like velvet. I pulse around his mouth when he sucks on my delicate skin, and when he puts my legs on his shoulders for a new angle, he hums, and I shudder.

"That's it, baby." His praise sends me to an entirely new level. "Look at you, letting me devour you. I knew you could be obedient when you wanted to be."

After another few seconds of him kissing, sucking, and licking, I'm gripping the blankets. He licks me clean with little praises here and there, and I'm in a daze when he towers over me with a smile full of arrogance.

"Give me one more."

I open my mouth with surprise, but I'm distracted when he plants his hands on my waist and spins me. My cheek falls to the bed when he pushes me face down. "This entire night is going in my spank bank, but we'll never talk about it again. You understand?"

"Yes," I pant.

His hand skims up the inside of my thigh when he leans over me. I feel how hard he is through his pants, but if he takes them off, it'll be detrimental. "At least now you know what to strive for with whomever you end up with. They need to make you lose control..." Ford sticks his fingers inside of me from behind, and it hits a spot I've never felt before. "Just like this."

A whimper falls from my lips when he pulls out, but he slowly glides them in again and again. It's torture, but it's the best kind. My hand is trapped in his when he interlinks our fingers together. He squeezes them hard and pushes our joined hands into the bed as his other hand works me over.

"Make this one good." He tugs on my ear with his teeth, and I'm delirious. "I want your come to drip down my fucking arm, Taytum."

A line of heat starts at my scalp and rushes to my feet. I thrust my hips upward, when he hits the spot again, and I'm a goner. He unclasps our fingers, and his forearm goes to my waist to brace my fall. He holds me steady, and to my surprise, he swallows my moans with his mouth. Our kiss lasts longer than my orgasm, and he doesn't break away until his fingers are out of me and I'm placed on my back.

We're both breathing heavily, but my eyes beg to close. Ford stares down at me from up above, and I have the urge to reach up to brush my hand over his sturdy jaw, but the act seems too intimate, so I do nothing but keep a hold of his stare.

"Sleep," he says, covering me up. "My phone is on loud in case your sugar jumps."

I nod and close my eyes. I bask in the calming warmth flowing throughout my body, and I'm so close to sleep that I hardly hear Ford say, "But first thing tomorrow, we're going to have a talk."

I don't have it in me to argue, so instead, I drift off to sleep, feeling completely sated.

———

I groggily reach up and brush the side of my face when something hits it. My eyes remain closed because there's a bright light coming from somewhere in the room, and I'm already annoyed by it. Rolling to my side, I wonder if I've imagined something hitting me, but then I'm pelted in the face again, and I know it's not a dream.

I rub my cheek and slowly peek an eye open, only to close it again. The sun is blazing through the window, and it blinds me. I move to pull the covers over my head, but I stop when I'm hit again.

"Okay, what the hell!" The blankets fall to my lap when I hastily sit up. I land on Ford right away, and unfortunately, the night hits me harder than whatever he's throwing at me. We make eye contact, and warmth bleeds into my cheeks.

"Five," he states.

My heart skips a beat when he talks, and that's the moment I realize that what we did last night is going to stay with me for far too long.

This is bad.

I flop onto my back and grab the blanket to cover my face. "Five what?"

"I was just counting how many glucose tablets I could throw at you before you woke up." I hate that I want to smile. "Five, in case you're wondering."

"I wasn't," I say matter-of factly.

I'm on high alert, all senses hypervigilant. My ears perk when I hear his footsteps against the floor, and my pulse thrums. He's as quiet as a mouse, but I feel how close he is to me. "Finger," he says.

Surprisingly, my glucose monitor hasn't gone off, but I know that I'm going to have to explain to him what's going on, and I really don't want to.

It's a consequence I was willing to pay last night, though.

Damn you, Taytum.

I pop an arm out of the blanket while still hiding under the covers. Ford chuckles and gently takes my hand in his and flips it palm up.

"Why are you taking my sugar like this when I have an automatic glucose monitor on my arm?" I mumble from beneath the blankets.

I hear the click and flinch when the needle pokes my sore finger, but then it's over and done with. "Sorry," he mutters.

The monitor beeps a few seconds later, and he sighs. "I'm making sure that the one on your arm matches this one because your levels are concerning."

I pull on my hand, but Ford doesn't let go. Silence fills the room, and sweat starts to prick at my hairline. I tug on my hand harder, but then he does something that shocks me so much I pull the blanket off my head.

My sore finger is in his mouth, and he's sucking on it.

We make eye contact, and the rush of last night flies through my head.

He drops my hand and grins. "I knew that would get you to come out of the little blanket fort you've got going on there."

I move to cover myself again, but I catch the quick flick of Ford's eyebrow, and then the blanket flies across the room. His eyes immediately move to my legs, and his neck bobs with a swallow.

He turns abruptly, stomps across the floor, and then I'm pelted in the face with my balled-up pair of jeans. I stare at his back, tightly covered by a gray BU t-shirt, and count the tensing muscles flicking underneath it.

"What?" I tease him while pulling on my jeans. "No panties? Oh wait! You destroyed them!"

Ford spins, and every time we make eye contact, my heart beats harder. Before, it would beat out of anger or irritation, but now, it's something else entirely, and it scares the hell out of me.

"If I remember correctly, you weren't complaining last night when I tore the delicate piece of scrap off of you." I stare at his hot smirk until he snaps his fingers and pulls me back to reality.

Our eyes catch, and he shakes his head. "Nuh-uh. Don't do that."

I swoop down and pick up my torn panties. "Don't do what?"

"Look at my mouth like that."

My stomach flips. "I didn't realize I was looking at it in a particular way."

He steps closer to me, but I stand my ground. My chin tips with defiance, but I think he likes that, because his eyes brighten with something enticing. "You were looking at it like you want it between your legs, and if I let myself taste you again, there's no hiding this from Emory."

My mouth runs dry. I have a brief–*insane*–thought that it wouldn't be that big of a deal if my brother knew, but I blink away the idea because it would absolutely be a big deal.

I admit that I don't know much about dating, but I'm not naive enough to think that just because Ford and I crossed the line, that we could be anything more. Friends with benefits, relationships, or even fake relationships aren't unequivocal by any means. One little misstep, stolen kiss, or lingering stare can turn things south—real quick.

Ford is a staple in my life.

He's Emory's best friend, and my parents consider him one of their own.

Ford and his boyish smile are in the giant family photo hanging in my childhood home.

There is no way he's going to mess around with something like that over some sexual attraction.

His voice scatters my thoughts. "What are you thinking about?"

I lie through my teeth. "How you owe me money for these." My ripped pair of panties dangle in between us, and I raise my eyebrows.

I expect him to smirk, but his face remains stoic. "You want to know what I'm thinking about?"

I shrug. "Not really, no."

He laughs sarcastically before reaching for his hockey bag and heading for the door. "Fine, I'll just tell you in the car."

I take advantage of his back to me and say, "Claire can just take me home."

Energy fills the space between us when he peeks over

his shoulder and shoots me a darkened look. His browline is a hood above his blue eyes, and his tense jaw is *hot*. "You're not getting out of explaining last night. I didn't mishear you when you said you'd taken too much insulin, so do as I say, Taytum, and go sit your hot little ass in my car."

I narrow my eyes and stomp past him dramatically, all while ignoring the dip in my belly at the half-compliment that followed his demand.

[28]

FORD

My car could run on the fumes of my rising anger with every second that passes where Taytum doesn't speak. I'm all tapped out on patience, and as soon as we pull up to her sorority house, she grabs onto the door handle to make a grand escape.

Too bad for her, I'm always thinking ahead.

The lock clicks, and her hair sways over her shoulder with a quick snap in my direction.

I should have made her sit in the backseat so I could use the child-lock feature. I put that little idea in my back pocket for next time.

"You want me to force it out of you?" I ask, leaning farther back in my seat to stretch my legs out as far as they'll go under the dash.

Taytum's soft sigh fills my car, and she crosses her arms against *my* shirt. "Fine." She rolls her eyes. "I forgot to eat. That's why my blood sugar dropped."

I laugh. "It's like you don't even know me." After last

night, she knows more about me than before, like how irresistible I think she is. "I probably know more about diabetes than you do, and you're the one who's been diagnosed."

She shrugs innocently. "Then you'll know that if I don't eat, my blood sugar drops."

"Taytum." I'm on the edge of anger.

"What?" If I were anyone else, she could get away with lying. But I know her better than she thinks.

"You're lying to me," I say. "You did the thing with your nose."

She instantly covers it with her palm. "What thing?"

"You know...the little scrunch, and then you dart your eyes to the left."

Her forehead creases, and I hide my grin by looking out my window. Each of her sorority sisters linger near the front window, and when I make eye contact with them, they all duck like they're synchronized swimmers. I imagine them all falling to the floor and trampling on top of each other to avoid being caught looking at me.

I break the silence in my car and drag my attention back to her delicate profile. "Why is your sugar all of a sudden all over the place?"

The app doesn't lie.

The glucose monitor on her arm pulls the same numbers I get when I prick her finger.

I drum my fingers over the steering wheel and wait for her to lie, but she shifts and turns toward me. Taytum's pretty blue eyes are bluer than normal from the gloss covering them, and the worry lines around them drive me to do something I promised myself I wouldn't do after last night–like touch her. I place my hand on top of her knee and give it a gentle squeeze. "It's just me," I reassure her. "Tell me what's going on."

"They can't afford it, Ford." She pales, and my spine straightens.

What?

Taytum's voice is clouded with a sadness that pulls me in closer. "The pump that everyone is so certain I need for better insulin absorption and because you think I'm careless." She looks at me through watery eyes. "My parents can't afford it. They can hardly afford my insulin now, let alone a pump. So, if I mess with my dosing just enough to throw off my readings, then Dr. McCarthy won't recommend the pump, and it'll at least save some money."

Christ. "I thought it was covered by insurance?"

Taytum shakes her head. "They're still fighting with insurance to cover my medical bills from last summer, and the deductible is insanely high because it's private insurance." She nibbles on her lip. "They're behind on everything. I found out when I went to refill my insulin prescription, and the payment wouldn't go through."

The more Taytum explains, the more my heart pounds. "Like how behind?"

She turns to me, and her chin wobbles. "Like tried three different credit cards until one went through to cover the full price of my insulin for this month."

Shit.

When I was younger, I used to think Jay and Mary-Ann were millionaires. As a child who came from poverty and ate off-brand SpaghettiOs every night because it was all my mother could afford, I thought their four-bedroom, two-bath house was a mansion. They both worked hard and continuously helped my Aunt Jo pay for the hockey gear I needed when she couldn't afford it. I know now, as an adult, that they were never millionaires, but they did okay. Taytum and Emory never went without anything they needed, and they extended their generosity to me as well.

To know that they can't afford Taytum's medicine is a low blow.

The guilt is tenfold, and I quickly try to recall what I have leftover in my savings account from the odd jobs I did as a teenager and how I can discreetly slip it into their bank account with no one ever knowing.

Taytum sniffs, and I eventually pull her into my shoulder. "Does Emory know about this?"

She flies backward and quickly wipes her eyes. "No, and do not tell him. Knowing him, he'll quit the team so he can get a job and pay for it."

That was my first thought too, but I'm realistic enough to know that now, more than ever, going pro is even more important than before. The cost of her insulin or a pump would never be an issue again.

I glance at the clock on my dash. I've gotta get to practice soon, but I'll be damned if she climbs out of my car under the impression that I'm okay with her messing around with her insulin to throw off the readings.

"So, basically, your solution is to not take the medicine that keeps you alive so Dr. McCarthy will think the dosage isn't stable enough to switch you to a pump?"

"No," the answer draws out of her mouth slowly, and I know it's because she's trying to come up with a more justified reason. Except, there isn't one. She knows it, and I know it.

"I'm still taking my insulin..." She looks away. "Just not the right amount every single time."

I twitch. "Well, that's not good enough." I'm slowly becoming more and more irritated over this issue. I know she thinks she's doing everyone a service by keeping the cost as low as possible, but doesn't she understand that she's gambling with her life by doing that? "That's why your blood sugar is all over the place. It's not being regulated by the medicine because you're not taking the right dose."

"I have it under control. Why do you think I took a drink of that guy's beer the other night?"

My jaw aches from clenching my teeth. Silence fills my car, and somehow, it's even more tense than before.

"Do you have a better option?" she asks. "I thought about seeing if Angie would let me pick up some shifts at The Bex since all the other jobs are taken, but I don't think a few shifts here and there will be enough to cover one pen of insulin, let alone four. And don't even get me started on the pump! Do you know how much it is? And then we'd have to somehow keep it from Emory because he'll wonder why I'm working, and then he'll tell my parents, and they're already concerned that I'm wearing myself thin and not staying on top of my health...and... and..."

Taytum is spiraling, so I squeeze her knee to steal her attention. "Take a breath, Tay."

Her mouth shuts, and she's breathing like she just ran a marathon.

"We will figure it out, alright? I have some money in my savings and–"

"Ford, I can't expect you to pa–"

I send her a look that shuts her up. "Take the right amount of insulin, Taytum. Or I'll tell them what you've been doing."

She tightens her lips and surveys my face to see how serious I am. I want to be on her side, and I want to be the one she trusts, but if I have to threaten her, then so be it.

I unlock the door, and her hand falls to the door handle. In an attempt to clear the air, I look her in the eye and try to reassure her. "We'll figure it out. You and me, okay? When are you due for more insulin?"

"I've got about a week until I need to fill the prescription."

I nod, and a call comes over the speakers in my car. We both look to see Emory's name flashing in green on the screen.

She opens the door, and before she can say anything, I put my hand up. "Relax. I won't tell him."

Relief smooths her creased forehead.

I can't help but add, "I've been keeping quite a lot from him lately. You know...like how you came all over my–"

The door slams so hard the loose change in my cup holder rattles.

I zoom off in the direction of the gym, chuckling, but as soon as Taytum is out of sight, my smile falls, and reality sets in.

[29]

TAYTUM

I'VE COME to terms with the fact that I'll always have diabetes.

That's old news to me.

Yet, I still find myself trying to come up with a solution to fix a problem that can't really be fixed.

Ford is certain that, together, he and I can figure everything out, but even he can't cure me from a lifelong disease, not to mention, we really shouldn't be left alone anymore.

I turn at the sound from behind and see a long leg climbing out of my bedroom window and onto the roof. A chill whips around me when Ford slinks down, and it takes no longer than a few seconds for him to pull off his thick sweatshirt and hand it over without saying a word.

After his warmth settles over me, I slowly lie back down and stare up at the sky.

"I hate when you come out here."

I smile to myself. He says the same thing every single time.

"That's why I do it." That's not true, but it is an added bonus.

Ford leans back and lies beside me. We're not touching, but I can feel his body heat pulsing next to me, even through the sweatshirt.

We haven't been alone together since the other day in his car, and the way my body relaxes with him near tells me that I need him more than I'd like to admit.

"Here." A brown paper bag falls to my stomach, and I huff out a breath. It crinkles when I grab onto it, and I immediately know what it is.

I pop to my elbows. "How did you–?"

Ford turns to me, and our eyes catch. His easy-going smile drives me insane. "Taytum, I can talk God out of Heaven. You don't think I can talk a female pharmacist into letting me pick up your medication for you?" His hand falls to his chest. "It hurts that you have such little faith in me."

I don't tell him that I have *all* my faith in him, because God knows his ego doesn't need to grow any more. I turn away and push the bag off to the side. My arms fall back to my sides when I lie back down, and we're almost touching. "Thank you."

I know he's looking at me, but I keep my gaze on the stars because I'm afraid he'll read every thought in my head.

"Wow, no jab? *And* I get a thank you?"

I try not to smile. "Give it time."

He chuckles, and more silence passes between us. It's a comfortable silence, though. The kind that you crave when you're all alone in a crowded room with nothing but your thoughts, and then you look across the room and see the one person that makes you feel grounded.

Ford shifts beside me, and I think he's getting up to

leave, but instead, he sends my heart into a tailspin when his pinky finger hooks over mine. A subtle gasp rushes from my mouth and disappears into the cool air from the perplexity of what I feel from the briefest of touches. We're connected by one tiny brush of our fingers, and yet, something I've never felt tumbles in and takes my breath away.

The feeling digs deep into my chest, and I'm terrified it's never going to leave. I'm even more terrified that I'll never feel this way with anyone other than him.

Out of pure panic, I blurt something that is wholly untrue and a complete and utter attempt at denial. "I have a date."

Ford's pinky clamps down over mine before he pulls his hand away. "You do? When?"

Shit. "Thursday."

I now have three days to find some guy on Bex Hex and coerce him into taking me out on a date so I can embarrassingly cover up my big fat lie to Ford.

He makes me stupid.

"With who?" He's suspicious. I can tell by the way the question draws from his mouth.

I play my part well and take it to an entirely new level when I turn and send him a flirty smile full of confidence. "Wouldn't you like to know."

Ford sizes me up, and my heart races. "I think, since I agreed to hide your dates from Emory, it means I have the final call. Remember? It's part of the rules."

I turn away because I feel the way my nose wants to scrunch with another lie. *He was right!* "You don't know him."

He scoffs. "All the more reason for you to give me the details."

I would, but there are none.

The faintest growl leaves him. "You probably don't even have a date. You just like to irritate me."

True and also true.

"I do have a date," I argue with full conviction.

He sits up abruptly and bends his knees. His arms rest over them as he stares at me. "Prove it."

FML.

I sit up just as quickly. "Fine. I will."

His eyes light up with the challenge, so naturally, I take it a step further.

"I'll make sure to send you a full bio and pair it with a photo on Thursday. Will that make you happy?"

Ford exhales slowly and repeats my question. "Will you going on a date make me happy?"

The question lingers between us for what feels like an entirety before he turns and starts to climb back through my window. I watch his steady movements and the way he swings his long legs through the opening with ease before he bends down and places his hands on the windowsill. He looks me dead in the face and says, "I'd love *nothing* more than for you to go on a date, Taytum. I'll be waiting for the photo to come through on Thursday."

He leaves me with a wink on the roof, all alone with my brown paper bag full of insulin.

When I hear his car take off from down below, I crawl back into my room, open up Bex Hex, and message every single guy that's swiped right on my photo.

Most of them respond within minutes, and I can't help but pick the one that I think will piss Ford off the most.

Professor Sterling.

Perfect.

FORD

I THROW my cards down onto the table, and Aasher does the same.

"I'm folding," I announce.

"Me too." He jumps up from the table before anyone else has a chance to lay their cards down.

"Eager much?" Emory snorts. He rolls his eyes and pushes his cards into the middle of the table. The poker game technically isn't over, but our little pre-game ritual is starting to become nonexistent now that Aasher is constantly rushing over to the apartment next door to hang out with the coach's daughter, leaving the rest of the guys to their own devices.

"You going home?" Emory asks after standing up and helping Berkley and Efrain pick up the poker chips.

"You better be," Efrain adds. "Tomorrow's game is going to be challenging."

He's right. Which is all the more reason I'm pissed at

Taytum for deciding that tonight was the perfect night to go on a fucking date with some guy I don't know.

I glance at the clock, and my blood runs hot. I told her I'd give her until 8:30 to send me that bio and photo she promised, or I was going to open her location and pull the stalker act.

I may do that anyway, depending on who she's with.

"You talk to Tay?" Emory throws on his coat as he flips through his phone.

If I was a total dick, I'd tell him no. That way, he can interrupt her plans before they even start, but things have become testy between us. Taytum can throw me under the bus just as quickly as I can her. "I think she's studying tonight." It's not technically a lie, because she was studying earlier. "There's not much going on around campus anyway. You know how it is the night before a hockey game."

It's unsettling that I don't even feel a blip of guilt from hiding something from him.

"True. Alright, I'll see you guys tomorrow."

As soon as the door shuts, I immediately pull out my phone.

She's got three fucking minutes.

Berkley clears his throat, and I quickly glance at him. "I'm leaving, I'm leaving," I say, throwing up my hands. "Relax."

He chuckles. "He's going to fucking murder you if he finds out that you're fucking his sister."

My head snaps up so quickly from my phone that the room spins. "What the hell are you talking about? I am not fucking Tay."

"But he wants to!" Efrain shouts from down the hall.

"We all want to," Berkley jokes.

I glare at him, and he laughs harder. "Look at you, all crazed over the thought of it."

"That's nothing new! Taytum is like a sister to me. Of course I don't want her with any of you fuckboys."

A sister. Yeah fucking right. I've never thought of her as my sister. Ever.

Efrain slides down the hall in his socks. "Who are you calling a fuckboy?"

I know they're kidding, and I need to lighten up if I want to keep up my charade of acting normal, but when my phone vibrates, I almost drop it before opening the message.

Absolutely not.

My fingers pound against the screen.

> So, what's his name? Grandpa?

I pull my hoodie on and rush for the door. "Later, fuckboys."

I'm safely tucked away in my car before I zoom in on the photo of Taytum. I scan the background and know right away that she's at the only pizzeria in town that offers a cauliflower pizza crust–which is her new go-to to help control her sugars.

Her text comes in over the speakers of my car when I'm pulling out of campus.

Patricia, my car's robot voice, says, "Actually, I prefer to call him Daddy."

I mute the speakers before muttering, "Shut the fuck up, Patty."

I spot her right away—looking all cute in her ripped jeans, white sneakers, and a light-blue sweater that just so happens to be hanging from her shoulder to show off some skin.

She's tucked in the back booth with a guy at least ten years older than her, and now that Taytum has kicked me off the Bex Hex app and changed her password, I wonder if she found him there or somewhere else. You know, like a fucking nursing home.

I ping-pong my attention from him to the menu several times as I stand in line to order.

When it's my turn, I'm faced with a pink-tinted teenager who is so shocked she stutters. "H...hi...how can I help you?" Bless her heart.

"I'd like to get an extra-large cauliflower-crust pizza with cheese."

I keep my hood up when ordering, just in case Taytum happens to walk by.

"Are you dining here, or is this to go?"

As if I'd take it to go when Taytum is on a date with some guy she says she's going to call *Daddy*. "I'm dining here."

"Okay, and it's...Collins, right? Or do you like to go by Ford?" The girl's cheeks burn brighter.

I grin. "Actually, the name is Walker."

She stares at me long and hard, probably wondering if I have a twin who plays hockey, but eventually, she accepts the name I've given her and hands me the ticket.

"Thanks." I slip a tip in the jar for her cooperation and head to the opposite side of the restaurant while making sure I still have a good view of Taytum.

I slink back against the booth, spread my legs out beneath the table, and cross my arms against my chest. It's too loud to hear anything she's saying to her date, but something breaks in my chest when I watch her throw her head back with laughter. Her cheeks flush, and there's a little glimmer in her eye that's always present when she flirts.

I hope her date chokes on the pizza he's about to bite into.

"Order up!" I push my hood off my head and stand. "For the name Walker."

I'm staring directly at her as I prowl toward the counter. The realization flickers across her face, and I brace myself for the impact.

Her eyes flare with heat, and I'm on fire.

My smirk deepens, and her smile falls.

Taytum wants to play games and go on a date with some guy who looks like he could be her father?

Not on my fucking watch.

She only allows me one bite of pizza before she heads in my direction. Every guy stops and looks, even the ones out with a date. Her swaying hips in those jeans are a lure if I've ever seen one, and I hate that she's so alluring.

I shove another bite of pizza into my mouth when she makes it over to my empty booth. The pink gloss on her lips draws my attention to her mouth, and I know it draws her date's attention too, which only irritates me more. I usher for her to sit with my hand, but she doesn't budge. Instead, she crosses her arms over her chest and seethes under her breath. "What the hell are you doing here?"

Her snippy tone forces me to chew slower, just to piss her off.

The ends of her perfectly curled hair brush against my arm when she leans into my space with flared nostrils. "Ford!" Taytum is practically foaming at the mouth, which is ironically how I felt when she texted me thirty minutes ago.

Once I swallow my bite of pizza, she repeats her question. "What are you doing here?"

I reach for my drink, but she snatches it away at the last second, causing me to laugh under my breath. "I'm eating pizza, obviously." I flick my chin toward her date. "What's he doing here? Robbing the cradle?"

I chuckle at my own joke, but Taytum doesn't find it funny.

Surprise, surprise.

"Professor Sterling isn't that much older than me," she states.

I grip the table. "*Professor*?"

Taytum's eyes widen. "I mean Augustus!"

I ask a question I'm not sure I want the answer to. "Is he a professor at Bexley U?"

Nope. Nada. Not happening.

She shifts on her feet uncomfortably and looks back to the table before swinging her attention to me again. "Yes, but he isn't my professor anymore, and he's only thirty-four, so chill."

I stare at her.

She stares at me.

We're having a silent argument, and I'm three seconds from picking her up by her waist, draping her over my shoulder, taking the pizza to go, and driving us home.

My cup clinks against the table when she places it back down. "You promised, Ford." Her eyes soften around the edges, and I'm a sucker because I fall for the innocent act.

I bite the inside of my cheek when she turns around and heads back to her date.

I did promise her I wouldn't interfere, and I rarely break my promises.

But Taytum has already become an exception, considering I've already broken a promise to her brother, and now I'm about to break another promise, because if her date so much as breathes in the wrong direction, he's dead.

[31]

TAYTUM

FORD HAS A GAME TOMORROW, yet he's five booths down, staring directly at me while I try to have a decent conversation with a man who *was* keeping my interest.

That ship sailed the second I heard the name Walker come over the speaker. The room tilted on its side when I snagged onto his knowing smirk, and my heart came to life. *Ugh.*

"You always made me laugh in class," Augustus says, pulling me back to the date.

I give him a look while ignoring Ford's lazy gaze from across the restaurant. "I did? You were always so serious. I don't think I remember you laughing."

"That's because you were always chatting with your friends, paying attention to them"—he shrugs—"while I was paying attention to you."

Before Ford walked in and ruined my date by watching my every move, that comment would have made me blush.

Now, though, all I'm left with is guilt, and I don't want to admit why.

"Oh, *please.*" I roll my eyes playfully. "Actually..." I push further back into the booth and hate that I have to forcefully keep my attention on him. "I think I remember you giving me a D on one of my papers that deserved an A."

He snorts. "Which you had no problem saying aloud when receiving your grade."

I give him a little shrug of my shoulders and grin.

After a long second, he crosses his arms and smiles. "I gave you a D to get your attention."

"Oh, is that right?" I ask.

He nods gingerly, and I try to find the same spark between us that I felt when he picked me up, but I crave to look at Ford instead. I flicker my gaze past Augustus's shoulder for a split second, and disappointment settles when I see that Ford isn't even looking at us.

Instead, he's buried in his phone.

Augustus clears his throat. "You never came to my office, though. I was hoping you'd come yell at me for a new grade."

I laugh. "Sorry to disappoint."

He brushes me off. "It was probably better that you didn't come to my office."

"Why?"

He leans further across the table and lowers his voice. "Because sitting across from you now, I know I wouldn't have let you leave my office after getting you alone."

I flush all over at his honesty, but I quickly cool down when I sense a presence approaching our table.

I glare at Ford. *What the hell are you doing now?*

Augustus leans away from me and quickly glances at

Ford before clearing his throat. "Can I help you, Mr. Collins?"

Ford hasn't been a student of Augustus's because he teaches in the arts department, and Ford's degree doesn't require those types of classes, but apparently, he—along with the rest of Bexley U—knows the names of the hockey players like the back of their hand.

Ford's rumbly chuckle is full of sarcasm. He takes his hands out of his hoodie pocket, and I tense when I see his clenching knuckles. "No, but you can help yourself not get punched in the face."

"Ford!" I'm shocked. My mouth falls open, and I admit that my plan was to irritate him, but Ford isn't one to pick a fight—irritated or not.

"Excuse me?" Augustus stares at him a little more intently, and my stomach fills with dread.

Doom is approaching, and I don't know how to stop it other than to drag Ford out of this restaurant and let him take me home.

"How many prior students have you fucked, Professor Sterling?" Heat radiates from Ford, and I'm pretty sure everyone in a ten-foot radius hears his strangled tone.

Augustus laughs uncomfortably. "None of your business, and before you try to say it's against the university's moral compass, it's not, if they're no longer my student."

"Yeah, but what about your wife's moral compass?"

I gasp, and my face stings like I've been slapped. The betrayal forces me to stand abruptly, and I look down at his ring finger to survey it. I blink several times, hoping the faint tan line on it is a fabrication of my brain. But it isn't.

"I see what this is," he says. "You're jealous that she's with me and not you." Augustus shrugs innocently. "I would be too. Just look at her."

I'm disgusted when his eyes rake over me.

Ford visibly shakes with anger, and I know I have to do something soon before he does. I round the booth and shove him away before turning, grabbing my cup of water, and throwing it right in my prior professor's face.

His mouth opens with shock before he takes his lying tongue and catches the dripping water droplets falling from his nose.

I slam the cup on the table. "Your wife deserves better."

Ford's hoodie bundles in my grip when I pull us through the restaurant and end up in the bathroom, away from wandering eyes. I back myself up against the door as a sort of barricade and watch Ford's chest climb rapidly while he paces in front of me.

"Will you calm down?" I plead. "It's not that big of a deal."

It's eerie to see him so worked up. I have never liked seeing Ford upset, and to this day, it still makes me uncomfortable.

"I know it isn't!" He puts his back to me but only for a second. When he spins, he levels me with a scowl. "If you're going to go on dates, you need to pick better guys!"

I huff and put my hands on my hips. "How was I supposed to know he was married?!"

He shrugs angrily. "I don't know! Maybe do a quick Google search! That's what I did!"

My shoulders drop. "I didn't think I needed to, because he wasn't a complete stranger."

Ford pinches the bridge of his nose. He's calmer when he speaks again, but now I'm the one that's all twisted. "How am I ever supposed to let you go on dates if you go on them with guys like that? Have better taste, Taytum!"

"Fine!" I shout.

I pull my phone out of my pocket and quickly open Bex Hex. Ford grunts when I shove it into his chest. His heart is thumping so hard I can feel it against my hand. "Look at these guys, and tell me who's good enough for me. I'll ask them on a date right now."

His eyebrows furrow. "No."

"Why not?" I ask with frustration.

Ford breathes heavily. "Because none of them are good enough for you."

I roll my eyes. "Same story, different year. You and Emory have been saying that since I entered high school!"

Ford's hand comes up to cover mine, trapping it against his chest. "Well, it's the truth."

I sigh and attempt to calm down. "Then who is good enough for me, Ford?"

His blue eyes bounce between mine when he opens his mouth. There's the smallest divot in between his eyebrows that mimics mine as I wait for his answer. My heart slows when he wraps an arm around my waist and pulls me in closer. The lights grow dimmer, and the air is full of unshed chemistry brewing between us, but then, all of a sudden, the room starts to sway. At first, I think it's because of his touch. But when I start to shake, I realize it's not.

"Tay?"

My phone dings, and his eyes widen.

We both reach for my purse on the floor. My fingers tremble against the zipper, but Ford swoops in and pulls me into his arms. He studies the number on the screen and curses.

"It's in my bag."

He quickly gets the pen ready with the right dosage without any direction from me. I slowly lift my shirt and flinch when he uses the alcohol pad to clean the area. His warm breath brushes against my skin until it's dry, and then I turn away and bury my head into his chest.

Ford handles me like I'm a piece of china. He's gentle, and I hardly feel the pinch. When the needle is inserted, I silently count to ten, then it's done and over with, and Ford's lips are brushing against my ear.

"All done," he whispers. I nod against his chest, and he brushes my hair away from my face. "You okay now?"

I breathe deeply. "I will be."

"Then let's go home." Ford doesn't let me walk. He keeps me cradled to his chest after putting all my things back in my bag and carries me through the restaurant like a walking billboard for embarrassment.

"Will you please put me down?" I ask.

"And risk you fainting? No."

I hide from all the staring and don't pull my face away from his shirt until I feel the cool air wash over my warm skin. I wiggle to my feet, but Ford tightens his grip until the passenger door to his car opens, and he places me inside.

"Was that really necessary?" I ask.

He stays quiet when he pulls the seatbelt down and leans across me to buckle it. I get a strong whiff of his cologne, but it's gone the moment he backs away and slams my door.

When we're on the freeway, with nothing but the sound of tires against pavement, I finally get the nerve to speak.

"You never answered me."

I feel the car pick up speed. "What are you talking about?"

"When I asked who was good enough for me." I stare at the blurring line outside of my window and wait for his answer. I'm afraid if I look at him and he sees my expression after he gives me the name of some guy, he'll see my disappointment.

I don't know when it happened, but no matter who gives me a second glance or swipes right on my photo, I immediately compare him to Ford, and the one who comes out on top is the one who doesn't *want* to be on top.

When we pull up to my sorority house, Ford puts his car in park and reaches for his phone. The light illuminates each of his strong features, and there's something so incredibly comforting knowing that Ford is there to take care of me when I need it. He visibly relaxes after he reads my glucose level.

I nod. "See? All better. And before you get angry, I haven't messed with my insulin since we talked."

He grips the steering wheel and stares out the windshield. "Good."

"You better go," I say. "You've got a game tomorrow, and Emory is going to kill you if you play like shit again from lack of sleep."

Ford turns to look at me. "Even on my worst days, I don't play like shit, and you know it."

I laugh quietly and open the passenger door to climb out of his car.

Once I slam it and round the car, I hear his window roll down. I keep my back to him, but I stop when he says my name. Butterflies flutter in my lower stomach, and the feeling is becoming tiresome.

"I didn't answer your question for a reason."

I hold my breath because there's a sincerity in Ford's tone that wasn't there before.

"Me," he says.

I turn slightly, in case I didn't hear him correctly.

"I'm the only one who's good enough for you." My heart skips. "But I guess I'll try to find a close second."

I stand on the porch with my back to him well after his car takes off.

The problem is that I'm not sure there will be a close second.

FORD

IT HURTS TO BREATHE.

My chest screams with the need for oxygen, but I'm on defense, and if I take my eye off the puck for even one second, I risk it flying into the net. Emory is a damn good goalie, but no one is perfect.

I should know that better than anyone, considering I almost pressed Taytum against the bathroom door last night and kissed her so deeply she forgot all about that loser she was on a date with.

See? I'm not even perfect.

I never thought I'd say this, but thank God for the spike in her blood sugar. Otherwise, my mouth would have been somewhere it didn't belong.

Shaking Taytum out of my head, I stare at the little black biscuit and put all my effort into the game. We've played hard, and we're on top by two, but if I don't send a sauce pass in Theo's direction, we may end up with a tie, and I'm sick of not getting what I want.

My jaw locks, and the opposing team is setting up plays like their life depends on it, and for some of them, it does. Hockey is their future, just like it is with me.

There are two players dressed in yellow, swarming together like bumblebees, and I swear time freezes. I watch their eyes meet for a split second, and I immediately start rushing down to the offensive zone with Coach screaming profanities in my direction. My team doesn't question my motives, though. I've always been one to know the outcome of something before it happens, particularly on the ice.

The crowd roars, and the echo ripples around the arena. I turn at the last possible second. I'm at a diagonal advantage of number seven, and I know he has plans to make a breakaway.

He won't, though.

I skate with vicious speed and block out the cheers. As soon as he winds his stick back, I slip in like a snake and steal the puck away. I carry it for a second and then pass to Berkley, who I know will be waiting. When he has possession, it isn't long before the puck is back to center ice, and Theo is firing it off into the net right at the buzzer.

The sound of the stadium comes rushing in like a waterfall, and our team is bunched together, celebrating. Emory slaps me on the back after ripping his mask off. His dark hair is stuck to his forehead with sweat. "You always have my fucking back, bro."

"How do you do it?!" Zeke, one of our younger players, is bewildered. "Only you could predict that the puck was going to squirt out for a breakaway opportunity, but then you swooped in like a feral vulture."

Theo wraps his arm around my shoulder. "Didn't you know he's part bird? Why do you think he's so fucking annoying?"

I elbow Theo in the stomach, and he bends over with strained laughter.

There's a loud, girly howl from the stands that catches all of our attention. We spin, and there's a huge group of girls howling like wolves with their Bexley U jerseys on. No surprise that Taytum is the ring leader–smack dab in the middle with the loudest howl.

My mouth curves with a quick shake of my head. I tap the guys quickly and flick my chin to the girls. At the same time, we all pull our helmets off and match their howls. Taytum's laugh is the loudest, and before long, the entire stadium sounds like a pack of wolves as we skate toward the other team to shake hands.

When I skate up to number seven, I'm not sure what to expect. Hockey players are hotheads–even me on occasion– so I wait for a lowball jab from him, but instead, he puts his ungloved hand out and shakes mine.

"That was a good game, man," he says.

I hold onto his hand in a tight grip and joke with him. "Thought you could squeeze one past me, eh?"

He snorts. "I tried and fucking failed."

We let go and start to head down the ice together. I'm certain the cameras are locked onto us, expecting some juicy hockey fight per usual, but instead, he drops his head and asks if there are any parties around campus tonight since they're not heading back until the morning.

"We don't usually party with the opposing team," Emory adds from behind. "But that game deserves to be celebrated."

"So, party at your place?" I quip.

"Fuck no."

I chuckle. "You can follow us over to the football house —that's the best party spot on campus."

"Good shit." Number seven throws up his knuckles. "See you in a few, but you owe me a beer for stealing that shot." Then he pauses. "Or maybe you can make it up to me by introducing me to one of those beautiful girls up there." He nudges his chin to Taytum and the rest of her sorority girls. My first reaction is to choke him out, but then Emory rushes past me to the locker room, and I do something drastic.

"I've got the perfect girl for you."

And just like that, there goes my winning high.

"You did what?!"

Taytum tries to smack me against the chest, but I catch her wrist mid-hit. She looks into the living room for Emory, but our sparring is nothing out of the ordinary. He probably assumes I'm reprimanding her for trying to grab a drink.

"Relax. I've grabbed your hand plenty of times over the years when you've gone to hit me." She looks for her brother again with the same expression she always wears when she's up to something. "But if you don't stop looking at him like that with my hand on your wrist, well then he might just find out that you rode my face the other night."

"Ford!"

I smile at the gritty way she says my name. The apples of her cheeks turn pink, and the *only* reason I'm toying with her is because I know she isn't mine tonight.

Or ever.

"What?" I shrug. "It's true."

There's a tug from her arm, and I finally let go. She

stumbles backward, and it forces me to steady her with a hand on her lower back. There's a quick gasp from her and a rising dick from me.

Goddamnit.

I turn and reach for a drink. Any drink will do at this point.

"Anyway, he's a good guy, so I set you two up," I say, sipping the booze.

"How am I going to get away with sneaking off with some hockey player from the other team with Emory here and what about rule number one? Remember? No sleeping with hockey players?"

She's skeptical and has zero trust in me. I lean on the island and let the granite cut into my lower back and say, "I meant that for *our* team and just watch."

The song changes, and there's a plethora of girls surrounding her brother. The females always want the grumpy, stoic one because they think they'll be the one to change him. It doesn't take long for him to take his pick by grabbing one around the waist and pulling her toward the door.

Taytum's face is full of disgust. Her pink lip is pulled into a scowl, and she rolls her pretty blue eyes. "He's such a pig."

"We all are until we find the right girl," Theo muses.

I look over my shoulder and see Theo leaning beside Claire on the other side of the island.

"Are you saying I'm the right girl?" Claire teases.

"You know you are."

Taytum sighs wistfully. "You two are annoyingly cute." Then she turns to me and puts her hands on her hips. "Fine, where is he?"

I chug the rest of my beer and nod in the direction of

Knox. He sees me pointing him out, and I instantly rethink my decision when I watch him stop mid-conversation at the sight of Taytum.

His eyes widen when he looks back at me. I reluctantly answer his silent question.

Yes. Her.

He blows out a breath and walks away from Efrain.

Right toward Taytum.

[33]

TAYTUM

I SHOULD BE MORE excited than I am.

Knox is attractive, and the look in his eyes tells me that he finds me attractive too, but where there should be butterflies flying, there's a pit instead.

The only thing that keeps me going is the fact that Ford is standing beside me, and I feel like I need to prove something to him—for instance, that he isn't the only guy who can make me blush or fill my head with dirty thoughts.

I need to prove it to myself too.

"We'll be right back." Claire pulls on my arm, and we leave the group of guys when they start chatting about their game.

We make a beeline for the back door. The wind whips at our hair, and she puts her hands on my upper arms, forcing me to look her in the face. "You're being weird."

"I am not," I argue.

But I am. I'm completely out of sorts.

Claire's hands fall from my arms, and I look up to the stars, taking a deep breath.

"What is going on with you? You've been so off. Even at practice."

My arms fall to my sides with defeat. "There's too much going on. Between school, dance, my parents, Ford, Professor Sterling..."

Claire steps forward. "Whoa, what? Back up...what are you talking about?"

Her eyes bug out when I give her the CliffsNotes version of the last couple of weeks, leaving out the part about my insulin because I don't need anyone else angry with me over that. When the back door opens and Theo's head pops out, she snaps her gaping mouth closed.

"Get back in here, you two. It's freezing."

"We're coming!" Claire pulls me back into the party but whispers in my ear before we make it over to Ford and Knox. "If Ford is pushing you toward this guy, I think you should go for it. He's either going to stand by and let you be swept off your feet, keeping his promise to you, or..."

Her sentence trails at the end. The guys stop mid-conversation, and I purposefully keep my eyes away from Ford because I think we both know nothing good can come from it. If he wants to push me toward some guy he approves of, then I'm going to take the bait. If anything, maybe it'll take him off my mind.

Knox and I snag eye contact, and I take my time checking him out. He's tall, athletic, and has a killer smile. I decide to let his hockey player arrogance go for now and smile softly. "Want to dance?"

He looks surprised, like he can't believe I would be bold enough to ask him. Before things got all messy with Ford, flirting and toying with a guy was my specialty. Dancing with subtle, teasing touches was the recipe for an exciting night, which would then be ruined by Ford and Emory. Unfortunately, I became a little too comfy in their interruptions, and it hindered me.

Knox steps forward. "I'd be an idiot if I said no."

I'm suddenly whisked into the middle of the party with a pair of steady hands glued to my jeans like they are one with the denim. It's easy to slip into normalcy and dance with him. The room spins before he dips me, and my hair flies past my face after he pulls me up. I'm trapped against his chest with his hand cupping the side of my cheek, and I laugh softly.

"Where did a cocky hockey player like you learn to dance?" I ask.

He smirks before spinning me again. "I had to take lessons for my sister's wedding last Christmas. It seems to have paid off in the long run."

I laugh again, and the song changes to a faster tempo, so I turn in his arms and start to move against him. His warm breath washes over my neck. "And where did you learn to dance?"

I grin. "Years of practice."

"Lucky me." His teeth grip onto my earlobe, and I tremble. *Oh*.

Claire and Theo are beside me dancing, and when she meets my eye, she wiggles her eyebrows. It's encouragement that I keep a hold of because when Knox spins me and puts his hands in the back pockets of my jeans, I catch Ford staring from the kitchen.

I'm grounded immediately.

The moment is short-lived. Ford abruptly pushes off the island, grabs some girl by her drunken hand, and they plant themselves right beside Knox and me.

No. I silently tell him. *You set me up with him, so deal with it.*

It's like he can read my mind, because he aggressively rolls his eyes and turns his back and starts to dance with the half-stumbling girl.

I glance around the party quickly and then back to Knox.

"Let's go." I grab his hand and pull him to the stairs. He trails after me willingly, but his eyebrows fall with confusion. "We gotta disappear before my brother decides to make an appearance and force us apart."

"Who's your brother?" he asks.

"Emory. The goalie."

I'm not worried about my brother even in the slightest. Instead, I'm worried about his best friend.

Knox puts on the brakes. "Your brother is Bexley U's goalie?"

I peer over my shoulder at him. "Yeah, are you having second thoughts?"

Ford comes to mind, and I hate him for inserting himself into my brain, whether it's on purpose or not.

Knox's face smooths. "Absolutely not. Lead the way."

[34]

FORD

I slap the top of the Uber and throw some money on the girl's lap before shutting the door. The Uber driver rolls his window down.

"I sent you the address. Get her home safely," I say.

"Will do, man. Good game tonight."

I nod to the older gentleman, then he's driving off with my drunken dance partner. I was half inclined to jump in the Uber with her to put some much-needed distance between me and Taytum, because I know what she's doing, and I have no one to blame but myself for the raging jealousy storm I'm in the middle of.

I stare at the football house. The white sheet that's hanging on the porch with a child-like painted wolf on the front is blowing in the wind, and I contemplate whether or not I should head back inside. I move my gaze farther to stare at the stars, hopeful that there's a hidden answer up there, but I stop at the bright light coming from the upstairs window. My breathing halts, and I stumble backward.

I blink once, then twice, and then bite my tongue so hard blood fills my mouth. My eyes shut tightly, and I curse God.

"Are you fucking testing me?" I ask him.

An owl hoots from the tree, and I stand there, completely dumbfounded, before finding the beady little monster. *Really?*

I can't help but look at the window again, hoping to God Taytum isn't still there for the world to see, but naturally, she is. My blood boils. He's touching her like he knows what she likes, and I hate to break it to him, but I know what she looks like when she's completely out of control with pleasure, and the face she's making isn't it.

Fuck. Just leave.

I turn around and stare at the car-lined street, but I can't move.

I'm frozen in place.

I can't have her.

I know I can't.

But I can't stand by and set her up with guys anymore.

I can't help her get laid.

I can't willingly watch her fall in love with someone who isn't me.

I should have never touched her, but unfortunately, I did, and now I'm forever fucked.

The party is in full chaos mode when I make my way back inside the house. Most of the hockey team has left, but the football players are still playing beer pong. Girls are slowly losing layers of clothes and dancing to music I can't seem to hear over my heartbeat. My attention shifts from the steps, to the dance floor, and then back to the steps. I climb them one by one with a hand around my throat and impulse driving my actions.

I might kill the innocent guy I set her up with if I go into the room and watch him touch what's mine.

So instead, I walk over to the bathroom that Rush doesn't let anyone use during parties because he doesn't want anyone "fucking in the shower" and praise my sperm donor of a father for giving me my height. I easily reach up, grabbing the key off the top of the door ledge, and shut it after I'm inside.

I can't fathom looking at myself in the mirror because I know I'm going to look so fucking almighty with my plan when I should feel like shit for it.

Taytum is reckless to my soul, so let it be damned.

The shower turns on, and it's set to every girl's favorite temperature—*hell*.

Steam billows around me, and it thankfully fogs the mirror so I don't have to face myself. When the air is too thick to breathe and sweat trickles down my back, I crack the door, and it rushes out like Niagara Falls.

I press onto the wall and wait. My hands fall into my pockets, and I cross my legs at the ankles. My heart beats harder with each bead of sweat that falls from my hairline, but when the fire alarm finally goes off, setting off the rest throughout the house, I push forward and turn off the shower. I open the door further to watch every bedroom fly open at the same time.

Taytum is two doors down, and it's the only room I care about.

Everyone is confused in their lustful or drunken state. Not much difference if you ask me. They stumble over to the stairs, half-dressed, with their hands covering their ears, and then I see Taytum following Knox.

She's fully dressed but looks a mess. Her shirt is crooked, and her hair is tangled at the ends. He looks back at her once and shrugs as they fall into the stampede of everyone else. The raging alarm is doing nothing but blending in with the fast thumping of my pulse, and I wait until she's walking past to grab onto her arm. I pull her into the steamy bathroom, and she gasps.

Once she registers that it's me, she surveys the room and lingers on the foggy mirror before shifting her gaze back to mine. I slowly close the door, and it cancels out some of the blaring beeps from the fire alarms that are slowly being turned off by Rush and his teammates.

"Are you kidding me?" Her question is obviously rhetorical. "You set the fire alarms off?"

Taytum pretends to be unbothered, but I linger on her neck and watch her pulse beat like a thunderstorm behind her skin.

I take a step toward her. "I did." The lack of control I have when it comes to her is pathetic.

She rolls those ocean-blue eyes, and I take another step in her direction. I reach forward and run my hand down her hair to smooth out the wild tangles.

Taytum flings my hand away. "Why set me up with someone only to ruin it just when it gets good? You're unbelievable, Ford."

"Gets good?" I scoff angrily. "I saw the way he was touching you. Don't forget, I know what you look like when you're turned on."

Her mouth flattens. "What do you mean you saw?"

I answer with one word. "Window."

She breathes heavily and then crosses her arms in that bratty way that I love. "This is the second time in one week where you have interfered with a date—and you forced me into this one."

"Date." I laugh but it comes out harsh. "You mean fuck session."

Taytum and I are head to head. She's glaring at me, and all I can think about is how I want to kiss her. I want to replace his mouth on hers with mine.

Goddamnit, what the fuck am I doing?

"Fine." I gaze at her mouth. "Date, fuck session, whatever you want to call it. Either way, why did you set me up with him if you were only going to sabotage it in the end?!"

I move fast.

I force her up against the bathroom door, and she hits it at the same time a heavy breath escapes her. I reach behind her and lock the door. The click breaks through the one fire alarm continuing to blare, and I slap my hands against the wood to cage her in. "Because!"

Taytum straightens her spine in defiance, and *God*, she's so fucking pretty. Not a single flaw covers her smooth skin and feminine features. Her lips are beyond kissable, and her body has always fit so perfectly in my hands that I can't help but crave it every second of the day. "Why, Ford?" she repeats. "Why set me up with someone if you're going to throw a fit afterward?"

My head is tangled with too many unsaid truths, and all I can do is blurt something without thinking. "Because if you don't run off with someone else, then I'll just be more inclined—" *Wait.* I grind my teeth to stop myself.

The glimmer in her eyes shines with a dare. "Inclined to do what?"

My palm finds its place on the curve along her waist, and it makes me question everything. "I'll be inclined to make you mine."

[35]

WE'RE in a ring of fire, and I see no way out.

Alarms are going off, *literally*, and Ford has a hold on me much tighter than he realizes. I could spend forever in this bathroom, with him looking at me like he can't control what he feels, and fall right for it. His hard chest presses against mine, and his hand on my face tightens with a fear that we both feel.

His heart beats against me like he just climbed off the ice at the end of a game, and I say his name. "*Ford,*" I warn.

There's no need to say it out loud. We both know that what we're doing is going to backfire.

His mouth comes closer, and I want to beg him to kiss me. His breath mingles with mine when he breaks the silence and says, "Call me Walker."

I grip his shirt, and he makes a throaty noise. My stomach dips when his mouth moves to mine, and I finally feel like I can breathe again. The kiss isn't urgent or rushed. Instead, it's calculated and steady.

And *hot.*

He pinches my waist, and I press against him. His hard length rubs me, and I shake in his grasp. My leg lifts, and I wrap it around him while he slowly moves his tongue over mine like he's trying to tell me something without using words.

"Fucking addicting," he mumbles, pulling back for a split second. He looks at me long and hard, his brow furrowed with confusion and maybe a little guilt, but he goes back for more, and I willingly give it to him.

His hand slides from my waist, and he cups me from behind at the same time he bites my lip. I whimper, and Ford pulls back to shush me. I don't realize the fire alarm has stopped blaring until he runs the back of his knuckles across my cheek bone while staring into my eyes. "Stay quiet."

I nod.

"But don't worry." He stares at my mouth. "I'll finish what he couldn't."

My head slumps against the door when Ford descends to the sensitive spot along my collarbone. His tongue is hot and wet with each slash against my skin, and a cry of pleasure threatens to escape.

The popping of the button on my jeans sends a spark in between my legs. I spread them, and with the way Ford kisses me deeper, I think he approves. Sparks of pleasure rush to my skin when his hand dips beneath my panties, and he rubs against the evidence of how turned on I am.

"You're so fucking wet. Tell me it's all for me," he whispers against my mouth. His thumb rubs against my clit, and the movement is so slow that I have to shut my eyes to keep myself present.

"What if I said it wasn't?" I ask.

He glides a finger into me. "Then I'd remind you that I know when you're lying."

My hips move, but he stops me with his hand on my hip. My eyes fly open, and to my surprise, he isn't wearing that dirty smirk I've grown to love. "I'm done helping you, Taytum."

Pleasure surges when he slips another finger in and plays with me. His fingers are teasingly distracting. "Wha... what do you mean?"

Ford's skin is becoming as flushed as I feel. His tongue slips out to wet his lower lip each time he pushes his fingers back into me.

Kiss me.

His Adam's apple bobs. "The dates. The one-night stands. I'm done helping you." He bounces his eyes between mine. "I'm too selfish. I want you all to myself."

I tilt my hips, and he hits the spot that makes me break. He shuts his eyes, and I feel myself tighten, wanting more. I'm selfish, too, because I know he's going to beat himself up for this later, and he's going to have a hard time looking my brother in the face come tomorrow, but it feels too right to stop him.

Ford confided in me once that his one fear in life is being abandoned, because of his mother's death, so I know, in the end, he isn't going to continue to risk ruining his friendship with Emory and destroy his own integrity.

He's had a place in my life, and my family's, since we were kids. How could things ever go back to the same if we started something and it didn't work?

It wouldn't.

Once we *openly* cross the line, there is no going back.

Which is all the more reason I should stop this. But

instead, I look him dead in the face and say, "I'm selfish too."

He tilts his head, but he isn't stopping. His thumb brushes against my clit, and my knees buckle. "How so?"

"Because all I want to do is tell you to keep me to yourself."

Ford's pupils dilate, and I prepare myself for the fall. He catches my soft whimper with his mouth, and we're both out of control. He touches me everywhere, and I do the same. My hands roam over his tight shoulders before I drop them and creep under his shirt. I love the way his warm skin feels against my palms and the way his palms feel against my body.

"There's nothing that compares," he says in between each kiss. "I've tried to find something, and I come up empty-handed every fucking time."

His teeth sink into my lower lip, and my body winds up with his quick movements in between my legs. I curve against him, and he encourages me by whispering in my ear, "You at my mercy is all I ever think about."

"Ah," I moan.

Ford's mouth covers mine, and his hot growl vibrates down my throat. It pushes me over the edge, and I come around his fingers fast and hard. He presses his forehead to my collarbone while pushing farther into me, and I'm dazed with pleasure. I finally open my eyes when I feel him staring at me. "I'm never going to be able to let another man see you come."

My eyes are heavy when he finally pulls his hand out of my pants. I reach forward and grab him by the collar and drag him closer, because I know the second we walk out of this bathroom, things are going to get complicated, and I want to play the game for a little while longer.

"Not yet," I beg. "Stay and give me more."

His nose brushes against mine, and I'm drunk from his warm breath. Knowing that Ford can't stand to watch me with anyone else because *he* wants me is an insatiable yearning on my end.

I feel alive.

My heart races when Ford moves his mouth to my ear. "I would, but I can't."

I slink backward just in time to see flashing lights outside the window. Ford's steady hands stay trapped to my waist, but he turns slightly toward the tiny bathroom window, and I swear he looks proud of himself.

"Oh my god." My hand covers my swollen lips. He turns back to me, and an air of arrogance follows him. "Look what your little stunt caused!"

I rush past Ford and peer out the window.

His breath is hot and seedy against my neck when he appears behind me. I glance backward, and he's grinning. "Whoops."

A beat of silence passes before I find myself smiling. I start to laugh at his insane tactic to get me away from Knox, but I stop as soon as I hear a familiar voice say my name.

"Shit." Ford immediately backs away. His eyes dart to the door before he looks at me with shame. It's a slap right to my face, and it hurts me even though it shouldn't.

The realization flickers over his face, because if anyone can read me, it's him. "Tay." He moves toward me, and his blue eyes, the same ones that were full of fire seconds ago, dull with desperation.

"It's fine." I shrug and pretend I'm unbothered. "We... we just got caught up in the moment."

Except, it isn't just one moment.

But with my brother shouting my name through the frat house, we're going to pretend it is.

[36]

FORD

I PASS BY THE FIREFIGHTER, the same one that keeps gawking at Taytum, and hear what he says to Rush. "Yeah, it must have been a fluke. I'd change all the batteries in the alarms to make sure it doesn't happen again."

I clear my throat. *A fluke.*

"Emory, I'm fine." Taytum is barely keeping up with Emory as he drags her through the empty frat house.

We thought fast on our feet when we ran into Emory on the stairs. His heavy browline furrowed as he looked between us, and I jumped into action. I lied and told him that I went to look for Taytum when the alarms started to go off and that I had found her in a sugar episode.

"Are you sure?" Emory asks.

I put my hands in my pockets and try to act casual as I trail behind them. Taytum rips her arm away, and Emory lets go willingly. "Yes. I know how to check my sugar and when I need to give myself medicine, *Dad.* Chill out."

"She's fine, Em," I add.

I make a conscious decision to keep my eyes away from Taytum, especially in front of him.

He doesn't look convinced. "Whatever. I'm taking you home. Let's go."

Taytum hesitates, and I want to step in so badly and tell him that I'll take her home, but that'll only make things worse. He'll ask why, and then I'll have to come up with another lie. There are lies all over the place at this point.

"I can make it home without your help," Taytum stresses.

"Go," he urges, opening the car door.

She hesitates again, and my body burns the moment she swings her blue eyes in my direction.

Don't do this to me, I silently plead.

I swallow my thick spit, keep my gaze as steady as I can, and say, "Later."

Later? Did I seriously say...*later*?

If I could punch myself repeatedly without causing concern, I would.

Emory looks at me oddly, but I quickly turn and head for my car, because honest to God, I can't make sense of my behavior.

When I'm tucked behind the wheel, I turn up the music to drown out the noise in my head. It's a cluster of dirty thoughts, cravings, refusal, and guilt. I had every intention of going back to my dorm room to put myself in a much-needed time-out, but instead, I end up at the rink.

It's just me, the rink, and the puck.

I swing my stick back, balancing on the ice, and shoot the little black biscuit into the net.

Swish.

Swish.

Swish.

I start to list every reason to stay away from Taytum halfway through my therapy session.

"Emory is your best friend, and he will kill you." *Swish.*

"You're too young to die." *Swish.*

"Plus, you're too good looking to die." *Swish.*

"You could lose everything." *Swish.*

"If things go awry, there goes any family stability you have in your life." *Swish.*

"You could lose her." *Swish.*

My chest heaves as I send the last puck flying over the ice. It doesn't make it into the net, which pisses me off. All my excuses to stay away from Taytum are valid.

Her family practically adopted me as a kid when it was most needed. Without them, I wouldn't be skating on this rink. Without Emory, I wouldn't know the true meaning of loyalty and realize that you don't have to be blood-related to someone to consider them family. And without Taytum, I wouldn't be half the man I am. I'd give up my life if it meant saving hers.

I rest my forehead against the glass and stare at the sin bin. That's where I should be. My hot breath fills the glass with fog as I take deep breaths from rushing over the ice, but it didn't tire me like I hoped.

I'm still out of breath when I get into my car. The dash says it's well after midnight, and campus has slowly begun to die down. The streets are empty, and it's just me, the moon, and the one window that's still lit up on the front of Taytum's sorority house.

My heart beats hard as I stare at the orangey glow from her bedroom. The window is open, and her curtain blows with the wind. I tell myself it's a welcoming gesture. I hiss when a piece of bark scrapes over my palm, but I continue to climb the bare winter tree until I'm eye level with the little slant of the roof.

To my surprise, she's not there, like I expected.

I should climb back down the tree, get in my car, and go home, but I have zero willpower when it comes to her.

Clearly.

With my long legs, I'm able to put one foot on the roof while I hold myself steady against the thick trunk of the maple tree. I creep along the shingles one by one with my heart in my stomach and use one lone finger to push the cottony drape to the side.

Relief settles my nerves when I see her prepping the insulin pen. Since she filled me in on purposely messing with her sugar levels, I've been worried that she hasn't been taking it when she's supposed to.

"I'm glad to see you're taking your insulin," I say, pushing one leg through the window opening.

She screams and drops the pen onto the floor. "Ford! What the hell are you doing climbing through my window?"

I glance back at the opening before pinning her with an obvious look. "It was open."

She pretends to be annoyed. She flings her freshly brushed blonde hair over her shoulder and shoots me a dirty look, which is only encouragement for me. After I close the window, I skim down her body and realize she's in her pajamas.

She looks cute.

Pink shorts and a loose, matching pink top with little red hearts placed haphazardly all over them. I swear to God, there are two hearts placed perfectly where her nipples are, and my mouth waters when I see that she doesn't have on a bra.

I pull my eyes back to her face when she crosses her arms.

"That's very stalkerish."

How fitting, considering I'm obsessed with her.

We keep eye contact the entire time I walk toward her. I bend with ease and swoop up her insulin pen. "I hope you're giving yourself the proper dose," I say.

She sighs, and I have to refrain from leaning closer to feel her warm breath against my mouth. I have to get my shit together. "I am."

"Let me." I keep the pen steady in one hand and slowly lift her pink pajama top, brushing my fingers against her soft skin like she's a drug, and I'm an addict. I don't miss the way goosebumps run over her flesh and how the rising of her chest matches mine. I gulp, pinch the tender skin on her belly, and ask her if she's ready.

Our eyes meet in the middle, and every single excuse I could think of in the rink disappears right along with my self-restraint. We keep a hold of each other while I press the pen into her belly and silently count to ten. My hand stays on her lower back well after I drop the pen to the floor, and I slowly pull her silk top down to cover her, but I can't let her go.

And by the look in her eye, I don't think she wants me to.

"You're going to have to tell me to leave," I admit, praying to God that she doesn't.

I'm shaking with a need I feel in my bones. Every single time I touch her, kiss her, *look* at her, it pulls me in a little bit more. I don't know how we got to this place, but the line was crossed the night I first kissed her, and I'm not sure I can cross back over.

Taytum presses up against me, and I feel out of control.

"What's the point in me telling you to leave? It's not like you ever listen to me anyway."

My chest constricts. I silently promise myself that this will be a one-time thing. I just have to get her out of my system, and then things will go back to normal.

"One time?" I ask.

I trick myself into thinking it isn't a lie, and she helps drive it further.

Taytum swallows. "What about your rules? I thought you said I couldn't fuck hockey players."

I twitch. "Fuck my rules."

Our chemistry heightens, and my blood screams with need. I pick her up, and she wraps her legs around my waist with ease. I stare up at her as I walk us over to her bed. "I just gotta get you out of my system."

She nods. "Same."

"Then get ready," I say as I lay her back, "because tonight you're not my best friend's little sister." Her wrists are trapped in my hand, and I pin them to the pillow. "Tonight, you're mine."

TAYTUM

HE LOOKS DANGEROUS, and I love it.

I lift my hips when his fingers hook into the waistband of my pajama shorts. He pulls them down with an urgency that I feel everywhere.

"Jesus Christ." His white teeth sink into his bottom lip when he sees that I have no panties on. "It's like you knew I was coming over."

I shrug shyly. Since we've both agreed that this is a one-time thing, I let the truth fly. "I hoped."

Ford exhales, and though I've always preferred his fun and flirty side, I can't get enough of his serious side. He looks at me like I'm a meal, and here I am, gladly feeding him.

I'm drunk with need. My legs beg to spread so I can feel his mouth between them again, bringing me to the edge of insanity. When his deft fingers fall to the buttons along my shirt, I pant. He slowly pushes each button through its rightful hole with a speed that makes me wither beneath him.

"Be patient," he warns. "I'm planning to take my time with you, Heartbreaker."

A rush of cool air blankets my chest when my shirt falls open. Ford slowly pulls it from my body, and I watch in awe as he shuts his eyes for a brief second. My fingers dive into his soft hair to tug on the ends, and I'm suddenly met with a blue flame when his eyes flare open.

"Not a single flaw on you," he mutters.

I arch when he hoists himself up and covers my mouth with his. A moan escapes at the first touch, but he eats it up by moving his tongue against mine with possession. I crave him everywhere—in between my legs, in my mouth, on my breasts. *Everywhere.*

After he's finished getting his fill of my mouth, he sits up slowly. I blush when he looks at every intimate part of my naked body, and when he catches me watching him, he says something that makes me burn. "Look at you so desperate for my touch."

I don't deny it. I am. My legs spread, and I give him the perfect view because I want him to remember how much he affects me, especially because I know, in the morning, we will both deny it.

He traces my swollen lips with his finger before he trails it between my breasts, over the dip in my belly, landing right above my clit.

"I want to hear you beg for it, baby."

He thinks I won't beg. I can tell by the familiar playful glint that catches the light from my lamp. I decide to turn his world upside down, like he's doing to mine.

"You want me to beg, Ford?"

He smirks and pushes my legs farther apart, thinking I'll refuse. "Yeah."

I bite the same lip he had pulled into his mouth a second before. "Do you want me to beg on my knees..." The bed shifts when he snaps to attention. "Or like this? Spread wide open for you?"

His smile fades, and a look I've never seen moves across his face.

"Touch me, Ford," I beg. "*Please.*"

I throw my head back with a quiet moan when two fingers enter me quickly. He slips them in and out slowly, and I curve to feel more of his palm against my clit. "*God.*" I'm breathless.

"Tell me how it feels." I barely hear him over the ringing in my ears. "I want to hear you say it."

"I c–can't talk..."

A hot thrill surges down my limbs. "But you can come..." he rasps. "Fuck my hand, Taytum." Ford presses his palm harder against my clit, and I move against it with desperation. The orgasm builds quickly. I push my heels into the bed and ache. "That's it, baby," he encourages. "Come for me so I can taste you after."

Oh my god.

Ford's hand slaps against my mouth when I start to moan. I roll my hips over and over again, riding the wave, until he pulls his fingers out and pops them into his mouth. I stare at his hollow cheeks while he sucks on them, and I quickly turn the tables on him.

I grip his wrist, pull his fingers out of his mouth, and pop them into mine.

His jaw slacks when I suck hard. The hem of his shirt is in my grip, and I shove it up and over his head after letting his fingers fall from my mouth. Every single muscle visible on Ford's body is toned. His abs teeter when he moves his hands to the button on his jeans. I stare feverishly at the veins along his forearms, pumped full of hot attraction.

The same hot attraction that's flowing in between my legs.

Ford has always been good looking. Golden hair, deep blue eyes, a smile that takes everyone's breath away, and not to mention, he's absolutely flawless on the ice. For the first time in my life, it doesn't feel unnerving to think these things with him looking at me like he is right now.

"For someone who has claimed they don't have enough experience in the bedroom, you're looking pretty damn naughty," Ford says, standing in nothing but his boxers. His hand reaches for me, and I willingly move closer. His thumb brushes against my swollen bottom lip, and something hot twists in my lower stomach. "Tell me what you're thinking."

My cheeks rush with warmth, and his eyebrows fold. "Now I really want to know what's going on in there."

I trace his strong jaw with my shaky finger and move it in between his well-defined pecs before I stop at the bulge in his boxers.

"Why don't I just show you?" I whisper.

I drop to my knees, and Ford's fingers immediately dive into my hair. He pulls on the strands until I look up at him.

He shakes his head before glancing to the ceiling. "Nope. On your feet, Taytum."

All I can see is the sharp angular part of his jaw wiggling back and forth, and I do what feels natural. "Wasn't it you that said to take what I want?"

He scoffs. "And this is what you want? To suck me off?"

I answer truthfully. "I want to make you lose your mind like you do to me."

He laughs sarcastically and finally looks down at me on my knees. "I'm already fucking there, Taytum. I haven't thought straight since kissing you in that stupid bar."

A truth I should keep to myself rushes to my lips. "I haven't thought straight since meeting you, Ford."

He mumbles something under his breath that I can't hear. In a desperate attempt to keep us in this make-believe, one night of bliss, I pull his boxers down and wait for him to give me the go-ahead.

All it takes is one look.

I lean forward and smile.

I'm about to kill him slowly, just like he's been doing to me for most of my life.

[38]

FORD

I DRIVE my hand into her hair to pull her to her feet so she'll stop, but instead, I keep her right where I *really* want her. Taytum's perfect lips wrap around my cock, and I can't see straight. Her hand might as well be wrapped around my throat because I'd rather die than stop now.

The restraint of never letting myself picture her on her knees in front of me is completely blown to pieces now that she's at my mercy, sucking on my dick like she's trying to kill me.

"You're so fucking hot I can't even stand to look at you."

She smiles with a mouth full of my dick, and a husky laugh leaves me. My balls tingle, and I go to move away, but she grips the backs of my thighs and pushes me to hit the back of her throat. *For fuck's sake.*

I tug on her hair and pull out of her mouth at the same time. There's a pop, and Taytum is left on her knees, pouting with glistening, swollen lips.

"Who the hell are you?" I ask, bringing her to her feet.

Her pretty eyelashes bat with a true innocence that I, along with every other guy on campus, crave to steal.

"You're..." Words escape me. I don't want to talk. I can't talk. I'll say too much. Taytum tilts her head to the side, and I zero in on her neck like it's calling for me. I suck on the delicate skin and pull one of her legs to hook around my back. Her pussy is wet, and when she rubs herself against me, I almost crumble.

I choke out one word. "Condom."

Could you fucking imagine if I got her pregnant?

I pause when I realize the thought of her pregnant with my baby isn't as terrifying as it should be.

I hurriedly grab my wallet and pull out a condom. Taytum watches with rapt attention as I roll it on. Then, I'm back to touching every part of her. "You're so wet that it makes me wild," I admit.

She's back in my arms and wraps herself around me. We're on the bed in record time, and I lean against her headboard so she can be in control. I'm not sure I trust myself with her at this point, and she's not as experienced as she pretends to be.

My hands glide to her ribcage, and I hold her steady. Her hair is a thick curtain around us when she slowly sinks down. My heart skips a fucking beat. We both stop breathing. It's so intimate that it should feel wrong, but it doesn't. It feels like I'm right at home.

Once she adjusts, she starts to move over me, and my hands fall to her hips. I dig into her soft flesh, and her little whimpers are the cries of every last one of my restraints breaking. "You're ruining me," I groan, brushing my thumb over her clit. She moves faster, and her pretty, pink nipples pucker. When she throws her head back with an orgasm, I'm completely enthralled. I watch her lose herself for me, and I am mesmerized. I selfishly hope she never feels this high from anyone but me, because I know I'll never get it from anyone but her.

Fuck her future husband.

Taytum is mine.

Her pussy squeezes me, and I can't help but move with purpose. She's flat on her back with her hair spilled out on the bed, and I'm railing into her without restraint. Her nails dig into my back, and I force myself to pause, afraid my possessive streak is too much, but she whimpers my name and says, "Please don't stop—"

I pick up the pace and seal our mouths together in the sloppiest, sexiest kiss I've ever experienced. I'm unwillingly giving her my all, and she's taking it without hesitation.

My hand clamps on top of the headboard, and I'm holding on for dear life when she comes around my cock again.

"*Fuck,*" I groan. Her cunt doesn't let me go, and I end up emptying every last bit of pleasure into the condom. I see nothing but her, feel nothing but her, and hear nothing but her.

Her gasp cuts through my haze. Her pussy gives me another squeeze, and my eyes widen when I almost go back for seconds. I quickly pull out of her because *what the fuck*.

Our eyes snag, and though we're both fully fucked and just scratched an itch that has been there for too long, there's something else brewing behind her baby blues that I know like the back of my hand.

There is no getting Taytum out of my system now.

She's there for good, whether I like it or not.

So warm.

My nose rubs against something soft, and the scent is so familiar that I go in for another whiff.

It smells like sunshine and flowers.

It's calming.

My chest expands when I feel her soft sigh against my chest. I peek one eye open and confirm that it's Taytum.

Though, I'd know her touch anywhere.

My body can feel her from a mile away.

I evaluate the situation slowly. It's early. The morning sun is just now peeking through the wispy curtain, and there's a thin streak of sunlight laying on top of our discarded clothes on her bedroom floor. As if I need any reminder of what we did last night, I stare at my hand as I absentmindedly rub it over top of her smooth leg that's hooked over mine.

She whimpers softly, and there's an uptick in my pulse. I adjust beneath her, and those perfect lips of hers brush against my neck. Taytum scoots closer, and her leg climbs higher. My teeth sink into my bottom lip as I try to hold back, but I can't.

My finger traces a line up the curve of her thigh, and her uneven breaths match mine.

"Let me have one more," I beg.

I don't bother hiding my desperation. I slowly push her to her back, and her sleepy eyes flutter with need. I sink a finger into her, and she comes alive at the touch.

"You're already wet," I rasp.

Taytum's long lashes brush against her skin, and I want to be the one to put the pinkish hue on her cheeks over and over again.

"*Ford.*" My name is a plea falling from her mouth. I dip low to kiss the moan that's about to come next.

"I'm not going anywhere," I say in between kissing her. "Come for me again." *God, please.*

Taytum opens her eyes, and they're glazed over with lust. I push another finger inside of her and watch with rapt attention as she gets all worked up. I sweat when she takes her hand and slowly snakes it down in between her breasts, landing at the apex of her thighs.

"Do it," I encourage her. "Show me how you'll touch yourself when I'm not here to do it for you."

Her middle finger rubs faster on her clit, and I'm salivating.

"This is better than my wildest dreams." I grip her chin with my free hand. "Now kiss me like you mean it."

Her tongue is devilish. My dick throbs, and I'm in a frenzy. I pull back to watch her touch herself, and she trembles against my finger. I push in a little farther and watch her break.

"Perfect," I mutter, in complete shock at how captivated I am. She's beautiful when she comes. It does something to me that I can't put into words.

When she's done riding her high, I pull my fingers from in between her legs. I bring them in between us and don't bother licking them off this time. Instead, I grip her chin hard and push them into her mouth. "Look at the mess you've made."

She sucks hard, and her doe-like eyes grip me until we both stop dead in our tracks at the knock on her door.

I fall off the bed, and Taytum sits up with her messy blonde hair flying past her face. "Are you okay?" she whisper-asks.

"Taytum!" We both turn to the voice on the other side of the door. It's one of her sorority sisters.

Whew.

"Your brother just pulled up and parked right behind Ford's car. I could be wrong, and maybe he's in one of the other girls' rooms, but if he's in there with you, and you're doing what I think you're doing, abort mission *now*."

My heart stops.

Taytum's hand flies to her mouth.

I fly to my feet and glide as if I'm on the ice.

I'm pulling my pants on, and Taytum is quickly buttoning her pajama top.

"Remember how well we worked together when we acted at The Rodeo Bar?"

She nods quickly and pulls her shorts on.

"Get ready to do it again."

[39]

WHEN FORD TOUCHES Bryn's waist and leans her against her bedroom door, I'm ripped to shreds. The jealousy I feel is completely insane.

I know it's a ploy, and she does too.

The only person who doesn't know is Emory.

Emory sighs loudly. "Okay, that's enough. Kiss her goodbye, and get in here."

As if I'm a glutton for punishment, I stay in the hall right in front of my bedroom door and watch Ford lean in to kiss Bryn. My stomach rolls when he pulls her in close and presses his mouth to hers. If I didn't already know before, I'm well aware of how consumed I am with him, because I could crumble to the floor with the ache in my chest.

When he backs away and shoots her a wink, I bite the inside of my cheek and push Emory out of the way. I stomp into my bedroom, knowing he'll follow.

"What the fuck was that for?" Emory says, his eyebrows furrowed with confusion while he waits for my answer.

Ford enters my room next, and I can't even look at him.

Oh my god. Get it together, Taytum!

"What was what for?" Ford asks.

Emory shrugs. "I think Taytum woke up on the wrong side of the bed."

Ford hums. "She looks well-rested to me."

I'm going to kill him.

I cross my arms over my chest. "What do you want, Emory? I have things to do."

And those things involve getting my shit together so I can stand to look in Ford's direction without losing it. My phone beeps, and I'm actually thankful for the distraction.

"We gotta go home," Emory says, following my every move. I check my sugar, and I'm surprised to find my blood sugar high, versus low. I reach for my pen, and out of the corner of my eye, I see Ford take a step toward me, but I shoot him a silent warning.

"Why do we have to go home?" I ask, prepping my pen.

Emory flops onto my messy blankets. Ford clears his throat as he leans against my closed door, and when I finally give him attention, I can tell he's trying to tell me something.

What?

He drops his eyes to the floor beside my bed. I follow his line of sight, and my knees give out. I grip my desk, and Emory sits up quickly. "Are you okay? Do you need one of us to do it?"

My hand shakes when his shoe lands an inch from Ford's used condom. Worry etches onto my brother's face, and he leaps from the bed and comes to stand beside me. I quickly flash a look to Ford while Emory insists he helps me with my insulin. By the time we're done, Ford is casually leaning against my window with an unreadable expression on his face.

"Are we all good now?" he asks as nonchalantly as ever.

My answer is clipped. "I'm fine." Then I turn to Emory. "Why do we need to make a trip home?"

Emory sits back on my messy bed. If he only knew what I did on it last night with his best friend. Ford is staring at the blankets and probably having the same thought as I am. Or maybe not, since he had no issues sticking his tongue down Bryn's throat a few minutes ago.

"Because something fishy is going on. I asked why they aren't coming to the game next week, and they were being cryptic."

Shame burns my cheeks. I know exactly why they aren't coming to the game. They can't afford it. And the reason they can't afford it is because of me.

"Don't worry," Ford jokes. "I'll root for you, *Emory Bemory*."

If I wasn't so worked up, I would probably laugh.

Emory is used to ignoring Ford's teasing, so he doesn't pay him any mind and continues explaining his plan. "We can drive down there after our practice, stay the night, and head back tomorrow."

No. "And do what? Scour the house for clues? Did you ask them why they're not coming?"

Emory scoffs. "Yeah, and they gave me the dumbest excuse."

"Which was?"

"They said they couldn't miss Lennie's birthday party."

Ford rakes a hand through his messy hair. "Lennie? Your dad hates Lennie."

Emory snaps a finger. "Exactly. Something is up, so we're going home, and we're going to get to the bottom of it."

"Em–" I start, but he interrupts me.

"You have to come. I'm supposed to be watching over you, remember?"

This again? "I'm not ten. I'm in my twenties."

"And you nearly died just a couple of months ago. I'm not leaving you here alone."

I look at Ford because if he stays here, I won't be alone, but he's silently begging me not to ask. There's a discreet shake of his head, and I sigh loudly before turning back to my brother. "Fine."

"Pack your shit, and don't forget your insulin. Meet us at the rink after practice, and we'll leave then." Emory is out the door before I can protest.

Ford and I stare at each other from across my bedroom, and defiance backs me up. "Too afraid to stay at Bexley U with me without the threat of my brother walking in on us?"

His eyes narrow. "You're playing dirty, Tay."

I cross my arms and shrug.

"What's the matter?"

"Nothing."

Ford's perfect smile catches me off guard. I grab my hairbrush and chuck it at his head, knowing he's fast enough to dodge it to begin with. His laugh echoes throughout my room. "I know what's wrong with you."

"You don't know everything about me," I jab.

He snickers, and it's the most sarcastic noise I have ever heard. "You didn't like my little show, did you?"

Damn him for knowing me so well.

"Better go. My brother is waiting for you."

Ford strides across my bedroom floor leisurely. He stops when he's right in front of me. I'm eye-level with his chest, but when he slips his finger beneath my chin, I'm forced to look at him. "If it makes you feel any better, the only reason

I don't want to stay here with you while Emory goes home is because I don't trust myself anymore."

He quickly backs away. There's an obvious line drawn between us now, and it gets thicker with each step he takes.

Before he leaves me alone with my thoughts, he grins. "And don't worry, you're a much better kisser than she is."

My jaw drops, and his laughter echoes all the way down the stairs and out the front door.

[40]

FORD

Coach points at Emory. "Fine, but you better be back before practice time tomorrow. I don't want any bullshit excuses about traffic either."

Emory nods and then skates across the rink toward the locker room. Coach yells for me, and I move across the ice casually before doing a little turn and sending him a goofy grin. "I know, I know. I heard you. Don't worry. We'll leave at ten."

"Ten?" Coach shouts. "That's only three hours before practice!"

I laugh. "I'm kidding. We'll leave at seven so we can beat rush hour. We'll be back by eleven at the latest."

Coach shoots me his usual you're-lucky-you're-good-at-hockey glare before turning his back and gathering his things. Aasher and Theo are the only ones left on the ice, and when I follow their line of sight, I slip. My stick flies, and they both turn to see what the commotion is.

What the hell is he doing here?

I bounce up like the rink suddenly turned into a trampoline and skate to meet them near the glass. My scowl deepens when I watch Knox smile at Taytum.

"Who let him in here?" I snap.

"Why does it matter?" Aasher looks over at me. "They're out of the Frozen Four."

"Yeah, Ford." Theo brims with amusement, and I want to crosscheck him. "Why does it matter?"

Claire and Riley are both laughing alongside Taytum, but when they see that practice is over, they descend down the aisle to come talk to us. Much to my disapproval, Taytum and Knox do the same.

Fix your face, Ford.

I smooth out my features and nod to Knox. After all, he thinks we're friends, since I was the one that set him up with the hottest girl at this university.

Too bad for him, she's mine.

"Hey, man." I choose to play it cool. "I thought you were heading back early this morning."

"We're leavin' soon," he says.

"And you thought to come check out our practice?" Theo asks.

He's a little skeptical, but I'm not. I know exactly why he's here.

Claire looks at her boyfriend. "Actually, he came by The Bex looking for Taytum and followed us over here since I knew where she was."

The ice is likely melting beneath my skates. My heart is pounding harder than it ever has, and the thought of Knox touching her again is enough to send me sailing over the glass to strangle him. Thankfully, I have *some* restraint.

I slowly shift my attention to Taytum, and she's looking right at me. I can read her like the back of my hand.

She's fucking with me, and I don't like it.

"Well, you found her," I announce.

Both my teammates rush to stare in my direction, but I can't stop glaring at Taytum. She blows me off, though, and turns to Knox.

I suddenly can't see straight.

"Gimme." She holds out her hand and wiggles her fingers.

Knox grins and pulls his phone out of his pocket. I'm sweating through my hockey gear. I don't miss the way their fingers brush, and I don't miss the way a rush of madness enters my bloodstream either. I look to the ice to see if the rink has somehow cracked from my anger, but I'm quickly brought back to the present when I hear Taytum say, "There. I texted myself from your phone, so now you have my number."

I make a mental note to change her fucking number, because I'm clearly unstable.

"Perfect. Want to walk me out?" he asks.

"No," I snap. "She can't."

Everyone turns to me, and I look directly at Taytum. "Come on." I nod to the rink opening. "Emory needs you to meet us at the locker room so we can leave."

"Emory can wait."

I growl under my breath. "If you make him wait, he'll just come get you himself, and you know how he is when you're seen with a guy."

Knox blows a puff of air out of his mouth. "I did hear some interesting rumors about your brother..."

Aasher and Theo both step in and back me up. "The rumors are true. Come on, girls. All of ya, on the ice."

Claire and Riley obey, but Taytum is a whole other

breed. I don't give Knox another second to breathe. I bang on the glass and point at her. "Get down here."

There's a little twitch of her lips, and I know I'm fucked up over her because, instead of letting her have her fun, I threaten her. "I will come up there and get you."

She crosses her arms, and I've lost my patience. I skate over to the opening and sit down on the first set of seats, drop my helmet, then start to unlace my skates.

I hear Knox say he'll text her later, and when I glance at her again, she's slowly walking down the steps in my direction. I *re-lace* my skates and wait for her to get closer. As soon as she's within my reach, I swoop forward, and she yelps.

I hold her tightly against my front, and she pounds my shoulder pads with her tiny fists. "Stop being ridiculous and put me down."

"You want to know what's ridiculous?" I ask while skating across the ice to the other side of the rink. "You playing games with me."

"I'm not playing any games!" she argues.

We're the only ones in the rink, and that's such a dangerous thing, considering I am completely unhinged.

We make it to the other end of the arena, and I do a quick scan, confirming we're alone before sliding her feet to the ice. Her ribcage extends in my grip.

"Admit it. You just gave him your number in front of me to get back at me for this morning." Taytum tries to look away, but I don't let her. Her sweet gasp hits me square in the face when I force her chin to stay still. I squeeze, and she pouts.

"That's not true. I gave him my number because we both agreed that last night was a one-time thing. Remember? You needed to get me out of your system."

Dwelling on what was said before I fucked her doesn't matter anymore.

"Of course I remember," I say. "How could I forget anything about last night?"

"You seemed to do a pretty good job forgetting when your mouth was on Bryn's a minute after it was on mine."

I knew it. It bothered her.

"I was trying to play it cool so your brother didn't find out that you were about to scream my name seconds before he came storming upstairs." I feel myself leaning closer to her. The minute I left her room this morning, I told myself I could never cross the line again, and yet here I am, bending in half to kiss her again.

Anyone could walk into the arena at any given second, but seeing her smile at Knox made me want to do wild things to her in front of everyone—just to prove that she's mine and not theirs.

"You make me crazy," I admit. "Look at me..." I drop my head and laugh sarcastically. "I can't even keep my hands off you when it hasn't even been five hours since I touched you last."

"And yet, you expect us to travel in a car together and stay at home with my brother and parents watching our every move?"

"I thought having their eyes on us would help me keep mine off you."

Taytum says nothing, and still, my fingers twitch to touch her in other places. "You're going to have to keep me in line, Tay. So stop fucking with me on purpose."

I promise myself it'll be a quick kiss. Just enough to curb the craving. But I know it's a lie. My hand falls to the crook of her neck, and I pull her in close. I suck the hushed words off her tongue and curse the sexy little noise she lets out.

I snap backward and glare at her.

"I'm so fucked," I admit.

I quickly skate to the locker room and leave her with my taste inside her mouth, praying her brother won't know that she's left me with hers.

[41]

TAYTUM

IF THE DRIVE back home is any type of foreshadowing for how the rest of the evening is going to go, Ford and I aren't going to leave my house unscathed.

My ears are bleeding from the volume of the music coming from my brother's speakers for the last two hours, and it did nothing to help block the inappropriate thoughts filling my head as I stared at Ford's talented fingers drumming to the beat the whole time.

"There they are." My mom stands on the porch with her hands on her hips. Naturally, Ford is the first one to greet her with a big hug.

Emory coughs from behind. "Suck-up."

I want to smile, but I'm too tense, so I brush past my brother to get the next hug. My mom squeezes me a little longer than she did Ford and pulls back without letting go of my shoulders.

I count backward in my head. 3, 2, 1...

"Are you feeling okay? What's your sugar level? Is the monitor doing its job?" Her blue eyes, the same shade as mine, scan me from head to toe.

"Ma." Ford puts his hands on my hips to steer me away. "You have such little trust in us. We've got Tay under control."

My mom playfully rolls her eyes and shoos him away. Emory swoops in to hug her, and in true Emory fashion, the hug lasts for half a second. He's suddenly right behind Ford and me, which prompts Ford to drop his hands from my hips. We briefly catch each other's eye, but he looks away, and I'm left feeling disappointed.

Oh my god, stop.

We end up in the kitchen, and I'm hit with the memories from my childhood. I breathe in the reminiscence as I stare at the wooden table over by the breakfast nook with four chairs that are the same shade of white and the one by the window that's a different hue. I still remember the day my mom added it to the table for Ford.

It hasn't left since.

"Where's Dad?" Emory asks, opening the fridge. He pulls out something in a glass casserole dish and grabs a fork from the drawer before he starts digging in.

By the looks of it, it's cold lasagna.

"At least warm it up!" my mom chides, pushing him off to the side. She scoops two hefty servings onto two plates and then turns to me. "Are you hungry, babe? What do you want? This is loaded full of carbs."

"I'm fine." I hate that my tone gives away exactly what I'm feeling because Ford slowly swings his gaze to me, and the look on his face tells me he knows what I'm thinking.

Nothing has been the same since I woke up in the

hospital last summer, and I have a big feeling that things are going to get even worse before the three of us leave tomorrow morning. That is, if Emory figures out what my parents are hiding from him.

The back door opens, and a gust of cold air flies in after my dad. "Hey, Dad–" Emory stops in the middle of his sentence and smiles at the short lady standing behind our father.

Ford stands quickly. He swarms his aunt, who has been his motherly figure–along with my mom–since his own mother died. "What are you doing here? I thought you were working."

Ford's at least two heads taller than his Aunt Jo. When he places her feet down on the ground, she pats his chest while peering up at him like he's a tall building. "And miss your random surprise visit home? I traded shifts, silly boy."

"I missed you," Ford speaks with a soft tone, and it's obvious to everyone how pleasantly surprised he is. For some crazy reason, my eyes begin to water. I quickly turn and blink the moisture away, trying not to focus too much on how fulfilling it is to see him happy.

"Well, get your cute little butt over here, Taytum Elizabeth!" I climb from my chair with a smile on my face. I wrap my arms around another added member to my family that isn't blood-related. "How are you doing? Are you keeping these knuckleheads in line at school?"

I laugh. "Trying my best."

Ford mutters something under his breath, but I hear him perfectly when I sit across from him. "More like us keeping her in line."

Emory helps Ford's case. "I do recall Ford having to go back for you after the fire alarm incident last night."

All eyes are on me, and I freeze. Sweat prickles my

scalp, and my face burns. I feel a swift kick to my shin and quickly snap out of it. Ford remains completely relaxed, but I know everything that's running through my head is running rampant through his too.

"Fire alarm? What?" My dad is concerned, but Ford quickly comes to my rescue.

"No big deal. Someone set off the fire alarms at the football house, and when I realized I couldn't find Taytum, I went searching." He starts to bite into his food. "She was checking her sugar. I stayed with her until she was good to go."

He sure did.

My mom reaches over and squeezes his shoulder. He looks at me briefly. "Thank you, Ford. If it weren't for you and Emory watching out for her, we'd have a heart attack with her at school by herself."

"I'm perfectly capable of taking care of myself," I remind them.

Emory snorts, and I almost throw a fork at his face.

Ford clears his throat and plays right into their hands. "Maybe we like taking care of you, little sis."

I raise an eyebrow. *Little sis?* Without so much as blinking, I go to kick him like he did to me, but with his hand underneath the table, he catches my ankle and holds on tight. I jerk it while trying to keep myself upright, but his grip tightens.

In an attempt to control the situation, I relax my leg and shift beneath the table. His hand loosens, and I scoot to the edge of my seat. My shoe brushes the zipper of his jeans, and I have to force myself to keep a straight face. "You guys don't want to take care of me," I say. "You want to control me. God forbid I give some guy my number."

Ford's fingers dig into my ankle.

"You shouldn't be focusing on a boyfriend, sweetheart. You need to get your health under control first. Level out those glucose readings so we can slap a pump on you," my dad adds.

My stomach falls. I want to reiterate that I don't need a pump, but with doing so, I'm afraid I'll spill their secret and everything will blow up in my face.

The room grows tense. Ford's aunt takes a step forward, and I wait with bated breath to see what she's going to say. *Does she know about their money issue?*

"You know," she says. "Sex is good for your health."

Emory chokes on his leftover lasagna, and Ford immediately drops my foot. To no surprise, I'm the only one who laughs.

My parents scold her jokingly, but I smile at her.

Aunt Jo has always been on my side, even when Ford is involved.

After my mom tells us all to go into the living room so she can make us a homemade meal from her new cookbook, *Cooking for Diabetics*, I move to sit beside Ford on the couch but think twice and sit on the opposite end. Emory and my dad are in the middle of a conversation about the guys' latest game, which prompts my brother into poking holes in their excuse of going to Lennie's birthday party instead of their next game.

Panic starts to make itself known in my lower stomach and forces me to leave the room. I can't bear to hear the excuse that's going to fall from my father's mouth next because I'm privy to the real reason they're not coming, and it weighs me down with guilt.

I feel Ford's eyes trail my every step, but when I do a quick glance back, he's turned all the way toward the TV where he, my dad, and Emory watch old footage of hockey.

He hoped that being back home around my family and brother would help keep his eyes off me, and I guess he was right.

[42]

FORD

MARY-ANN PATS EMORY on the shoulder as she sits down on the arm of the couch. "Dinner is almost ready."

"Alright, Mom," he says without taking his eyes off the hockey footage he's been watching for an hour. I started off watching it but quickly shifted gears and started to make note of the subtle changes around the house.

I'm an observant person—which is how I know that Taytum has gone upstairs to check her sugar and inject her insulin if needed since we're about to eat—and it's how I know that something isn't right around the house. Things are misplaced or missing. Things like their family portrait that has been hanging on the wall for the last four years and Taytum's senior ballet photo where she stands alone on the stage in nothing but a leotard and flimsy tutu that shows off her long, toned legs.

I push off from the couch and walk into the kitchen to see what else is missing when I find my stand-in mom setting the table.

"Move it," I say. She hands over the plates and sits on the chair to watch me take over setting the table.

"You're such a gentleman," she teases.

I grin. "You raised me right."

She laughs through a raspy cough that I'm not happy to hear. "You raised yourself."

"Not true," I correct her. "And you need to stop smoking."

With the same green eyes as my mother, she levels me with a withering stare. "Fine. I'll stop smoking as soon as you admit that you and Taytum are sleeping together."

The fork in my hand slips and falls to the floor with a loud clang. I drop down like a shot was fired, and my aunt laughs under her breath when I stand back up. I point with the fork, prongs facing in her direction, and deny it until I'm blue in the face.

It's no use, though. She doesn't believe a word I say.

I continue setting the table with her knowing little grin following me around.

"Alright, Miss Know-It-All..." I place the last utensil down and look her square in the eye. "I'll admit it if you tell me what's going on with this whole ordeal." I twirl my finger around the kitchen.

"What are you talking about?"

It only takes one look at her face to confirm what's going on. *Damnit.*

"They're selling the house, aren't they?"

She shushes me, and I sink into a chair.

"Is this because of their financial problems?"

Talk about being pelted with guilt. Maybe if they didn't spend their life savings on putting not one, but *two* of us in youth hockey and giving Emory, Taytum, and me every-

272 / SJ SYLVIS

thing we needed for Bexley U, they'd be able to afford Taytum's medical bills, insulin, and fancy pump.

"How do you know about that?" We both turn at the sound of Mary-Ann's voice as she stands with her arms down by her sides. She comes closer and grabs the back of the empty chair separating me and my aunt.

She looks to Taytum's empty chair and sighs. "Does she know?"

I gulp. "She knows you're struggling to afford the insulin on top of the other medical bills." I keep my word to Taytum and don't let on about her messing with her levels to push getting the pump.

"There weren't any issues with the last pick-up, though. As far as I know, the credit card went through."

I look away in the middle of her sentence.

"Ford...?"

Silence fills the kitchen, and it doesn't take long for me to break.

"I paid for it, okay?"

"What?" The two women in the room speak at the exact same time.

I shrug. "It's the least I can do. Look at all you've given me. Both of you."

"Stop that right now." Mary-Ann's hand comes down onto my forearm, but I refuse to look at her. "We've got it under control. We're still fighting with our private insurance, but once we sell the house and make the equity off of it, we can pay off the credit cards and bills to get back on our feet. The most important thing is making sure she gets her insulin every month and that pump."

"I couldn't agree more," I say. "But you don't need to sell the house."

The depths I'm willing to go to for Taytum tells me much more about myself than I'm willing to admit.

"It's already on the market."

"Well, take it off," I demand.

She takes a seat, and her head hangs low. "Trust me. If there was another way, we'd take it. But there isn't."

I unhook my grip on the table and bang my knuckles on the top with frustration. "Well, whatever you do...don't tell her yet." Not until I figure out a way to save the day.

"Don't tell her what?"

All eyes are on Taytum. My heart stops, and I pray that her mom can come up with something on the fly, but I know the moment Tay and I are alone, she'll bat those thick eyelashes and it'll pull the truth right out of me.

I can't lie to her.

I can't even keep my hands off her.

My aunt sits up a little taller and catches my eye. I already know what's about to come out of her mouth, so I send her a death glare, and she rolls her eyes but zips her lips.

"What's going on?" Emory rounds the island and looks at Taytum. "You okay?"

Taytum tucks her hair behind her ear and gulps.

Jay enters the kitchen next and ping-pongs his gaze around the room before looking at his wife. "Oh, did you tell them?"

"Tell us what?" Emory crosses his arms.

I look at Taytum, and she's already staring at me. The blood starts to drain from her face, and I'd pretty much do anything to put the color back on her cheeks. I gently shake my head and silently tell her that everything will be fine.

"We're selling the house."

Emory is shocked and immediately asks why. When his

parents don't answer, he starts prodding even further, demanding to know why they're not coming to the game next week and why they'd go to Lennie's birthday party when we all know they hate the nosy lady to begin with.

I'm locked on Taytum listening to everything going on around us. She's frozen in the middle of the kitchen, listening to her parents explain to her older brother how they need money to pay off the medical bills and such. When Emory starts to come up with the most ridiculous plan to get a job and help pay–as if he can fit that into his busy schedule–Taytum starts to visibly shake. I'm on my feet, following every one of her backward steps. No one but my aunt notices our departure. She quickly grabs onto my hand, gives it a gentle squeeze, and then I'm off.

It's funny how everyone is so worried about Taytum's diabetes that they tend to forget about her.

I don't, though.

I should if I knew what was good for me.

But deep down, all I want is for her to be good for me.

[43]

TAYTUM

I'M TREMBLING, and the cold winter air isn't helping. My chin wobbles, and chills cover my skin, but I'd rather be outside in my stupid little hideout than inside where my entire family is trying to figure out a solution to a problem that isn't even theirs.

I run through my options, and they're almost as ridiculous as Emory threatening to quit Bexley U's hockey team to get a job. As if I'd ever let him do something like that for me. Sure, he's ruined a lot of good moments in my life—like every date I've ever had, my senior prom, multiple friendships because god forbid I have an attractive older brother and girls blame *me* for his refusal to date them—but I'd never take away his future because of something completely unfair to not only me but to everyone else too.

"One, two, three, four..." I glance behind me and see a head full of sandy-blond hair. Ford continues to climb the rickety ladder we built when we were ten and finishes his sentence. "I declare a thumb war."

"Sorry, I changed the password," I mumble. "You can't come up."

There's a long pause, and when I peek back again, he shoots me a dazzling smile that I feel in my chest. "Mmm... girls rule, boys drool?"

In complete disbelief, I turn toward him. "How do you even remember that one?"

His crooked grin reminds me of the boyish version of him that used to sit up here with me on summer nights. "I remember everything about you...even the dumb passwords you came up with in fifth grade."

I roll my eyes. I don't have time for his cutesy remarks. I know he's just trying to lighten my mood, but this time, it's not going to work.

"I also remember that your favorite color is blue, which makes sense because it's the same color as my eyes."

I scoff dramatically. "That is not why my favorite color is blue."

Ford climbs up another step of wood nailed to the tree trunk. "I remember what you wore on the first day of high school, and on the first day of your sophomore year, and on the first day of your junior year, *and* lastly, I remember that damn dress you tried to escape the house in on the first day of your senior year when you thought Emory and I had already left for Bexley U."

They stopped me from going into the school and made me change in the back of my car.

I hated them for it.

Ford's fingers drum against the bark of the elm tree, and I spin on the creaky old wood, letting my legs dangle off the edge. The treehouse is pathetic with its old plywood as a floor and nothing for the sides. I wouldn't even call it a treehouse, but when we were young, it was all the rage.

"I also remember that every time you've ever been truly upset about something, you climb this outrageously tall tree and give me a heart attack."

It makes me feel alive. It always has.

"You're welcome for keeping your heart healthy." I turn away. "A higher heart rate is good for endurance."

Ford finally hauls himself up and scoots to the very far edge of the plywood. He doesn't let his feet dangle, though. Instead, his long legs sprawl out in front of him, and he traps me in between them. I glance down at his leg in my lap, but I don't attempt moving it. "Fuck endurance. Your little stunts are terrible for my heart, Taytum."

"I'm beginning to think I'm terrible for everyone's heart," I mumble.

Ford slowly rests against the sturdy tree trunk, and we have nothing but the moonlight separating us. "You know what else you're terrible for?"

"My parents' wallet?" It's not funny, but it is fitting.

He sighs. "My willpower."

"I didn't ask you to follow me."

"And yet, here I am."

It makes me feel better that he's up here with me, but I won't admit it. I look through the bare branches of the tree to stare at the backside of my house. *They're selling our home.*

"Tell me what you're thinking about."

I swing my feet back and forth, and Ford's leg tightens against my stomach. "I'm thinking of ways to pay for my insulin and past medical bills."

Ford's smooth voice settles me. "Alright, let's hear 'em."

I smile on the inside. "I could drop out of college and become a stripper."

The plywood beneath us bends a little as Ford leans closer to me. "What did I tell you before we left the rink?"

"Before or after you kissed me?" I tease.

"Stop fucking with me," he mumbles under his breath. "A stripper. Yeah, fucking right."

I laugh quietly when he grunts but shut right up when he quickly reaches forward and pulls me in closer. His legs spread over the plywood, and I fit in between them with my back against his chest. His heart pounds against my spine when his arm traps me to him. "You love to get a rise out of me, don't you? You are not stripping."

I roll my lips together. "Your possessiveness is showing again."

His lips brush over my neck. "It only comes out to play when you're involved."

My arms fall to his as he holds us steady over the make-shift floor.

"What else have you come up with?"

I shrug. "Feet pics."

Ford's chest rumbles with laughter. "I've seen those ballerina feet. You ain't makin' money off those."

I elbow him in his right abdomen. "Rude."

He laughs. "What's next?"

He told me to stop playing games, but I can't help it. Ford brings out a side of me that no one else can. "I think my best bet is to marry rich. Maybe a doctor." I snap my fingers. "Rush's brother. Remember him? He's in med school. It'll be a two-in-one. My parents will love that. I'll be under the care of a medical professional at all times *and* be able to afford my medication."

Ford tenses from behind. His muscles lock, and I hear the way his teeth clank together. "You think you're funny, don't you?"

The corner of my mouth quirks. "I think it's funny to get a rise out of you."

Ford's hand glides over my thigh, and I'm suddenly hyperaware of his every movement. "I think you like to test me," he whispers, pushing on my thigh. It falls open just wide enough that he can run his finger up the inseam.

"I should tell you to stop," I say. "Weren't you the one that told me to keep you in line?"

I don't know what we're doing or how we found ourselves in this position, but it's too enthralling to stop. I'm not sure if he's trying to distract me or if he feels as uncontrollable as I do, but being up here with him feels like some sort of survival. He refuses to let me carry my burdens myself, and to me, that's huge.

Ford's hand is steady on the inside of my thigh, and it leaves a sensitive tingle behind. "You won't tell me to stop. You like me touching you just as much as I like touching you, don't you?"

My lungs fill with air, and I nod against his chest. His teeth sink into my earlobe, and he pulls on it at the same time he unbuttons my jeans. "I can't help myself when it comes to you," he admits. I shut my eyes when his fingers slip underneath my panties. "This wasn't my plan when I came after you."

"What was your plan?" My question is clipped when I feel his finger tease my entrance.

Ford holds me steady with one arm around my waist as the other explores. He breathes hard in my ear before whispering, "To take care of you."

I arch back to look up at him. "You are taking care of me."

[44]

Taytum is mine.

She doesn't know it, and I'm not sure when I'm going to tell her, but this girl is mine.

"Keep doing that," she tells me, resting further onto my chest. I watch my hand move inside her pants, and it's so fucking hot that I can't seem to care that we're balancing on a dry-rotted piece of plywood.

We could fall to our death in seconds, but it would be a death worth dying for.

"I like the thought of taking care of you," I admit, pushing another finger inside of her. My thumb rubs her clit achingly slow, and I know it's driving her nuts. I crave to feel her around my dick again.

"*Ford....*" she breathes my name out like I'm her lifeline, and I'm obsessed with the thought of being the only guy on this planet that gets to have her.

"I've gotta tell you something," I whisper, pulling on her other earlobe and wishing it was her pussy.

She whimpers and tries to move her hips against my hand. My forearm tightens around her waist to hold her steady because we truly might die if we move too much. "Okay, tell me." Her back arches, and I'm so infatuated with her body that I want to kiss every single inch of her skin.

"You're not marrying some fancy doctor."

"Ah." Her lungs rush to fill with oxygen, and I creep my mouth over to her neck to trail kisses up all the way to the corner of her mouth. "You're so good at touching me."

"That's because your body was made to be mine." I rub her clit faster and hook my finger a little further in until I know I hit the spot that she's been trying to reach. "Which is exactly why you're going to be my wife someday. Not some doctor who wouldn't be able to make you come, especially when he sees your parents looking out the kitchen window to find you."

"Wait, what?" She tries to sit up, but I don't let her.

"Do me a favor..." I hit the spot with my finger again, and she bucks against my hand. "Say my name when you come, baby."

Taytum's head falls back onto my chest, and her orgasm face is too much for me to handle. I can't help but plunge my tongue into her hot little mouth. I catch my name falling off her lips, and when she's done riding my hand, I pull it out and lick it clean—like always.

I button her jeans, and she sits up, freshly finger-fucked and looking at me like she wants to do it again.

My cheek lifts, and I'm in heaven when she puts her hand up to her mouth to hide her laugh.

Something warm settles in my chest that can't even be taken away when I hear her brother shout her name from their back deck.

"Oh, shit." Taytum's smile falls as soon as her hand

does.

I shake my head to ease her concern and reach out to gently rub her chin with my thumb. "Do you trust me?"

Her eyes say a thousand different things, but all that matters is that she nods slightly.

"Then let me take care of you. Don't worry about the money, alright?"

She opens her mouth to say something, but I quickly press it closed.

Emory is closer now, and Taytum and I both look down to the yard when he calls to us. "I know you two aren't in that unstable treehouse."

"Wanna come up?" I shout down through the branches. Taytum's mouth twitches with a hidden smile.

"And die? No thanks."

Taytum peeks over the edge, and I hold onto her waist so she doesn't fall. "It's perfectly stable."

I snort, and she snaps her eyes to me. I lower my voice so only she can hear me. "Stable enough to withstand some finger-fucking, for sure."

"You're terrible," she hisses.

"And you're terribly addicting," I counter.

She looks at me long and hard but pulls away when there's a cluster of snapping twigs from below. "Get down here, you guys!" Emory shouts.

Taytum tenses. "I'm only coming down if you promise not to threaten to quit hockey to pay for my medication. That's absurd. You're the best goalie in your division."

"I know I am." Taytum rolls her eyes at her brother's arrogance. "But fine, you have my word. I'm not quitting. Just get down here before you leave Mom and Dad another medical bill."

Taytum shouts as she crawls over to the ladder. "Oh,

fuck off, Emory. You're not funny."

"Ford thinks I'm funny, don't you?"

Taytum's raises her perfectly arched eyebrow in a challenge, and I can't help but show off my straight teeth with a cocky smile. "I admit...that was a good joke."

The glare I get from Taytum sends me reeling with excitement. I follow after her and Emory as we all head back through the yard and into the house. I grab onto Taytum's hand at the very last second, before we are met with her parents' concern, and give it a slight squeeze.

"It's going to be fine."

She looks forward, and I stare at the side of her delicate cheek.

"You said you trusted me, so prove it, yeah?"

Our gazes meet in the middle, and I silently beg her to let me in.

She slowly lets go of my hand, but I don't miss the way her eyes fall to my mouth or the quick nod of her head as we walk into the kitchen.

I'm going to fix this, and then I'm going to make her mine.

━━

The number of times I've lain in this exact bed and fantasized about Emory's sister is something I always said I'd take to my grave, but now that I've actually touched her, there is no way I can lie here for another second without having her.

Emory took entirely too long to fall asleep.

I ball up another tissue and throw it at his face, wondering if he'll stir again or if he's actually fully asleep.

The little white ball flies through the air and lands on his closed eyelid. I hold my breath and wait to see if he brushes it off his face or if he stays still. My stomach fills with relief when he doesn't stir, and I slowly slide out of bed, making my way to his side of the room. There are fourteen crinkly tissues on the floor in between our beds that I quickly brush into one big pile and shove under his.

Mary-Ann will find those eventually and probably think they're under there from him beating off, which is just an added bonus. I laugh silently and walk over to our closed bedroom door with my blood full of wild anticipation.

After Taytum, Emory, and I made it back into the kitchen where the news was spilled about the Olsons selling their house, my aunt put her foot down and demanded we talk about anything *other* than Taytum's diabetes and her parents' finances.

When I gave her a hug goodbye after dinner, I whispered my gratitude in her ear, and she squeezed me extra tight. But I got a text from her shortly after I laid in bed that I can't get out of my head.

> I know what you're planning. I don't think it's a good idea, but if you're willing to do it for her, then I was right all along about you two.

The thought makes me tense, but I know as soon as I'm with Taytum, the dread will disappear, and I'll quickly be reminded of my reason why.

I pause when the door latches behind me. My hands go up like I've been caught robbing a bank, but after a few long seconds no one comes to question what I'm doing in the hallway at one in the morning with my heart racing out of my chest.

Her bedroom door is only a few yards away, and I keep my sights set on it, as if it's going to disappear into thin air. My fingers tremble when I grip the doorknob, and I'm flooded with fear that someone is going to see me sneaking into her room in the middle of the night.

It feels an awful lot like I'm crossing some imaginary line, but I can't find it in me to care. I also can't, for the life of me, remember all the reasons it was a bad idea to sleep with my best friend's sister behind his back.

Not when she's *this* close to being in my hands again.

The door unlatches, and my chest loosens.

My eyes quickly adjust to her dark room, and I find her on the bed. The faint glow from the night sky shows off each and every curve begging for my attention. I lock the door with a single flick of my thumb and sink onto her bed.

Her sleepy sigh does something to my dick, and I wrap my hand around her waist to pull her in closer. She nestles into my chest, and I brush away her blonde strands to give way to her ear. "How could you sleep knowing that I was just two doors down, thinking about all the ways I wanted to touch you?" My voice is so low the sound is unrestrained, which is pretty on par.

"Who said I was asleep?" she asks.

I follow her quick movement like a lost puppy when she pulls herself up and leans her head on her palm. Her smile is mostly concealed by the dark, but it doesn't matter—I'd know that flirty tone anywhere.

"Were you waiting for me?" I ask, trailing my finger over the curve of her cheek.

"See for yourself."

What?

Words lodge in my throat the moment she grabs my wrist and shoves my hand under the covers. She places it right between her legs, and...*fuck me*. She's bare and soaked.

"Taytum Elizabeth..." I chide, rubbing my fingers through her wetness. *My God.* "Were you touching yourself while you waited for me to sneak into your bedroom?"

My dick is so hard it hurts. The things I want to do to her are dirty and ruthless. I want to fuck her in every position, make her scream my name, and watch her come over and over again until the end of time.

I have never demanded a girl say my name while she came before Taytum, but all I want to hear is my name falling from *her* mouth.

Taytum moves against my hand, and I can't stop picturing her touching herself underneath the covers while she waited for me. It's so hot I might make her do it again, just so I can watch.

"I actually wasn't touching myself," she shyly admits.

My hand stops, and I try to make my eyes adjust in the darkness so I can see her better. "You weren't?"

"No." Her mouth comes closer to mine, and it takes everything in me not to kiss her.

"Are you saying that you are this wet from the thought of me coming in here?"

I am going to mark every part of her body in her childhood bed, because I have zero willpower. I always thought that the older I became, the more controlled I'd become, but that was completely obliterated by Taytum and her hot little kiss.

Her sweet breath brushes against my lips, and I'm a goner.

"If I say yes, will you stay?"

I chuckle against her mouth. "I'd stay even if you said no."

[45]

TAYTUM

His lips are greedy when he kisses me, and I'm obsessed with the urgency that backs every one of his touches.

"God, I can't get enough of you." He pulls away briefly before going back for more. Ford's calloused hands brush against my ribs when he shoves my oversized tee over my head and drops it to the floor.

I straddle him from above and push his shirt up next. I eagerly touch every tight ab along his stomach and feel the burn scorch my insides.

"Do you know how many times I've thought about this moment? Sneaking into your room late at night to make you mine?" He's out of breath, and it does nothing but excite me.

I push at the waistband of his loose sweats, and he takes them off, all while keeping me steady on top. His hard length is in my palm, and I'm lost with lust when his hand snakes down his chest to cover my hand gripping him.

He gets harder, and I've never felt so untamed before. There's a need pushing me to do things that I've only ever imagined.

"I thought about you back then too," I admit, shimmying down his legs.

Ford groans quietly. "What did you just say to me?"

I lick my lips. "I said I used to think about you too."

"Fuck, Taytum."

All of a sudden, my feet hit the floor. Ford's hands tighten around my hips, and he breathes down into my space. "You can't say stuff like that."

"Why not?"

"Because I have a hard time controlling myself when it comes to you, and with your mouth that close, all I want to do is feel it around my cock."

I fall to my knees instantly, and he curses under his breath. I grip his thighs, and the sound he makes fulfills every single fantasy I have ever had.

My bedside lamp clicks on, and he's gazing at me like I'm the most irresistible thing he has ever laid eyes on. He looks at me like this isn't just some space in time where we touch each other in secret, behind closed doors.

He looks at me like he wants to keep me forever.

His hand cups the back of my head, and I lick my lips. "I don't think I can hold back with you tonight." There's a tug on my hair, and my nipples harden. "Not with you looking at me like that while you're on your knees."

I answer by gripping him around the base of his length and putting him in my mouth. His hips tilt, and his fingers tangle in my hair. My stomach dips with eager anticipation every single time he plunges himself in farther.

"Jesus Christ," he mumbles. "I don't even want to know

how you got so good at this when I've tried to stop every guy from even looking at you for the last several years."

I pull back and smile. "You think you're the only guy I've ever snuck around with?"

Surprise makes me yelp when he picks me up and throws me onto my bed. He glares down at me in a hot, jealous rage that I can easily become obsessed with. "You and your fucking games."

My legs are spread wide, and he's in me before I take a breath. "I'm the only guy you can sneak around with, got it?"

I nod through the twisting in my lower stomach and meet him halfway when he thrusts into me. My eyes shut with every lasting tingle he leaves behind.

An orgasm is right around the corner, and I know he can feel it, because he won't stop hitting the perfect spot. His hot whisper skims my ear, and I shake. "Oh, and Taytum?" He glides in slowly and pulls an orgasm from me. His hand slams onto my mouth to drown my whimper when he whispers the rest of his sentence. "Delete that fucking app. You won't be going on any more dates."

I come so hard that he pulls out of me half a second later and comes on my bare belly.

We stare at the mess he's made without muttering a word.

I can hardly stand to look at him as I shove the rest of my eggs in my mouth. A little bit of the yolk drips to my chin, and when I reach up to wipe it away, I hear him gulp from across the table. I finally get the nerve to look up at him, and he's staring directly at my mouth.

My tongue rolls over my lips slowly, and his nostrils flare.

We're lucky no one caught him going back to his room this morning. To my surprise, Ford didn't leave right away last night. After we cleaned up and got dressed, he pulled me into his arms and laid with me until my alarm went off at four. He grabbed my chin, kissed me hard, and then snuck back into the room he shared with my brother until they left for college.

Neither of us have touched on what we're doing, or what it means, but part of me doesn't want to. There's fear lingering there whenever I think about it, and for once, I just want to *be*. I don't want to worry about the future or what will happen if my brother happens to walk in on us, or what my parents will think if we tell them that we're seeing each other. I especially don't want to think about what'll happen if we do start something real and it doesn't work.

Not to mention, I have a good amount of baggage that he's well aware of—like medical bills, a lifelong disease, and possible hospital visits, which just so happen to trigger him into panic attacks.

I snap out of it when Emory walks into the kitchen with damp hair and his backpack all ready to go. "Hurry up and eat," he demands, biting into a fluffy waffle my mom wouldn't let me have, despite the fact that I haven't had any carbs today. "Coach will make us skate laps if we don't get back in time for practice."

I roll my eyes, but at the same time, I stuff the rest of the egg into my mouth. Hockey coaches aren't the only strict mentors–Professor Petit has demoted the star of a show before because she thought they were slacking when, in all reality, they weren't.

"Chill. I'm ready." I slide out from my chair.

My mom rounds the island and lowers her voice. "Did you give yourself a shot today? The right dose?"

I immediately look at Ford, and his brows furrow as he tries to read my expression. The shake of his head is discreet.

I test the waters with my mom but tread lightly. "Why wouldn't I?"

"I'm wondering the same," Emory adds. "Of course she took her insulin."

Ford stands up and collects our plates. "I think we'd know if she didn't," he says through an airy chuckle. He turns the water on at the sink and starts to wash our dishes before my mom sends him away and finishes. "It would be obvious because she'd probably pass out or go into DKA. It would be totally unsafe, and she wouldn't do something to jeopardize her own health. Right, Taytum?"

I narrow my eyes. *Is he testing me?*

"Right," I answer, letting the word pop out of my mouth with force.

My mom dries her hands on the towel and sighs. "Okay, but after last night, I just worry that you'll do something rash because of the cost of your medicine. It's not for you to worry about. Just take what you need, and if you need to change your medication, we will figure it out."

"But that's where you're wrong," I argue. "It's *my* medicine. Of course I'm going to worry about it." I leave out the part where I feel absolutely sick over the fact that they're selling my childhood home to afford everything.

"Taytum," my mom stresses.

I sigh and decide to let it go. "Okay. Let's just drop it."

She grabs my hand and squeezes three times, *I love you.* "We've got it figured out. You just go to the pharmacy when you're due to fill the prescription, and it'll be taken care of. We need to get your levels straightened out."

I look over at Ford briefly, and he's staring directly at me with a flexed jaw. I pull my attention back to my mom and fake a smile. "Okay, Mom. I love you."

Her hug lasts for a long time, and behind her shoulder, I watch Ford leave the kitchen to follow after my brother, who is likely already in the car, waiting for us to scramble inside so he can get to practice on time.

"I'll let you know when we get in," I say, turning the corner.

I'm almost to the front door when a hand lands on my elbow and tugs me into the foyer.

"What are you doing?" I ask, looking from Ford to the hallway that leads to the kitchen.

"Do I need to start checking your injection sites to make sure you're actually taking your insulin? I checked your levels, and they're still all over the place." His calm demeanor from last night is long gone, and in its place is my brother's overprotective best friend.

I snatch my arm from his grasp. "Did you tell my parents?"

He pulls back, and I recognize the tiny slip of hurt that flashes across his face. "I told you I wouldn't."

My brother blares the horn, and both Ford and I look toward the window and see him in the driver's seat of his car, waiting impatiently for us. "I know. But then she acted like–"

Ford steps closer, and I stop talking. His thumb goes

under my chin, and he tilts my face to his. "You have my word, Tay. I'm not going to ruin your trust by telling them something you asked me not to. You *are* taking your insulin, though, right?"

I nod. "I am. I don't know why my levels are wonky. I'm trying to correct them."

"You know why she asked you that?" he asks.

I shake my head.

"Because you're *you*. You're selfless, loyal, and your heart is the size of Texas. I've never met someone who can care so much for others until I met you." I open my mouth to deny his claim, but his grip on my chin tightens. "You should have hated me my senior year after I ruined your prom night."

Oh God. I still hate when anyone brings up that godawful night.

"Except, you were the only one who attempted to snap me out of my panic, just hours later, when we were at the hospital." He laughs under his breath. "I used to think it was your need to prove something to someone. Like you wanted to show the world that you could be the one to bring me out of my panic attack, but that's not why you did it. It was because you cared about me."

My heart slips. That night was the start of Ford Collins latching himself onto my soul. He's been there for years, and I've refused to admit it aloud, but it's true.

Another sound of the blaring horn makes us both jump. His hand falls away, and the wall goes back up. But before we walk out the front door and pretend like there's nothing going on between us, he hooks a finger into my belt loop and pulls me backward until I hit his chest.

"When you're ready to admit it, say the word."

"Admit what?" I ask.

"That you care about me as much as I care about you." He lets go of me and starts to walk past, but I stop him.

"And what if it doesn't work? You and me? Then what? Everything will get messed up, Ford. *Everything*."

Ford shrugs. "It's a risk I'm willing to take."

FORD

> Taytum: Do not pull the same stunt you pulled for Riley's tryouts. Wear something nice.

> Me: What do you mean? You don't want the hockey team to write each letter of your name on our stomachs and do the wave during the recital?

> Taytum: Do not. I'm already nervous!

> Me: Oh, come on! You're no fun.

> Taytum: I'll lock my bedroom window later if you come up to my show without a shirt, Ford.

I'd just use the front door, but whatever.

> Me: Fine!

Taytum: Thank you.

Me: Maybe I'll just come naked. That's a nice view, right?

Taytum: FORD!

I smile until my phone disappears and is flying through the locker room doing multiple flips. It lands on the tiled floor, and my heart falls to my ass when I see Emory grinning. He reaches for it, and I go old-school on him. I give him a quick jab in the neck before diving down, snatching my phone, and putting it in my boxers so he'll think twice about grabbing it.

"Wow," he muses. "You must be texting someone good if you're willing to pull that move."

Theo whips his attention in my direction, but I can't look at him because he knows I'm messing around with Taytum, and I know he disapproves.

He doesn't care that I'm with her, but he does care that I'm hiding it from our goalie.

As captain, his job is to make sure the team dynamic is a ten out of ten, and if his beloved, hot-headed goalie finds out that his best friend is fucking his sister behind his back, well...things are going to get heated.

"Go on," I joke. "Grab the phone." I thrust my hips at him, but there's sweat trailing down my back at the thought of him finding out like this.

I told Taytum to say the word and I'd come clean to Emory.

But she's hesitant, and we have bigger things to worry about right now.

Like the phone number I snagged from my aunt that's burning a hole in my conscience.

"You're so desperate for anyone to touch your dick that you're going to trick me into it?" He chuckles. "We've gotta get you laid."

Thank God Theo steps in, because all I can picture is his sister, naked and withering beneath me.

"What time are we meeting?" Theo asks, pulling off his practice jersey.

"Seven," Emory states.

"See you guys then. I gotta go and wish my girl good luck." Theo throws up his fist, and we give him knucks before breaking apart to go our separate ways.

I turn around to put the rest of my gear away but stop when I eye my jersey hanging in my locker. After making sure Emory is gone, I pull my phone out of my pants, and I quickly text Taytum.

> Me: Don't worry, Heartbreaker. I'll wear the most expensive thing I own.

"What the hell are you wearing?" Theo asks.

Emory is laughing from beside Theo, and I can't help but crack a smile.

I look down to my hockey uniform. "Oh, this old thing?"

Theo looks at me disapprovingly. "Are you ever serious?"

I can be...in certain situations. But this? It's not one of them. Taytum needs a laugh. I know it because I know her. She's nervous and cagey, just like she always is before a show, and the fact that her parents aren't here because they're trying to save money isn't helping.

"Listen, I'm here for comedic relief. Take it or leave it."

Theo sighs and turns to walk into the auditorium. Emory is still chuckling from beside me, and the moment we sit in our seats, I feel a buzz from my phone.

> Taytum: Are you kidding me?

Emory is engaged in a conversation with Theo, so I quickly type a text back.

> Me: No. And stop texting me while I'm sitting a seat away from your brother, if you're still holding out on telling him.

I wait impatiently for her to text back while the other seats begin to fill up. My leg bounces up and down as each minute passes without a message, and when the stage lights blink twice, signaling that the show is going to start soon, I stand up.

"What are you doing?" Emory asks.

"Takin' a piss," I announce. "Wanna hold my dick?"

An older woman gives me a dirty look, but I ignore her as I shimmy past. Theo shakes his head, so I ignore his silent disapproval and walk up the aisle, garnering looks from random people in the audience at my choice of attire.

I pass by the bathroom and eye the door that leads backstage. Since the show is about to start, no one notices me as I slip inside and head down the dark hallway where dancers are running about.

I spot her at the very end of the hall in her black leotard and wispy skirt that barely covers one of my favorite parts of her body. Her neck lengthens when she raises to her tiptoes to look at something on the stage, and all I want to do is reach up and undo her ballerina bun so her golden locks bounce along her back.

"You don't like my outfit?" I ask, startling her.

She falls to her flat feet and spins with wide eyes. "Ford! What are you doing back here?"

I shrug. "You stopped texting me."

Her sweet gasp makes my mouth water. "I'm a little busy!"

I can't help but grin at her stressed state. Taytum never shows when she's frazzled or nervous, except with me. "I just wanted to tell you good luck."

A rustle of tulle and quiet feet catch my attention, and I step back to put space between us. A cluster of ballerinas rush past, all looking at me briefly before Taytum squeezes every one of their hands and tells them good luck.

Once they're past the threshold of the door and on stage waiting for the lights to shine upon them, she peeks at me and checks me out from head to toe.

"I can't believe you wore your hockey jersey." Her arms cross over her tight leo, and I can't help but watch her lungs expand beneath the material.

"You said to wear something nice. This is the nicest thing I own."

Her mouth twitches, and I poke her in the side. She laughs and swats my hand away. "You're stupid."

"I made you smile, though," I point out.

Her cheeks are rosy, and I have never felt the way I do when I see her smile. Something comforting settles in my stomach, and my hands beg to pull her in close because it feels wrong not to.

"Go sit down. You're distracting me." She brushes me

away, but I grab onto her hand quickly, and she flies into my chest.

I catch the yelp on her mouth with a quick kiss before backing off so no one sees—though I want the entire world to see.

"Break a leg, Heartbreaker." I wink and start to walk away but stop at the last second. I spin and see her staring at me. "Do I need to check?"

She acts confused, but I know she knows what I'm referring to. "Check what?"

"I'll peel that flimsy tutu off your body right now and check to see if you've had a recent injection, Tay."

She bristles at my tone. "Do you think I want to pass out on stage in front of everyone? I checked my sugar, and it's fine."

I exhale. *Good girl.*

There's no point in checking her levels because they've been all over the place lately.

"Now go! I have things to do."

I laugh under my breath. "I do too...but unfortunately, she's busy."

The music starts to fade as I walk down the empty hall, but before I get too far, I hear, *"Pst, Ford!"*

I pause, spin, and look at Claire like she has ten heads. "Um, aren't you supposed to be on stage?" I ask.

She quickly shakes her head, and the shimmer on her cheeks catches the light when she steps forward. Her hand lands on my arm, and she pulls me around the corner. "I go on in ten, so we have to be quick."

"Quick?"

"We need to talk about Taytum," she says.

"Ah." I nod. "You think we should tell Em too."

Claire eyes my outfit. "Why are you wearing your

hockey uniform?" She shakes her head. "Never mind, not important. And no, I don't think it's a good idea to tell Emory. He'll go ballistic if he knows her sugar is high. He'll probably storm on stage in the middle of the show."

I snap backward. "Wait, what?" I pull out my phone to go through her levels again.

"I watched her take her sugar before the show started. I saw the number, and yet..." We both turn to her name being called. "She looked worried. I confronted her, and she assured me that she was fine. Is she?"

I pinch the bridge of my nose and shut my eyes. "She will be." *But she better have used her insulin.*

"I gotta go," she mutters.

I catch her eye before she rushes off. "Meet me in the dorms after the show. We need to talk."

She nods quickly.

"Don't worry," I assure her.

Claire's smile hardly reaches her eyes before she's scurrying off to leap onto the stage.

If there's anyone that can help prepare me for meeting up with a long-lost parent, it's Claire. And if there's anyone who can give me a fucking heart attack, it's Taytum.

[47]

I SMILE when I hear the familiar sound of my window closing. My heart leaps, and my stomach fills with butter-flies. Ford's footsteps are slow and steady as he walks across my floor, and though I am exhausted from the show, I still planned to stay awake until he showed up.

My bed dips, and it takes everything in me not to roll to my back.

His finger hooks around a wavy piece of my hair, and he sweeps it off to the side, giving way to my bare shoulder. I clench my thighs when he places a soft kiss to the hollow part of my collarbone, pulling a shaky sigh from my mouth.

With every trailing kiss against my skin, a round of chills follows closely behind, until I can't take it anymore. I move to my back and latch onto his shadowy figure hovering over me.

"You said you trusted me," his whisper floats to my lips.

My eyebrows furrow. "I do," I confirm breathlessly.

There is something unhinged in his voice. It's almost unrecognizable.

"Do you want me to trust you?" he asks.

What? Where is this coming from? "Yes..." I answer him hesitantly.

I jump when the covers are abruptly pulled from my body. Ford's finger falls to the space in between my breasts, and it leaves a fire behind as he trails it all the way to the apex of my thighs. I'm breathing heavily from the touch, but he turns the fire to ash when he pulls away.

I'm suddenly confused. "What are you doing?"

He remains silent for far too long. My heart beats faster, and I'm suddenly aware of how still he is.

"Punishing you."

The room tilts, even in the dark. "Punishing me? For what?"

"For lying to me."

I huff with anger and move to get up, but it's short-lived because Ford grabs my hips with a tight grip and traps me below him. "You promised me you wouldn't mess with your insulin again."

I jerk with denial. "I haven't."

Ford's mouth is so close I can almost taste it. His warm breath is minty, and I've never craved something as much as I've started to crave him. I even crave his anger and so-called punishment. "Then why are your sugar levels all messed up?"

"I already told you that I don't know!" I admit. "Maybe the few times I did take the wrong amount, it did more damage than I thought." I try to hide the fear from my voice, but there's a deep-rooted concern in the pit of my stomach every time an alert goes off on my phone.

"Damnit, Taytum!" Ford's voice is hoarse, and I don't know if it's from anger or fear. "I can't lose you."

My hands curve around his biceps, and for a brief second, I wish he didn't care about me as much as he does, because what if something happens? What if my organs fail or I unknowingly fall back into DKA and end up in the MICU again? The panic would take him under. I've only seen it happen once, but it was traumatic to watch.

"You won't lose me," my whisper floats into the silence that surrounds us.

Ford's arms wrap around my waist, and he pulls me in close. "Promise me you'll always put yourself before anyone else."

I pause. "That's asking a lot."

He shakes against me. "Not to me it isn't."

Ford reaches across me and flips on the lamp. I suck in a breath at the look on his face. His blue eyes are hardened with unyielding emotion, and he looks at me like he's afraid I'm going to slip right through his fingers. "I can't lose you," he warns. "Especially if it's the same way I lost her."

He's referring to his mom, and I feel sick.

My chin quivers, and I can't help but feel everything all at once.

I want to go back to our secretive flirting, when things were lighter, but we're too invested at this point. We know each other too deeply, which is why the room is suddenly filled with desperation.

"Promise me, Taytum. Please. Even if you and I are never more than what we are tucked away in this room, I need to know that you'll always put yourself first."

My chest constricts at the validity in his tone, and I crumble. Ford is quick to wipe away my tears. He grips my cheeks, and his thumbs work in overtime to fling away the moisture. "I promise," I finally say.

A tiny divot carves in between his eyebrows. "And promise you'll let me take care of you. No matter what."

I sniffle. I'm not sure he'll always want to take care of me, but I still nod. "I promise."

His fingers disappear into my hair, and he brings my forehead to his mouth. The kiss is tender, and the room settles. I grab onto his wrists, and he pulls back to peer into my eyes.

"Ford?"

His forehead creases. "Yeah, baby?"

I feel incredibly vulnerable. More vulnerable than I've ever let myself be. "Will you take care of me now?"

He briefly looks at my mouth. "I thought you'd never ask."

[48]

FORD

I LOVE her so much it terrifies me.

I wish I could lock the feelings away, but I'm so physically bound to her that it would destroy me to leave her in bed like this. Her tears have dried, and her chest no longer rushes with emotion. Instead, she's trembling beneath me as I kiss her like it's the last time.

I sit up and take my clothes off. They end up in the same pile as her clothes that she stripped from her body, knowing I would be slipping into her bed at some point. I say nothing as I cover her body with mine and kiss her again.

It starts off gentle. I nip at her mouth, and she presses the softest kiss to my lips. My hand cups the side of her face, and I go in for more. I deepen my strokes and let my body show her how much she means to me. It's an uncontrollable, unhinged kiss and she whimpers.

Her warm hand presses against my chest, and I roll over when she climbs on top to straddle me. My hands fall to the small of her back, and I touch every inch of her bare skin while she rocks against me.

Our lips never unlock when I slip inside. Her gasp is shaky against my mouth, and I glide in and out with my hand crawling up her back to grab onto her hair. Sex was always a tool I used as a distraction or a way to get off, maybe even to build my ego, but with Taytum, it's so much more.

It's grounding, but thrilling.

It's intense, but sensual.

She has me in the palm of her little hand, and I'm not even sure she knows it.

I break away from her kiss to watch her move over me. "You feel too good." I swipe my thumb against her clit. I watch in awe as her eyes roll into the back of her head. *Goddamn.* "Tell me you're mine," I demand.

She moans. "I'm yours."

"But only behind closed doors, right?" I ask, feeding off every bit of displeasure I have not showing the world that she's mine.

Fuck Emory's disapproval.

There's no one better for her than me.

"Ford." Her blue eyes flare, and her pupils dilate. I have never seen a hotter sight. I'd destroy the entire world for her right now if she asked me to.

Her tits bounce in my face when she starts to pick up her pace, and I immediately tug on one of her nipples with my teeth. When I slowly raise to look her in the eye, I spot the rosy color covering her skin. She's flushed with need, because of *me*.

A hot, lustful sigh flies from her mouth when I tug on her other nipple.

"I love the way you look when I touch you." Her whimpers and moans will send me to the grave one day.

Taytum's eyes flutter open, and she glances at my mouth. "I love it when you touch me." Her voice is raspy and breathy, and I'm going to fuck her so hard she can't help but feel my possession over her.

Because that's what this is.

Possession.

"Tell me you're mine again," I say.

She doesn't hesitate, and there is nothing in this world that can take away the feeling it gives me. "I'm yours, Ford." She stares down at me. "I think I've always been yours."

I gaze at her long and hard before flipping her on her back. "I'm done waiting," I say, settling on top of her. I don't have to explain. She knows what I'm talking about.

Her chin is so small in my grip, but I hold it steady and pound into her. She rasps out a feverish breath, and her pussy instantly tugs against me.

Mine.

Mine.

Mine.

Possession scorches my skin when I pull back to push into her again.

"After the game," she rushes, meeting me halfway. She's close to coming, and it's hard for me to register what she's saying. I slam into her again while holding the headboard steady with my hand for support.

"What?" My question comes out winded.

"We can tell Emory—but after the game."

It was the right thing to say but at the wrong time.

My mouth falls to hers so hard I may have busted her lip. I fuck her harder. I continue to move in and out of her with speed until her perfect little pussy grips me and she's moaning against my mouth.

We started off slow, but things are ending sloppy. She's like a drug to me. The more she gives, the more I want, and there's no hiding how much I love her after this.

"After the game," I confirm.

She nods against me.

"Good, because I love you so fucking much that I'm not sure I can take not claiming you in front of everyone for a second longer." She stills. "You heard me right. I love you, and I always have, but you don't have to say it back." I enter her one more time before groaning the rest. "I already know you love me too."

I pull out and come so hard I collapse on top of her with my come on her stomach.

Neither one of us moves for a long time, but eventually, I get up and clean us both off. I don't bother with clothes. Instead, I pull back her covers and climb into her bed. Her bare leg slides over top of mine, and her head rests against my steady heart.

Sleep sweeps in quickly, but I know I'm not dreaming when I feel her warm breath against my chest. "I've never loved anyone the way I love you," she whispers.

I wait until my throat unclogs with emotion to say, "I know."

The energy in the arena tonight is out of this world. Coach confirmed there are more scouts lining the stands than at the start of the season, and it's important now, more than ever, that I continue to play the best defense I ever have.

Pro hockey has always been the holy grail.

When you're on a team like Bexley U, your only ambition is to make it big, but my goal has never been to prove something to myself or make it big to inflate my ego. It's always been about making the sacrifices from my aunt and the Olsons worth it. Being an orphan is a mind-fuck, you learn at a very young age not to take things for granted.

Only now, instead of wanting to prove a point to the people that raised me, I'm striving to make it pro so I can support the girl in the stands whose eyes follow my every move on the ice.

If I don't make it pro and get some stellar entry-level contract with a team, I'll just have to find a job.

"Keep up the D," Theo says as he rushes past me to head out of the locker room for the second half of the game. "And don't get distracted."

I nod, knowing that he's referring to our chat in his room the night before.

Theo, Claire, and I damn near had a therapy session, and although I left with not one, but two solid plans in tact to ease the Olsons' finances and take care of Taytum's medication for a while, I still can't fight the worry concerning her sporadic sugar levels.

I'm the last to leave the locker room. I'm not even halfway through the threshold when I decide to rush back to my locker and check her levels for peace of mind. Maybe then, I can focus and play the game of my life.

I open the app as a bead of sweat trails over my nose, and a rush of panic rains over my body. Her sugar isn't where it should be. I send her a quick text, throw my phone back into my locker, and rush toward the arena.

Coach meets me in the hallway. "What the fuck are you doing? The game is starting."

I say nothing and move past him quickly to reach my starting spot. Theo shoots me a look, and I nod, telling him that I'm fine.

The buzzer is about to sound, so I swing my attention to Taytum in hopes that it can give me some type of silent indication that she's okay, but seeing her unravels me instead. Her light hair is a curtain covering her face as she holds her phone in her hand. It sends a flood of relief into my bones, but then Claire looks to Taytum's phone, and her jaw slacks. She bends quickly and pops back up with Taytum's insulin pen.

Is she okay?

"Ford!"

My name breaks the dam of silence, and the roaring crowd floods back in. I turn in panic because the game has started, but within a split second, I'm paralyzed with shock.

Oxygen vanishes from my lungs, and my helmet glides through the air as we both soar over the ice. I land like an avalanche, and I know I should shield my head without the protection of my helmet, but I'm a little too late.

[49]

TAYTUM

I wince when I press the pen into my stomach and breathe out of my nose slowly. It's the best place for me to insert it, but the skin is becoming tender, and I have the brief thought that maybe a pump *would* be better–if it wasn't thousands of dollars.

"Oh no."

I turn toward Claire. "What?"

There's a wave of concern that travels amongst the hockey fans, and my resolve falls when I follow their line of sight.

Number twenty-two is sprawled across the ice, and my heart is right there with him. My hand flies to my mouth, and everything slows around me. Claire says something to me, and Riley rushes to the glass to get a better view, but I stay rooted in place with my insulin pen in my hand.

Ford.

He isn't moving.

My skin crawls.

I drop everything and make a beeline for the opening to the ice. The only thing I hear is my pounding heartbeat, and the only thing I see is Ford lying on the ice, motionless, with his helmet feet away and his stick nowhere to be found. I'm running as fast as I can, but he still seems so far away.

My foot touches the ice, and suddenly, arms are around my waist, jerking me backward. "Taytum, no. You can't go out there!" I try to peel Aasher's hands off my body, but he's too steady on the ice, and his hold on me is too strong.

"Let me go," I plead. "He isn't moving!"

He puts my feet back on stable ground and blocks the opening. A few more hockey players skate up to help him, but their backs are to me as they watch a stretcher move toward Ford.

Aasher looks me dead in the eye, and there's remorse there. "I know, but you have to stay back."

"Aasher!" I'm shouting through the panic, and my stomach clenches with nausea. "Please!" *Why isn't he moving?*

"Taytum!" Emory skates over to me in his goalie gear and pulls off his helmet. "Go to the hospital. Now."

"Is he going to be okay?" I look past his wide shoulders to get a better look. I'm paralyzed with fear, and it hurts to breathe. Ford is on the stretcher, and they're taking him down the tunnel, out of my sight.

I don't wait another second for Emory to answer me. I turn and race up the stairs where Claire is waiting with her keys and my purse.

"Let's go." She grabs onto my hand and drags me down the emptying hall. I hear the sportscasters on the TVs talking about Ford and how he was still unconscious when they placed him onto the stretcher. Sirens blare when we make it outside, and I watch in terror as the ambulance races by.

"Claire," I choke, catching her eye.

"It's going to be fine. Get in."

My door isn't even closed, and Claire is pressing her car's accelerator to the floor.

I press back into the seat and realize pretty quickly how daunting it is to care so deeply about someone, knowing just how fragile life can truly be.

I'm frantic.

Claire drops me off at the ER while she goes and finds a parking spot. I don't even think I shut the passenger door.

The lights are bright, and everyone is staring at me like I'm the one who needs a doctor, and honestly, I probably do.

"Where is he?" I ask the receptionist.

She gives me a dirty look. "Who?"

I sigh with frustration. "The hockey player they wheeled in here a second ago! Where is he?"

"Ma'am, you can't just—"

I spin and head for the doors. I know exactly where to go, and no one is going to stop me from being there when Ford wakes up.

What if he doesn't wake up?

My mouth dries even more with a wave of nausea. There's a pounding in my head that I'm forced to ignore because suddenly there's a security guard in front of me. "You are way too gorgeous for me to detain you. Can you please just calm down?"

I want to kick him in the balls and scream at him to move. "Are you hitting on me?!"

"What? No!" His cheeks ripen with heat. "It's just... You're..."

"Taytum?" I turn and latch onto Dr. McCarthy.

It's the first time I've ever been happy to see him.

"Are you okay?" he asks. "What's going on?" His white coat flies behind him as he moves toward me. I tremble with relief.

"If I say no, will you let me go back?"

His confusion lingers, but he nods slowly. "Yes."

"I'm not okay." I look around at the bystanders. "It's my sugar."

It isn't a lie. My sugar is all over the place lately, but at the moment, all I care about is Ford.

"Come on." He brushes off the security guard and the receptionist who is practically lying on the desk to watch the scene unfold.

When the swinging doors shut behind us, I stop walking. "It's Ford. He got hurt in the game, and I need to see him."

He shakes his head, but I cut him off before he can tell me no. "You don't understand." I'm talking so fast I'll be surprised if he can keep up. "He gets panic attacks in hospitals! He wasn't even conscious when they brought him in, and if he wakes up, hooked to machines, all alone? I have to be there!" I grab onto Dr. McCarthy's arm, and he stares at it for a second before sighing.

His hand lands on mine, and he pats it. "Just sit still, and I'll see what I can find out. Go over there." He flicks his chin to the nurses' station, and I hurriedly rush over.

I recognize one of the nurses from when I was here last,

and she purses her lips. "Well, if it isn't Miss I-Can-Take-Care-Of-Myself."

Usually, I'd smile and give her some quippy comeback, but I can't do anything except focus on my breathing.

Crash.

Both of our heads whip at the commotion.

My ears perk. "I have to go." I rush toward the sound of Ford's voice.

He's awake.

"Get some midazolam!" someone shouts.

My hair is stuck to my face, and I'm a mess of fear and anxiety, but when I slide in front of the room Ford has been placed in, I shout his name, "Ford!"

His blue eyes are wide, and he's gasping for air. He's shirtless, with nothing on but the bottom half of his hockey uniform.

"Hey, it's okay. It's okay." I enter the room as the nurses scold me, but I ignore them. I fling myself onto his body and wrap my arms around his waist. "I need you to breathe. Deep breaths."

"I gotta get out of here." His chest heaves, and I squeeze him tighter.

"Remember last time," I whisper against his skin. "Breathe in and then out. Match my breathing, Ford."

"Taytum, I need to go–" Ford sways, and I'm too small to keep him upright, so I push him toward the bed, and he falls clumsily. His arms and legs move sluggishly, and he sucks in a heap of oxygen again, gasping for air.

"I'll stay with you, but you have to calm down or they're going to sedate you." *Like last time.*

I palm his face, and he stares up into my eyes. There is an undeniable amount of fear and anxiety there, but if there is anyone who can reach him in this state, it's me.

I've done it before, and I'll do it again.

"Breathe," I demand.

He brings his clammy forehead to mine and takes a few deep breaths. *Whew.*

I eye the nurses, and I mouth, "He's fine."

They nod, and we all exhale deeply.

In between another deep breath, Ford asks, "Are you okay?"

I straighten my spine. "What? Am *I* okay?"

His arms tighten around my waist before he pulls back and stares up at me. "I looked at your levels when I went into the locker room... Then I saw you in the stands..." He looks confused. "Then I ended up here."

Emotion chokes me, and all I do is nod against his forehead. "I'm fine, Ford. But we need to let them check you out. Okay?"

I slowly try to back away, but he doesn't let go. "Not without you beside me."

My heart flips. I turn to look at the head nurse, Dorris, and she gives me the okay with a quick nod.

"I'm not going anywhere," I say, pushing back on his bare chest. I keep my hand pressed to his heart, because God knows he has his hand on mine.

FORD

SHE HASN'T LEFT my side.

Taytum's legs are hooked over mine, and her hand holds on tight to my arm as fluids rush through my vein in the other. I'm still cagey, and my heart still beats too fast for the athleticism that I possess, but without her, I'd probably be in a straightjacket from the Hulk-like strength I seem to possess when I'm in distress.

I hate hospitals.

The smell.

The fluorescent lights.

The depressing energy that seeps from everyone.

The memory of watching my mother die.

"You definitely have a concussion, and you need a CT due to how long you were unconscious."

Taytum stiffens, and suddenly, I'm the one comforting her.

"I feel fine," I say.

It's partly a lie. I'm nauseated and weak, but the thought

of being wheeled into a CT scan without her sends another line of stress down my spine. The sound of wheels against the tiled floor scratches a memory in the back of my head that I hate to think about.

"Ford." Taytum sits up and peers down at me with a flushed face. "You need a CT."

"Do I, though?" I ask with doubt. "My head is perfectly fine."

She purses her lips. "That's debatable. Even more so now that you have a concussion."

The doctor chuckles and doesn't give me an option to decline. "They'll be up soon to wheel you in. If it checks out, you're free to go home with a few precautions for the next couple days."

Taytum thanks the doctor, and I lie back on the bed, trying to calm myself. The heart monitor beeps like crazy until Taytum snuggles back onto my chest and breathes a sugary sigh in my direction.

"Calm down," she soothes.

I nod and take a deep breath. My arm tightens under her grip, and I rest my hand on her thigh. The room is quiet except for my heart monitor, but eventually, it slows. The longer she lies here with me, the calmer I become.

This moment proves that she came into my life exactly when I needed her to. Even though she started off as a friend-turned-crush, then turned into my favorite target to tease, and now to *this*...I know that she and I have always been something more.

Always.

"Thank you," I rasp.

She tilts her head to look up at me. "For what? Making you stress about me so much that I distracted you during a game, and you plummeted to the ice?" She is full of sarcasm. "You're welcome."

"I'm never going to apologize for caring about you, and I never want you to feel guilty for it either."

She lays her head back down, and I let my words rest in between us. Her finger starts to draw on my bicep, and I flex it to make her laugh—except, she doesn't.

"Tay?"

"I get it now."

"What do you get?" Hopefully how much I love her.

Her forehead creases. "How afraid you must have felt when I ended up in the hospital last summer." I grab her wobbling chin and ignore the sting of the IV in my arm. "Or how frustrated you were when you found out that I was messing with my insulin. I get it now, and I'm so sorry, Ford."

"Hey..." I try to stop her from getting too upset. "It's okay. Stop crying." I angle her face to mine and press our lips together. She tastes like sugar, and I can't help but deepen the kiss. I pull away at the sound of my heart monitor going wild and send her a dark look. "See what you do to me?" I ask.

A soft smile falls to her lips.

"And knock it off. There's only room for one of us to have an emotional breakdown tonight, and if you have one too, we're both going to end up in the loony bin."

"At least we'll be together." She laughs, but I catch it on her lips and kiss her again because I can't help it. When we break apart, I decide now is the perfect time to fill her in on my plans to ease her worries over the insulin.

"Plus"—I keep a hold of her face—"I think I found a way to afford–"

Our heads swing to the door, and my smile falls.

Emory stands there, still in his hockey uniform, with sweat dampening his hair. His jaw is tense, and the look he gives me is downright lethal.

"How long?" he snaps.

Taytum locks every one of her muscles. "Em–"

He puts his hand up to stop her all while keeping his glare pinned to me. "How...fucking...long?"

Fuck.

"That depends on what you're asking," I say slowly. "If you're asking how long I've loved her, then I could answer with years."

His jaw clenches. "How long have you been *fucking* my sister behind my back?"

Well, this is going to go over well.

"Emory!" Taytum sits up and gapes at her brother. "Seriously?"

He ignores her. "Answer the fucking question, Ford."

I answer without any added jokes. "A couple of months."

His jaw falls before he quickly regains the ability to speak. "*Months?*"

"Not months!" Taytum corrects, looking over at me. "We didn't have se–"

"Spare me the fucking details," Emory interrupts her.

My heart monitor starts to beep again, and Taytum looks at it, then to me, and then to her brother.

I sit up a little taller with my best friend's sister beside me and try to take the fall for it. "We were going to tell you."

Emory crosses his arms, and he is in full defensive mode. "I don't give a shit. You're not fucking my sister anymore."

Taytum climbs to her feet, and I hate that she acts like a pillar between us. Anger rushes through my veins, and I fling the heart monitor off my finger because my pulse is only going to continue to get higher.

"Emory, you're being ridiculous. You can't honestly expect me not to date anyone for the rest of my life!" She throws her hands up. "God! That's how this whole thing between us started!"

He runs his hand through his hair with frustration. "This is not about that! Don't you get it?"

"Get what?" I ask.

Emory's arms fall to his sides. "How the hell do you think you can take care of someone like her? You can't even sit in a hospital without the doctors threatening to sedate you." He points to the door. "Yeah, they told me you woke up and lost your shit like before. Have you ever thought about how you'll be there for her when she ends up here again? Because we all know how shitty she is at taking care of herself." His hands go to his waist, and the longer I hear him tell me that I can't take care of her, the more my blood pressure rises. "You can't even take care of yourself."

Taytum steps in front of her brother. "I am perfectly capable of taking care of myself, Emory!"

"You are not! You can't even take the right dose of insulin!"

Taytum's eyes snap over to me, and through the whizzing of her hair, she looks devastated. I answer her silent question right away. "I didn't."

"And then there's this bullshit! You two with your little secrets!" Emory yells. "What happens when you realize you don't want her anymore, Ford? Huh? I lose you as my best friend, or I lose her as a sister? I've seen it a thousand times before. You say you're into someone, and then the second it becomes real, you back away and mutter some stupid joke."

I get up from the bed with the stupid fucking IV pole

following me like shadow. "It's always been real with her, so don't you dare come in here and spew some bullshit that I'm going to be the one to hurt her. You think I'd risk our friendship or risk disappointing your parents for some casual fling? Do you truly think that little of me, Emory? We grew up together. You know me better than anyone." I briefly look at her. She's breathing fast, and her eyebrows are pulled taut. "Besides her."

"Guys! Just stop." Taytum tries to step in between us, but Emory quickly moves her off to the side.

"Taytum, go," I urge.

She stomps her foot. "I am not leaving you two in here like this! And get back in the bed! You have a concussion."

"Go!" Emory barks, keeping eye contact with me.

Taytum crosses her arms in defiance, but I still try to plead with her. "Taytum, please."

"And let him hit you? You have a concussion, Ford. I'm not leaving."

Emory feels betrayed. I get it. But how could he ever think I'd hurt her like that?

"You can hit me if you want," I say to him, "Disown me as a friend. Tell your parents some bullshit, and get them to hate me too. But it won't change anything, Emory. I love her. I have always loved her, and deep down, you've always known. I wouldn't risk everything for just anyone."

Emory grabs me around the neck, and my head instantly throbs. Taytum screams, and I hold up my hand. "Go!" I wince, glancing at her while Emory presses his fingers in harder. My back hits the wall, and the IV pole falls to the floor. "Trust me." My voice is strained, but I stare at her. "Please."

Emory knows me, but I know him too.

He has to get his point across.

He has to come to terms with this.

"This is ridiculous, and this is exactly what I was afraid of." She turns to her brother. "I knew you'd react like this. If anyone is ruining anything, it's you, Emory."

Then, she briskly leaves the room, and I'm alone with her slightly unhinged brother, who is no longer looking at me like I'm his teammate. What's even worse is that he's no longer looking at me like I'm his best friend either.

[51]

TAYTUM

I PRESS my back onto the tiled wall beside the restrooms and try breathing through my nose. I can't seem to catch my breath. I start to pace back and forth as my hands shake. My headache gets worse the more I think about Ford and my brother essentially fighting over me.

We should have told him.

It's my fault.

I wanted to wait because I was afraid of the outcome, and well...here we are.

My mouth is drier than the desert.

Why am I so fucking thirsty?

I start to pace again.

My stomach rolls.

I hate that my brother said that Ford couldn't take care of me.

He's been taking care of me for weeks.

He's taken care of me for far longer than I've given him

credit for, and I know he'd do anything for me. I feel it every time we touch.

I laugh quietly, in disbelief, when I think about the fact that he was willing to help me date other guys just so I could have some freedom, all while he was lusting over me. There has never been a moment where I thought that Ford would put someone else over me, even himself or his own wants.

Emory has it wrong.

I turn to stomp back into Ford's room because I refuse to let Emory ruin anything else of mine. Their teammates are starting to pile into the waiting area, but I duck behind a nurse and follow her down the hall to avoid questions.

There's no time for that.

My parents are likely to arrive soon because I'm certain Emory called them, and I am determined to get this straightened out before they get here. They're under enough stress as it is. They don't need to witness Emory punching Ford because of me.

I lean against the wall for a second and try to catch my breath.

My heart feels slow, and the hallway becomes distorted. I press my hand to my face, wondering why I feel so sluggish. I'm hot to the touch, but I'm shaking like I'm cold.

I lift my shirt and look at my injection site.

My memory is muddled, but I know I gave myself insulin before Ford fell.

What's wrong with me?

I need to check my sugar.

I take a step forward toward the room, but my knees buckle. The hard floor bites into my skin, and I wince. My eyes droop, and I try to shake myself awake.

Insulin.

I feel for my back pocket, and the empty denim scrapes against my palm. *Where is it?*

Panic stuns me. *Oh my god.*

It's last summer all over again.

Only this time, I know what's wrong.

"Help." My voice is so faint I can't even hear it.

My eyes refuse to open.

Shit.

The hallway comes into view, but it narrows right away. I push myself up on my palms to make it to the bend in the hall so someone will see me, but I know it's too late.

I close my eyes before I feel the sting of the floor meeting my cheek.

52

FORD

"How COULD you keep this from me?" Emory's eyes drive into mine, and although we're almost the same height, his tone tells me he's looking down at me.

I chuckle sarcastically. "Do you know how long I've refrained from admitting to myself that I love her? Let alone confide in you about it?"

Emory grips me tightly. "I'm talking about her not taking her insulin!"

"Because she trusted me!" I stress. "And I had it under control. She stopped messing with her doses the second I caught on! Do you even want to know why she was messing with them?"

Emory scoffs, and I'm instantly frustrated.

"She was trying to make it to where her levels weren't stabilized so the doctor wouldn't give her the okay for an insulin pump."

"She's so insecure about it that she's willing to risk going into DKA again?!"

I shove his hand off my neck even though the movement makes the room tilt. "No, Emory! She found out that your parents were struggling to pay for things. The pump is thousands of dollars. She..." I try to calm down. "She was trying to delay the process until she found a way to pay for it herself."

Emory's eyebrows are furrowed with anger, but I refuse to back down now.

"And you can act like I'm not good enough for her, but I know that I am. No one will love her like I do, and no one is more loyal to her than I am, so just fuck off, Emory." I push past him, and he tries to stop me, but I'm seething. "I even attempted to go to my father to ask for money so I could pay for her pump and future doses—and to save your parents' house—so tell me again that I can't take care of her, because the lengths I'm willing to go for her are beyond what you could expect."

Emory's mouth slams shut, and I flex my jaw. I pull the IV from my arm and toss it to the ground. Then, I stomp over to her purse and grab it. "I'm sorry we didn't tell you right away about us, but I'm not sorry for loving her. I'm not sorry for keeping her trust and for constantly watching out for her...even if that means keeping something from you and your parents."

He steps forward. "Where are you going?"

I throw my hands up and raise my voice. "I'm going to find her because she needs her phone to track her sugar levels, and she probably needs her insulin!"

I open the door, but his solemn voice stops me.

"Why her? Why now?"

I peer over my shoulder at my best friend. "How could there be anyone else when she exists?"

My heart aches with the truth, and I turn to go find her.

I step out into the hallway, but I quickly move backward when I'm almost run over by an empty rolling bed. I follow the rushing nurses and glance down the hall.

Emory bumps into me, and I grunt.

"What's going on?" he asks.

It's chaos.

A doctor follows the commotion, and an alert comes over the intercom.

"Code blue on floor one. Code blue on floor one."

Anxiety rises to the surface.

There's a flashback tapping me on the shoulder, but I ignore the debilitating memory and run toward the mayhem.

Emory calls after me, and he probably thinks I'm trying to run out of the hospital to avoid another panic attack, but I'm not. The hallway sways, and a wave of nausea almost takes me down. I'm not sure if it's fear or the concussion, but either way, neither of those things stops me.

"Taytum!" I shout.

Dr. McCathy turns and is shocked to see me. I dump Taytum's purse out on the ground and look for her insulin. I scatter everything around. I fiddle with her manual glucose monitor, the strips, and even her glucose tablets, but I can't find her insulin pen. "Where the fuck is it?"

I shake my head. *Never mind that.*

I enter her phone's password and search for her last sugar reading. Doctor McCarthy takes it, and his brow furrows. "When was her last injection?"

"I don't know. I think she gave herself insulin right before I got hit. So...fuck, I don't know. An hour ago?"

Dr. McCarthy spouts off a list of instructions to the nurses, but I hear nothing. The blood drains from my face when they lift her lifeless body onto the gurney and rush her down the hallway and behind the swinging doors. I want to follow after them and hover over their shoulders to make sure they're doing everything they can, but I stay with Dr. McCarthy and tell him everything I can think of that will help.

"Her sugar has been all over the place." I'm certain he's already aware, but I add it anyway. "She was messing with her insulin dosing a couple of weeks ago and—"

"Wait, what?" Shock ripples over his face. "What do you mean?"

I try to slow my words. "She's taking the full doses now, but up until recently, she was spacing them out and not taking as much as she should. Or taking too much." I shake my head. "She found out how much the pump is, and her parents have been struggling to pay for her insulin, so—"

"Jesus!" Dr. McCarthy starts to walk away. "Okay, that's helpful. She's probably in another DKA episode."

"What? I'm coming with you. I'll wait outside her room. I don't care, but I'm not just going to go sit here when you have the love of my life in some room while she's in a possible diabetic coma!"

Dr. McCarthy spins around and grabs my arms. "You have a concussion. You're shirtless and frantic. I promise you she's going to be fine. I will fix her."

He turns, and I know I'm only going to add to the chaos if I fight it and follow him, so I go the opposite direction and meet Emory.

He's paralyzed with fear. He's in the same spot I left him in, even with some of our teammates standing around with worried looks on their faces. They likely saw the entire thing.

I bypass them and snap my fingers in front of Emory's face. "Emory!"

He meets my eyes slowly, and my bare chest is covered with goosebumps.

"Call your parents. Tell them it's an emergency."

Theo speaks up. "They're already on their way because of your concussion."

Fuck my concussion.

Claire runs over to me from the nurses' desk. "She's on floor se–"

"Floor seven," I finish for her. "The MICU. I know." It's the same floor my mother died on. But regardless, I'm going up there.

"Someone get me a fucking shirt!" I shout.

Three of my teammates rip the shirts off their backs and hand them to me. I grab one, pull the cotton on over my head, and haul Emory over to the elevator. The door closes, and for the first time since being in this hospital, I'm not panicked because of the past.

I'm panicked because I might lose the love of my life.

"What?" Mary-Ann's hand covers her mouth in shock.

Dr. McCarthy briefly looks at me standing ramrod straight beside Emory and Taytum's dad. "She's going to be okay. We're pumping her full of fluids, and we've got her blood sugar leveled with insulin. She's woken up a couple of times, but she's drowsy." He lowers his voice. "But we need to discuss the reason why she's back in the MICU."

Taytum's dad scrutinizes him. "What do you mean?"

Dr. McCarthy looks at me briefly, and I step forward. "Let me."

He ushers his hand out. "I'll be over here to give your family some privacy."

Family.

I'm less on edge than before with the confirmation that Taytum will be okay, but there's a weight on my shoulders that doesn't let up when I stare her parents in the face. Jay is the one who taught me hockey. He was the one who took Emory and me to practice, and his encouragement still lingers in the back of my head from time to time. Mary-Ann always made sure I had a warm meal at night, a clean uniform, and enough love to make up for my shitty parent situation.

They're both going to feel so betrayed.

"A few weeks ago, Taytum almost fainted."

"Again?" her mom asks.

I nod. "That's when I found out that her blood sugar was completely out of sync. She admitted that she wasn't using the right dosage because she found out that you guys were having a hard time affording it. She was trying to screw up her levels so that Dr. McCarthy wouldn't push the insulin pump yet."

"Oh my god."

I keep my gaze locked with Jay, even with Mary-Ann muttering under her breath. His neck is gradually becoming redder with anger, but I'm willing to deal with it for Taytum.

He inhales sharply. "And you didn't think to tell us?"

"I did. I even threatened it." I shake my head with frustration. "I thought I had it under control. I even injected her myself with the insulin from time to time. I went to the pharmacy and filled the prescription for her." My voice begins to shake, and I pinch the bridge of my nose to keep myself grounded.

Mary-Ann starts to cry, and I wince. "You should have told us! How could you not tell us? After everything?"

"Because she trusted me. I wasn't going to betray her trust."

"Well, we trusted you!" she interrupts. "You were supposed to be watching out for her. Both of you were!"

Emory remains quiet, and I don't dare look at him for help. He hates me more than they do at the moment.

"I know. I understand why you're upset with me." I shut my eyes for a second to regain my confidence. "But if I have to pick between her trust and yours, I choose hers."

Both her parents are shocked, and I attempt to stick up for Taytum, because I know they're probably just as angry at her as they are with me. "I'm sorry, but Taytum was just trying–"

Emory steps forward. "Stop!"

We all turn at his sudden outburst. Emory's fists flex by his sides, and the veins along his hands stick out further when he bounces his attention in between the three of us. I know what he's about to say, and it's only going to add gasoline onto the fire. *They're going to fucking kill me.*

"Taytum would probably be dead if it weren't for him." Emory moves his attention to his parents. "How can you be angry with someone who has done nothing but be there for Taytum since the very moment he met her?" He laughs sarcastically. "Did you guys know that Ford researched diabetes for twelve hours straight the day after she was diagnosed? Or that he went to the store and bought us both glucose tablets and a blood sugar monitor in case something happened while she was with us and didn't have hers?"

I'm dumbfounded that no less than an hour ago, he was threatening my life, but now, he's sticking up for me.

Emory catches my eye, and although I would never

consider him to be a *soft* guy, the look he gives me is close enough. "He's even attempted to call his father for money so he can pay for her medicine and save our house."

A zip of unease rips up my spine. It's not something I want credit for, especially when it has to do with my father.

Jay and Mary-Ann whip their attention to me. "What?"

"Don't look at me like I'm a hero," I add. "Not until Emory tells you the rest."

"The rest?"

Emory's hand falls to my shoulder, and I stagger with confusion. "He loves her. He loves her so much that he's willing to contact the one man he hates more than anything just so he can take care of her." He pauses. "And us."

My throat is tight.

Emory sighs. "She loves him too. When she's in trouble or scared, she turns right to him. And he's *always* there. Of course he isn't going to betray her trust. Why would we want him to?"

They remain quiet, and we all just stand and stare at each other until Dr. McCarthy interjects. "Maybe now would be a good time for you to go get that CT."

"Oh my god, your concussion!" Mary-Ann covers her mouth with her hands again.

"I'm fine," I reiterate to the doctor. "I'm not leaving until I see her."

"Well, then go see her, because you need to get your CT. I've seen you sway three times while standing here." He puts his hand on my shoulder. "Taytum is going to be okay. DKA is serious, but we've caught it in time. We know how to treat it, and you sped up the process by telling me about her missing doses."

"She never should have missed them in the first place," I say with guilt.

Jay steps forward and nudges me toward the door. "Go see my daughter, Ford. Emory is right. Your name has always been first out of her mouth when she needs someone, so I'm betting she wants to see you."

I'd be a fool to question him.

So, I walk off with Dr. McCarthy to lay eyes on my girl.

53

TAYTUM

I DIDN'T SEE this coming, and I feel so ignorant.

Emory was right. It's obvious that I can't take care of myself.

Even after listening to Ford and coming to the realization that messing with a few of my insulin doses wasn't safe, I still missed the signs that I was in a diabetic crisis. I should have known better. I should have made an appointment with Dr. McCarthy instead of waiting until the one at the end of the month.

My eyes open as soon as I hear the door. I blink through my drowsiness but wake right up when I see Ford and his crooked smile heading toward me.

"Are you okay? How is your head?" I ask, sitting up.

He chuckles with a shake of his head. His dusty-blond hair is messy, and the color on his face is lacking—yet he still looks handsome. "Are you really asking me if I'm okay right now?"

I pause. "Well, are you?"

"I'm fine." He intertwines our fingers, locking them together. "Considering."

My mouth quirks. "I'm glad to see Emory didn't kill you."

He laughs tightly. "For a second there, I thought your parents were going to kill me too. You'll be surprised to know that Emory was the one who changed their minds."

My forehead creases, but his hand tightens on mine before he says, "Don't do that to me ever again."

My breath is shallow, as he tugs on our joined hands and places them over his heart. "Do you feel this?"

The muscle in his chest thumps hard and speeds with velocity. I nod.

"It's yours."

My eyes burn, and I feel a fullness that wasn't there before. One tear slips over my cheek, and he swipes it away.

"I know that for years I've called you Heartbreaker..." he whispers, "but don't you dare break my heart, Taytum. You got it?"

The tiniest smile slips onto my face. "I can't make any promises."

His eyes narrow. "You and your fucking games," he mutters. "Scoot."

I make room for him on the bed, and he takes me in his arms.

There's a lot going on, and I'm hit with guilt knowing there's going to be even more medical bills my parents will have to face on top of what they're going to think about Ford and me, but I know, with him by my side, it'll be fine.

It's me and him, against everyone else.

"Ford?" I whisper.

"Heartbreaker?" he whispers back.

I settle in closer. "I love you."

His heart beats faster against my ear. "I love you too."

I turn, and his mouth is already there, waiting for me. His hand sweeps my hair away from my cheek, and I'm in a world of bliss when he kisses me. I feel right at home with each caress of his lips—so much that when someone clears their throat, I almost don't pull away.

Ford and I break apart, but he keeps his back to Dr. McCarthy.

"*Ford.*"

Ford grumbles under his breath.

I meet Dr. McCarthy's disapproving look. and he sighs exasperatedly. "Will you tell him to go get his CT?"

My jaw drops. "Ford Collins!"

He sighs. "Ugh, fine!"

I watch him drag his feet all the way to the doorway before he turns and reassures me that he'll be right back. Then he says, "Oh, and by the way, I figured out a plan to afford that pump. That way, this"—he points back and forth between me and my IV— "will never happen again."

He winks and saunters out the door.

EPILOGUE

FORD

I STAND and stare at the masterpiece I've hung above the fireplace like it's a fine piece of art and smile to myself. I'm all alone in this big ol' house that I grew up in, and it feels weird to know that the deed is in my name instead of Jay's and Mary-Ann's.

All their belongings are still inside, and they're due back soon after meeting with the realtor and lawyers to finish the selling process.

They refused to accept my offer to get them caught up on bills and to purchase Taytum's insulin pump as well as future medications. Jay's exact words were, "You can pay for Taytum's medical expenses when you're married and she's on your insurance. For now, it's not your problem."

I took that as an excuse to propose, but *apparently,* running across the living room and kneeling in front of Taytum three seconds after the words left her father's mouth wasn't what anyone had in mind.

After I had filled Claire and Theo in on what was going

on with Taytum and how I was going to contact my father after nearly fifteen years of not speaking and take the money he had offered me after he learned of my mother dying, Claire came up with a much better plan.

At the time, I wasn't sure it would work.

But thanks to her close proximity to some high-up people in the pros, I was quickly granted an agent, presented to multiple pro teams that already had their eye on me, and several offers were on the table within days. Each came with a signing bonus that I could choose to receive over time, like most players, or right away.

Naturally, I went with the highest one, and the money was in my account as soon as I signed the papers.

It was enough to buy the Olsons' house in secrecy and purchase Taytum's insulin pump out of pocket, plus take care of some other expenses.

"They're going to kill you."

I spin at the sound of my Aunt Jo's voice. I smirk and point to the frame behind me with a black-and-white photo of the hockey god Bobby Orr—only, I've photoshopped my face where his would be. "Do you like it?"

She scans the picture and furrows her brow. "Is that Bobby Orr?"

I pretend to be wounded. "Uh, no. It's obviously me."

Her raspy laugh fills the living room as she comes over and smacks me on the back of the head. "What am I going to do with you going all the way to Pittsburgh next year?"

I shrug. "Not laugh as much."

She fixes the frame for me, making sure it's straight, before taking a seat on the couch. "I'm proud of you," she says with watery eyes.

The croak in her voice makes me uncomfortable. "Stop it," I warn.

Typically, she listens to me and will stop giving me compliments. Not that I don't enjoy when someone inflates my ego, but it's different with her. Her praise means as much to me as if my real mother were the one saying it.

Only this time, she doesn't stop. "I'm proud of your maturity."

"I am the most immature twenty-three-year-old there is." That's what Coach says, at least.

Aunt Jo shakes her head. "That's not true. I don't know many twenty-three-year-olds who would be willing to call up the man they hate the most to ask him for money for something incredibly selfless."

I glance away because not only do I hate thinking about Henry, but I hate talking about him even more.

"He would have given you the money," she notes.

"I'm sure he would have, and I'm sure he would have used it as an excuse to slip back into my life or, if anything, used it as a way to rid himself of the guilt over her death."

My biological father didn't kill my mother with his own bare hands.

He wasn't charged with murder, and he didn't end up in some high-security prison.

But he did leave us with nothing, and when she got sick and begged for his help, he took too long to show up.

She died, and when I found out that he could have saved her all along, I wanted nothing to do with him.

I didn't want his money, because if it couldn't bring back my mom, what difference did it make?

But for Taytum, I was willing to stir up a shit-ton of baggage if it meant helping her and the Olsons.

Four car doors slam, and I push up off the wall. My aunt stands, and we walk to the front door to break the news to Jay and Mary-Ann that they don't actually have to move.

Her hand falls to mine, and she squeezes it. "I'm still proud," she whispers.

I elbow her gently. "Stop being mushy..." The door opens. "But thanks, Mom."

Her eyes well. I've called her Mom from time to time, and I know it hits her hard.

"Well?" I ask, pulling Taytum to my side when she and the rest of the family walks through the front door.

"It's done." Jay claps his hands once. "Now we just have to figure out where we're going to go."

Mary-Ann launches into a whole spiel, discussing some smaller houses that they've found and possibly even just renting an RV and living in it for a while.

Taytum tenses.

I rub my hand down her back and whisper, "Relax. I have a surprise."

"Your surprises never go over well," she says.

She isn't wrong.

But this one is different.

"I have a surprise for you guys." We're all standing in the foyer, and I start to lead them into the living room. My aunt can barely keep a straight face. "Well, I have two surprises."

Emory is the first to notice it. There's a giant crease in between his eyebrows. "What the hell is that?"

I smirk. "What?"

"That." He points to the photo above the fireplace and moves closer. "That's not even you."

"Is that Bobby Orr?" Jay asks, scrutinizing the photo closer.

Taytum is amused, but she's also confused.

Just wait, baby.

"It's part of the surprise."

"Your face photoshopped onto Bobby Orr's body is part of a surprise?" Emory asks. "This oughta be good."

Mary-Ann looks at me with skepticism. "Why is it hanging above the fireplace?"

"Well, because it's a housewarming gift."

I meet Taytum's squint. Her blue eyes swim with questions as she continues to silently ask me what's going on.

Emory scoffs. "You're supposed to get a housewarming gift when someone purchases a house. Not when they sell it."

"Obviously." I roll my eyes. "I got it for myself."

The room falls silent.

The Olsons blink several times, and I'm prepared to defend my case. I pull my phone out, open the text from my realtor, then hand it over to them.

Congratulations! The paperwork has been signed. The house is yours.

"Now, before you get mad...it's already done. I bought it with cash, and I did it for you. It's yours."

Taytum gasps. My eyes fly to hers. Those perfect, kissable lips part, and I'm having a hard time abiding by her brother's ridiculous rule that we don't kiss around him.

"You were the private buyer?" Mary-Ann asks in awe.

I nod. "And my *only* request..."

Emory cuts me off. "Here we go..."

I point to the photo behind me. "Is that you keep my photo up."

Jay chuckles, and Mary-Ann can't wipe the smile off her face. Emory comes up in front of me and pulls me into a hug. I'm shocked until he adds, "You suck at photoshop."

I laugh, and then Taytum is crashing into my chest and wrapping her arms around my torso. She's warm to the touch, and I know it's from being worked up with emotion. My hand traps her face to my chest because, knowing her and her stubbornness, she's trying to wipe away her tears so no one knows she's crying.

I know, though.

I know everything about her.

Jay and Mary-Ann grab hands and look at me from across the living room. I shake my head at them because I don't want their gratitude, nor do I want their argument.

It's a done deal.

The house is bought, and now they can use what they've made on the sale to catch their bills up. Taytum's sugar is finally regulated with her new pump, and the cost is covered.

"Thank you," Taytum whispers against my chest.

I turn us around and put my back to everyone. Our only audience is the photo of Bobby Orr with my face poorly photoshopped overtop of his. "No." I grab her cheeks and bring her face close. "Thank *you*."

"For what?"

I stare into her blue eyes that I fell for when I was too young to even know what love was. "For letting me take care of you."

The End

AFTERWORD

If you have enjoyed the Bexley U series and love college sports romance like me, make sure to preorder the first book in my brand new sports series on Amazon!
mybook.to/wilderuone

Haven't read the first two books in the Bexley U series? No worries! Head to Amazon and download book one here:
mybook.to/weakside

ALSO BY SJ SYLVIS

Bexley U Series

Weak Side

Ice Bet

Puck Block

Wilder U (Coming 2024)

Untitled

Shadow Valley Series

Sticks and Stones

Untitled (2024)

English Prep Series

All the Little Lies

All the Little Secrets

All the Little Truths

St. Mary's Series

Good Girls Never Rise

Bad Boys Never Fall

Dead Girls Never Talk

Heartless Boys Never Kiss

Pretty Girls Never Lie

Standalones

Three Summers

Yours Truly, Cammie

Chasing Ivy

Falling for Fallon

Truth

ABOUT THE AUTHOR

S.J. Sylvis is an Amazon top 50 and USA Today bestselling author who is best known for her angsty new adult romances. She currently resides in Arizona with her husband, two small kiddos, and dog. She is obsessed with coffee, becomes easily attached to fictional characters, and spends most of her evenings buried in a book!

sjsylvis.com

ACKNOWLEDGMENTS

I'm not going to attempt to hide the fact that Puck Block was insanely difficult to get out on time—not because of the book itself because truly, Ford and Tatum flew out of my fingertips effortlessly (*I am obsessed with them*), but life in general was chaotic. We're talking sick kids, major surgery for my husband, an er visit right when my book was due to the editor, spring break for my kids right after that, plus more. BUT, with the help of the most supportive family and friends, I was able to make it to the finish line with tears in my eyes. I am *so* proud of this book and series!

I am so thankful for each and every one of you who played a part in this journey. From my amazing friends who were there to help with my kiddos, to my husband who was still recovering from his surgery yet continued to encourage me, to my mom who flew all the way to Arizona, to my alpha/beta readers who read quickly, to my *amazing* editors who hustled to get this book back on time despite me turning it in late, my PA who picks up the slack without me even asking her to, my cover designer for always coming in clutch, my PR company for keeping me organized, and more. I could not have done this without you. Thank you so much for being you. I am forever grateful for everything you do and it does not go unnoticed!

To my author and reader besties - we are in this together and I am so happy to have you by my side whether it's a shared post, a vent session through facetime/voice messages

(Emma & Laura—I'm looking at you, haha), or a mile long text history. I love you so much!

My readers—how I love you all so much! Thank you for your patience when it takes me a little longer than most to release a book and for your continuous excitement over these characters. I hope to continue writing *all* the perfect book boyfriends for you to swoon over! If I accidently miss a share or a message, or I don't personally thank you, please know that I love you dearly and am so thankful for you and your shares!

Xo,

SJ